St. Croix: the gift

St. Croix: the gift

William A. Wright

Dale Ann Edmiston

Brave Knight Writers

St. Croix: the gift

By William A. Wright and Dale Ann Edmiston

Brave Knight Writers

www.braveknightwriters.com

Editor: Deb Hall (thewriteinsight.com)

Cover Design: Jennifer Fleming

Cover Images: Unsplash.com/@ hasselossius ;
Unsplash.com/@ aessuproduction

St. Croix: the gift/Wright & Edmiston. —1st ed.

ISBN: 979-8-9877319-5-6

ISBN (e-book): 979-8-9877319-6-3

Other Titles by the Authors:

Havasupai: the novel

Paper Alley

Above and Beyond: radio silence

Instead, by Grace: from dark to light

Instead, I cooked: you do the dishes

St. Croix: the novel

St. Croix: through the wall

For the unborn

A person's gift opens doors for him
and brings him before the great.
Proverbs 18:16

Preface

What breaks us? Infidelity, lies, death, fear, loss, broken dreams, loneliness, rejection, and hate wreak havoc on our spirits. These factors can overflow into our physical wellbeing, but the pain generated lives in the spirit. We are spiritual beings.

Jim Fisher's genesis lay in sorting scrap, a salvager by nature. As we walk with him, he never loses that quality. His story began with the crushing death of a young son and a spouse who let him down. Even though he had risen through the ranks to become one of the controllers of the electrical grid, he was broken. Storm after storm took down the grid, while Jim fought one storm too many. As a dropout he sought paradise on an island and became an artist. But fate laughed, launching different plans for him and his talent to salvage and rehabilitate. A gift from his dying son holds the key. A gift of courage and bravery is his gift to pass on.

Psalm 103:13-14 tells us, As a father has compassion on his children, the LORD has compassion on those who fear him. For he knows what we are made of, he remembers that we are dust.

St. Croix: the gift is the final story in the trilogy. It takes the reader on a fantastic journey through a self-convicted world. A world where the human spirit is repressed in the name of equity. Such an existence was never meant for the flesh, let alone the spirit. Freedom comes in surviving storms. The ancient world chiseled their beliefs and laws in stone to stand against the elements. Such practices became shunned by the modern ethos, who saw it far better to write in mutable space. Before the apocalypse came a great deception, as mortals created a new and improved god, promising to serve those who submit.

"Human beings are born with different capabilities. If they are free, they aren't equal and if they are equal they aren't free." Solzhenitsyn.

Humans exist as flesh and spirit, one cannot exist without both, this is why we must allow our spirit to be filled with the Holy Spirit. Then we feed our spirit with the words of God, with worship, and with fellowship in the family of God. Our flesh is born to slavery and drudgery, our spirit to power and liberation. The fruit of the spirit is love, joy, peace, patience, kindness, goodness, faithfulness, gentleness and self-control. The fruit is the opposite of what breaks us. Although the Bible lists nine segments, they support and intertwine to become one. Gentleness does not designate weakness, instead it is strength controlled by wisdom to serve God and others. A gift from God grants a combination of strength and wisdom as our spirit grows with the Holy Spirit. Love, as the nectar of the fruit, draws on the other qualities to hint at true paradise. Sadly, too many turn back from the promise to return to slavery. As it was in Numbers 13:31-33.

The characters in *St. Croix: the gift*, come to terms with the new world where the spirit has been dismissed. An adoptive father guides them to freedom.

"There are things you cannot know without suffering. God has special tutorials in tribulation for his shepherds. Do not begrudge the seminars of suffering. His aim is to make you, like Jesus, a sympathetic shepherd. It's scary. Paul prayed that he would share Christ's sufferings and become like him in his death (Phil. 3:10). God answered him. He was forsaken at his last trial (2 Tim. 4:16), and the Romans took him out. We are not playing games." — **David Mathis**

"The longer I live the more I realize the impact of attitude on life. Attitude, to me, is more important than facts. It is more important than the past, than education, than money, than circumstances, than failures, than successes, than what other people think or say or do. It is more important than appearance, giftedness or skill. It will make or break a company . . . a church . . . a home. The remarkable thing is we have a choice every day regarding the attitude we embrace for that day. We cannot change our past... we cannot change the fact that people will act in a certain way. We cannot change the inevitable. The only thing we can do is play the one string we have, and that is our attitude... I am convinced that life is 10% what happens to me and 90% how I react to it. And so it is with you... we are in charge of our Attitudes" - **Charles R. Swindoll**

St. Croix Series

St. Croix is designed to entertain as it takes the reader through the process of salvage.

Join the adventure!

St. Croix: the novel

St. Croix: through the wall

St. Croix: the gift

ONE

Atanase (Ah-tah-NAH-seh)

I perched on the driver's bench of the buckboard. With a vantage point from one of the many rolling hills, I gathered my thoughts. Though I survived, I still couldn't wrap my head around the brutality of man. In such a beautiful setting, they killed her and left me for dead. The horses I had unharnessed munched on the grasses while secured by long lead ropes to the rear of my wagon. The view made this moment special and my heart ache.

We shared so many good times. She'd been gone a year, a lifetime.

In the valleys between the soft mountain ridges, small runs of water trickled their contribution to the Susquehanna as the river raced over ancient boulders which never yielded to the torrent. How long, I wondered, had the process been going on, and yet was today just another of ten thousand or a million?

A flock of wild mallards rose above a long tranquil expanse between quick currents. They didn't appear dispatched, just ready to move on. High corn belts separated bands of golden wheat where men in blue shirts and black trousers with suspenders swung their sharpened scythes in choreographed rhythms.

With seemingly little effort, they layered their harvest in neat stacks as women and children in pale blue tied them into sheaves, then placed them in stacks. The distance prevented any form of visual detail, but I was aware of everyone, and my mind filled in the blanks.

A cloud moved and the sun's warmth felt like her embrace. A gentle breeze, like tickling fingers, reached up from the valley. With my eyes closed, the softness caressed my face and arms. Choose an eternal moment? Today would have been mine. If my wife was here.

This scene, bearing no hint of the alterations that had been caused by power-hungry entities seeking to control all aspects of life, was idyllic. All horrors of humanity cleansed by God's creation.

The Susquehanna flows by Harrisburg, through Lancaster, and on toward the Chesapeake, where clear mountain water mixes with brackish waters that pulsate high and low with the world's oceans. Clarity vanishes in murk and becomes impossible to swallow. Built on the banks of the Chesapeake stands a barren city. Laid waste by greed, pride, and hate, its buildings were left to crumble from natural entropy. None believed it could happen. To question the process was to become labeled with indignant ridicule.

The process of removing rights granted by the Creator began in subtle movements by individuals, but as the fervor increased, the men in power joined forces to strengthen and increase their operations. Plausible denial of intentions was all a corrupt politician needed to cover their tracks.

City after city fell to the same plight. The name of the city isn't worth a mention; it would only bring derision to a man whose name it bears. The past matters little.

Today, beauty healed my heart. Where my thoughts drifted revealed the pitiful flows of humanity, with no impact on the rocks of truth. My wife's favorite Bible verse, Philippians 4:8, came to mind. She used to prod me with it during all our travels. Now it was where I set my sights and my heart. The God of Peace was certainly with me. What I saw before me was reassuring me that the pettiness of men has little effect on the rock of truth.

A giggle broke my train of thought, and as I swung about, I caught sight of a bonnet dropping behind the wagon's tailgate. The horses whinnied, almost as if laughing at the fun. Without a sound, I dropped off the bench to the ground and leaned forward as I crept around the side of the buckboard. In a sprint, I rounded the rear of the wagon, catching sight of a bouncing bonnet racing to the front of the wagon, then stopping in a giggle. My eyes caught hers as she peered over the top of the worn sideboards, her strong fingers gripping the sides of her head, the bonnet hiding her beautiful blond hair. Her eyes smiled as I shouted, "Gotcha!"

She dropped from sight in a mist of giggles. So sweet, so innocent, my sidekick for the last year. Her laughter helped heal me from my tragedy. She exuded life and wonder about all things. In her own words, she thought, "everyone is special. I love and appreciate the smallest of wonders."

It made my leaving much more difficult, but sometimes we don't do our best; we do what must be done. I chased her around and around the buckboard until my wind had left me; she ducked underneath for a shortcut to the other side when I got too close. At thirty-five and still stiff in places from my wounds, I couldn't manage the shortcuts.

In final desperation, I fell flat on my back in the soft grass and closed my eyes. She stood over me, tickling my face with a long tiller of wheat. Before I squinted to open an eye, I grinned, and she giggled. The game over, I helped her onto the driver's bench and rested beside her, fielding questions about everything and anything her ten-year-old mind was thinking. Many of the questions I had answered before, but I answered as if they were fresh. It was communication, conversation, ten-year-old style. In this moment, nothing in the world seems to have changed from the beauty I once knew. Children do that for us. Sometimes we need the reminder that it's best to stay childlike, innocent.

I had memorized Luke 18:17, which tells us, "Truly I tell you, whoever does not receive the kingdom of God like a little child will never enter it."

Funny, I never had what anyone would call a childhood. I lived in the streets of Romania, ate out of garbage cans, and slept on piles of rags in alleys populated by rats. I suppressed the memory so I could better enjoy Katy's childhood, the now of it all.

"When are you leaving?" Katy asked in sudden seriousness.

"In two days."

"But why?" she asked in desperation, not for the first time.

"My time has come, I'm strong enough to travel now and I'm on a mission. I'm only here because of a misfortune. The whole thing is a miracle, a miracle I want to share."

"Pa says you should be dead. He said when he found you, you were."

"I can't remember anything from the first couple of months I was here."

"I remember. I remember you just lying there. All the women came to help care for you. I remember the gatherings where the women all came at once to cook and work together while they waited for something to change. We were told you were a secret, not to let the English notice you . . . or they would kill you. Oh, Atanase, I love you. I don't want you to leave."

Speechless, I stared off across the fields and kept telling myself there are some things we must do. Her pleas continued, but I tuned her out. She loved everyone and everything. I was nothing more to her than anyone else in the community, but I worried my leaving might make her bitter. I could be the first one to hurt her, to change her. She was so precious. The last thing in the world I would ever want is to inflict pain or damage on such a sweet child.

"Katy, you wouldn't keep a bird caged or tie a dog to a post, would you?" I scrambled for a way to find damage control. "You have your family and community. You'll grow up, marry some fine Amish boy, and forget all about me."

My words received no response except sniffles until she blurted, "Boys are stupid. They smell like horses . . . and I hate you!" Her last three words came out in a yell as she jumped from the bench and ran down the hill toward the valleys, where she could hide from the world and sob.

I felt pain in old scars. I didn't belong in an Amish community; they call me English, even though I was born in Romania. To the Amish, everyone outside the community was English. They respected me; I respected them and their ways, but I was still an outsider, and of late there had been hints. Though I was indebted to them, nothing would ever remove the last two holes in my heart. Katy would grow into a fine woman, mother, friend, and wife. The death of childhood can be every bit as painful as any death.

On my return to the barn, I walked the horses out before leading them to their stalls for grooming. Katy's father, Levi, entered as I put the curry brushes away. Levi had a fifty-pound feed sack over each shoulder, which he lowered to the ground when he saw me.

"Levi, you are amazing."

"Why do you say that?"

"The English took your lands, and you keep working as if nothing happened. Pretty amazing to me."

"Only a fool believes he owns anything. I ask you, can you own the water flowing in the Susquehanna? Show me how it can be. If you go down and try to claim it as it flows by, everyone will laugh. If you dip in a bucket and snatch some from the flow, you must dump it out or it evaporates. If you put a lid on, it is useless, and what becomes of it if you drink it?" Levi said and laughed.

"Yeah, but we're talking about the land," I replied.

Levi lifted the feed sacks onto a half-full pallet of like sacks. He had more to carry in from the wagon, and I walked with him to carry the rest. Outside in the light of day, he took off his straw hat to wipe his brow.

"The English changed the rules. They outlawed their money. It wasn't our money, it was theirs, and then they said the new money was all digital, and to keep track of it, you had to accept becoming a part of their database and tracking system. Some plain folk accepted this. But those of us who refused couldn't pay our taxes, and the English took possession of the farms. The English, being so distracted and lazy, had no vision of what to do with the land, so they said we could stay and sharecrop it. We are shepherds and stewards; we care for the flock whether we own the sheep or they belong to the landlord. In the end, God owns it all. Nothing changes except the hearts of man. Some hearts become blackened, marked for eternity. For their lifetime, they may boast about what they own and flaunt their power. They are silly men who fool only themselves."

"Like I said, you are amazing," I told him.

"We are plain. We do not differ from some of the English who defy the new ways. You are one. So we barter and trade and call it illegal. The biggest outlaws are the ones who make the laws."

We each hefted two sacks on our shoulders and carried them into the barn. After we placed them, I stopped Levi from going back for another load.

"I must confess, my friend, my leaving is causing great pain to your Katy."

"Ah yes, her mother and I have spoken. It grieves us. She is so soft-hearted, but it must be. There is no other way. You are a good man, a special friend, and your leaving pains us all. She will be fine. The same will happen when the old dog dies."

"You're killing me. I rate with the old dog," I replied.

"Don't be so prideful, my friend. Yes, the old dog."

Levi and I laughed. We both understood Scripture. Some more serious things about their plight went without saying. We both needed a little tension relief, and bantering provided it. The Amish community was practicing biblical advice. To hold on to worldly treasures leads to death. Neither of us spoke about it. I, of the same mind, saw my future in such a way. The incident that had brought me to this place was lost to me. A lot of my past was sketchy. Strong was the memory of my adoptive parents and my wife. Levi and I carried in the rest of the feed before dinner.

Levi's wife, Elizabeth, and five of his daughters bustled about prepping for dinner as the menfolk washed the toil from their hands and arms. I realized Katy was absent, and I pointed it out to Levi. Darkness had crept into the valleys as the sun ducked behind the rolling hills. Elizabeth gave orders to the older girls to finish prepping. No one would dare eat until Levi, Elizabeth, and I returned with Katy. We all grabbed oil lanterns off the front porch and headed for the valley where I had last seen her.

A run of trickling water whispered in the already darkened wood. The three of us separated, and I walked the center, crisscrossing the small stream by stepping on stones. Levi to my right and Elizabeth to my left walked along the halfway points of the embankments of the creek, moving toward the river. Elizabeth and Levi called out to Katy, but I remained silent, listening for her sobs. The last thing I wanted her to realize was I might find her, since I had caused her flight.

Halfway to the river, the terrain produced sizable boulders, and my progress slowed because of a need to check hollows and crevices where she might be hiding. The sounds of Katy's parents' calls signaled they had outdistanced me. Then a sniffle caught my ear, and I moved toward the sound of a more defined sob. Holding the lantern above my head to increase my field of vision, I spotted her, hunkered between a large tree and a house-sized stone. Her arms, folded, rested on her knees, and her head was bowed forward.

"Katy," I ventured.

"Go away." Her face was hidden in her arms.

"Katy, everyone is worried about you. Your mamm and pa love you. We've been looking for you." I spoke in a gentle tone. "What are you thinking?"

"You didn't have parents. You lived on your own. I can do the same and become just like you." Her words were punctuated by sobs.

"It wasn't by choice; I did what I had to do. It wasn't fun or anything good." No one ever told her this part of my history; she must have been listening when adults talked.

"I just want to experience your world."

"Katy, my world no longer exists. The world of the English has fallen into chaos. So you overheard the part of my story of living on the streets? What about the rest of the story?"

Katy lifted her head, taking a deep breath, then shook as she released it. Even in the dim light, I could see her swollen eyes as tears glistened on her cheeks. With the lantern lowered to the ground, I came to rest on a rock near her, my back against the enormous tree.

"When I was about ten, a wealthy woman rescued me and took to the ocean. A wonderful couple snuck me to America and finished raising me. They were amazing people. They taught me about love by loving me. Just like your mother and father. Did you overhear anyone speak about this part of the story?" As we sat, I shared my need to see my adoptive father and siblings. An empathetic Katy seemed to take solace in the sacrifice of our imminent parting.

Katy breathed in a normal pattern as she listened. In a few words, I told her of my adoptive parents and the manor they reconstructed. Their home became a place where misplaced children found love and warmth from the cold streets. I wanted to alert Levi and Elizabeth that I had found her, but I also wanted to bring peace to her heart.

"When we try to make things happen by our own will instead of God's will, well, in the long run, it can make things worse. We need to find your parents. Are you ready to go home for supper?"

Katy's only response was to stand with me and walk toward the river. Several calls echoed through the trees before Katy called out to her mother. When we gathered near the river, everyone shared hugs, but few words were exchanged. We all understood without them.

***

Two days later, I pushed my forty-five-year-old Harley out of the barn near the road. Levi and Rudy had secured five gallons of gasoline—no easy chore; it had been a two-month process. Filling my tank, I wondered how much the world had changed during my year here with these simple folk. Things had already gotten tight, as a third civil war in Mexico had flowed across the unsecured border with California and Arizona. Over the course of many years of hostilities in the old Southwest of the United States, fifteen million people had died. The supply chain to noncompliant citizens had been cut off. Digital money was required for all purchases, and small business owners had long given up their dreams. America's homeless population had grown to near 50 percent in the major cities, and crime ran rampant everywhere. For sure, the unknown lay before me. Here in Lancaster, rumors roamed, and several witnessed the occasional highway robbery, but hard news had been shut down nationwide for the last twenty years. After all, it had been a carload of thieves who killed my wife, Lisa, and left me for dead.

Levi and his friend watched as I filled my tank, checked my oil, and made sure all my stuff was secured to the rack over the rear fender. The morning sun returned to the dew, to the gentle breeze flowing up the Susquehanna. A flock of mallards squawked while traveling with the wind. They were in pairs, with females making the most noise.

The whole end-of-the-world thing wasn't playing like a Hollywood apocalyptic movie with nuclear war, zombies, and the walking dead, but conditions weren't good for the peasants. There had been a period of conditioning in the beginning. Everyone enjoyed the conveniences technology offered; then came the wave, a tsunami of tech changes where everything became scrutinized and judged. Social credits and demerits became keys to who could do certain things, like travel or make purchases. The big change, digital money, came with an expiration date of three years. It was no longer possible to save money to gain any independence. All these thoughts ran through my head as I prepped my bike as best I could. My plan was to head toward New England and pray I found some of my adopted siblings.

"Take care, Atanase, and watch out for the Acceptors." Levi grabbed my arm with one hand before he jammed his other meaty hand into mine for a solid, powerful shake.

The Amish used the term *Acceptors* to define the English who bought into the digital economy and were blind to the dark side. The Acceptors referred to anyone who resisted the controls of the new society as a Reprehensible. To Levi, I was an English Reprehensible, and I called him an Amish Reprehensible. We took pride in the label. Both my pistols were loaded and concealed. Illegal to own, both could get me a life sentence. To not carry was more likely to get me a death sentence, so I weighed the risk. My favorite is the KelTec, but the .380 is smaller, easier to conceal. Most of my ammo is twenty years old, purchased before the Constitution was repealed.

No one target practices; ammo needs to be saved for good purposes.

"Levi, I hope to be back someday. I just need to find my people—my father and siblings. I'll be praying for you and Elizabeth and the children. You know, I think Katy sees and knows things the average person walks by."

Levi gives my hand an extra squeeze and closes his eyes. He assures me, the whole community has me in their prayers.

TWO

Atanase

Lancaster sat west of my first destination by less than half a tank of gas through quiet rural areas. During my lifetime, such a trip had gone from a pleasantly quick hop to a dangerous, life-threatening enterprise. The unknown rested in the road conditions, as most people no longer were free to travel. Roads wandered into oblivion, as vegetation crept across long stretches of blacktop, and bridges rested in creek bottoms. Compared to highways, the farm roads offered safer options. The back roads avoided population centers between Amish country and the Brandywine area. The solitude allowed time to reflect on both the past and the future. It was twelve years since I last saw my father. He never got to meet my Lisa. The incident happened as Lisa and I were heading home to where I was raised.

Funny, Wilmington is only two hours from Amish country. With reports of several roving gangs and fuel shortages, in my weakened state it might just as well have been another continent. Drone patrols and checkpoints brought many areas under government control. The efforts eliminated a lot of the gangs but also restrict movements by the Reprehensibles. No fan of the current government or their laws, I was a renegade. The main difference between the gangs and the government: the latter claimed legitimacy.

A prayer cried in my heart for a drone to eliminate the ones who killed Lisa. How many times had this popped into my head? Don't be bitter, Scripture says, but my heart argued.

Amish country roads, not well maintained, were clear of obstacles. Good enough for buggies and the trailer trucks who came to collect the harvest. My first barrier presented itself as downed trees, utility poles, house rubble, barn debris, and a tangle of wires blocking my path. The entire mess was covered by snarled vines and brush, indicating it was old damage. Many rural areas came under attack during the great food shortages. This snag is on Village Road south of Lancaster, as I was avoiding troubled urban areas. Lancaster's population had dropped to 25 percent of its all-time high, fueled by food searches. Now, the Amish reported the area was a gang land.

At rest, I looked about. To my right, a bypass through the woods around the snag, nothing more than ruts worn by horses, wagons, and cattle, I supposed. Not an ideal track for a six-hundred-pound Harley, much better suited for a dirt bike. The silence was unnerving as I sat viewing the area. Rich in mud and ruts, long stretches of standing water reflected the trees above. I parked the bike to walk the bypass to assess the viability of a run on it. I can't risk getting laid up. A sudden drumming and flash stopped my heart as I spun in a defensive posture. A lone grouse in sudden flight, nothing to fear. A good two hundred yards in length, the trail offers a challenge. At the far end stand three burned-out houses, five white tail deer grazing on the lawn. For a moment they lifted their heads, then returned to feed. There was no sign of human activity.

My odds weighed, I returned to my bike and struck out at half throttle. To dare a rest stop under these conditions would have been a mistake. The motorcycle sashayed through the deep ruts. A rooster tail of water and mud spat from the rear tire. Spinouts and rock bumps didn't slow me too much; my outstretched legs saved me from losing my balance as I muscled the bike upright. Back on the road at the other end of the bypass, headlight to taillight, head to toe, every inch was caked in mud. In my burst onto the crumbling blacktop, the little deer herd scattered, as frightened as I was by the grouse. The next obstacle was quick to come into view: the collapsed bridge which should have crossed over Pequea Creek.

The bridge's road surface rested in the creek. Water a foot deep washed over the slabs. Probably the only opportunity I'd have to rinse the mud from my ride. Hitting the water caused a power wash to spray in all directions. The worn banks on each side of the creek afforded my access. Without a pause, I regained the roadway on the other side.

Not a house along Village Road was occupied or livable. The homes stood as ruins of dreams and monuments to a loss of heart. Greed, corruption, and international interests at the highest levels had done a job on the nation. As with Rome, Greece, and Egypt, the United States had collapsed under her own weight as its founding pillars cracked. Conspiracy? No, human nature brings on cultural collapse. Blame placement accomplishes little. We can't label it, then wrap it in pretty clothes; it simply all boils down to black hearts and selfishness. These conditions exist under every label, even some who claim to be Christian.

Strasburg served as an encampment for UN troops called Peacemakers. The UN roamed the United States at will. As the rule of law crumbled, many local militias had formed. The sitting president declared martial law and requested UN troop deployments. Most of the foreign troops came from Asia; none of them embraced American values or the rights of individuals.

Once declared, no one rescinded martial law. Now, eighteen years later, foreign troops still enforced the new laws of the land. The troops acted with displays of total disrespect and contempt for the citizenry.

I avoided town by traveling on Hagers Road, as I prayed for no outlier checkpoints. Only travelers with proper vaccination documentation, travel papers, and an Acceptors ID could travel. All others suffered at the mercy of the UN troops. Their treatment of women was unthinkable. Men just vanished, and if caught with a concealed weapon, disappearance was guaranteed. Mobile crematoriums prevented accurate body counts. Twin Elm Road proved clear sailing. A couple of runs on one-lane roads put me on Georgetown Road heading southeast without an encounter of a checkpoint. My thoughts drifted in the mix of the Harley's engine drone and the deserted road.

The manor where I grew up was a wonderland of art and music. Mother played the piano and sang almost every afternoon during one of our homeschool breaks. Father taught all the kids art, either painting or sculpting, depending on a child's interest. There were eighteen of us in all. Eight boys and ten girls, all adopted from disparate world cultures. We came to the manor at various ages, some in their midteens, all homeless street urchins. We kept to ourselves and didn't mingle with the children from town. Each of us would go on month-long travels to exotic destinations to learn about the cultures of other places. We had aunts and uncles, not by blood, who would escort us on these adventures. Our homeschooling included intense instruction in languages. We were privileged children; there appeared to be no money issues. The dinner parties always included new faces, and the men would disappear into the study for whispered meetings and drinks. When mother died, the fun began to wind down and father lost interest in most things. We all began to leave, some for college, some to travel. I wondered who, if anyone, would be there. I didn't even know if the manor still stood. I know there were other manors around the world with the same mission, the same network of benevolent providers checking in from time to time. Dropping into lowland, I felt a chill, a sign of fall's approach.

The devastation in the Ninepoints area resembled the aftermath of a tornado, and I slowed to avoid debris scattered on the road. A ghost town, there was no sign of life. The houses were rubble, and the vehicles along the street and in the driveways rusted in place, some intertwined with vegetation. Nature reclaims its territory fast when men no longer fight it back. A coyote stopped in the road in front of me, just for a moment, then bounded behind a rubble pile. If not for the threat of the human population, I figured I could learn to love the new order of the world. The slow pace and the wildlife have appeal. This was the intent—to cut back on the world population, not for the benefit of the peasants but for the elite and wealthy. The threat was real: I was now an outcast, a disposable.

Most of my siblings had left the manor before the great upheaval of tech controls. We had been taught to expect the world to change, to be outsiders. We were also given instruction on how to survive and certain tools to help. One was a credit card of sorts, which we could use without being legitimate or in the database. My father's friends Michael and Joaquim knew how to maneuver in the cyber world of finance. Their money flowed in and out of the world markets without a submission or acceptance to the world data bank. "Don't ask how, just benefit from their genius," I was told.

Homeville, Russellville, and Forestville were all in the same condition as Ninepoints. Russellville had an exception: I saw two people in the distance walking with a dog. I know they saw me; my bike startled them. I didn't dare stop to talk to them; these were not the days to trust anyone. The friendliest people could be snitches, or worse. The best I could do was crank on as a fast as I could. People had developed a new way to think, for a struggle for survival will always bring on change. America had always been a land of plenty and opportunity, whereas the third world had been where people struggled with life-and-death issues. Now those conditions existed in a crumbled America. The new American dream was to live—not live well, just live today.

Just before Forestville, a new issue arose: the overpass had collapsed, and barriers blocked both ramps onto Route 1. There was no way to get through, so I muscled my bike around and went back to turn right onto Penns Grove Road. A trailer truck backed out of the lot at the first building on the corner to block my path. As I came to an abrupt stop a short distance from the truck, two men with rifles ran toward me from the building. They weren't shooting, but I wasn't going to wait for them to start. Bullets were a premium; I knew they wouldn't pull a trigger unless they had a good reason and a good shot. Being a moving object was my best chance. In a spin I redirected back the way I came, on Newark Road. With my helmet on and with the roar of my bike, I couldn't hear the shots, but one shattered the mirror on my right, and another burned its way through the calf of my right leg. Must have been the adrenaline rush, but I didn't even consider slowing to check it. There would be time down the road. I leaned until my crash bars sparked on the surface and sped down Webb Road.

At Pusey Mill, I took another right and cranked out to 90 miles per hour. At West Baltimore Pike I turned left. There were people sitting, walking around along the road, more people than I had seen in years. They all turned to see me charging full-out down the road; there were no other operating vehicles in sight. I knew a little about the area from years ago and needed to get out of the population zone to check my leg. It had begun to throb. Just past Jennersville I made a hard right on a small farm road. West State Road took me back onto Newark Road where I continued my original route, still cranking out to 90 miles per hour. Appleton Road led to a more isolated farm area where I could stop to assess my wound. On a lonely stretch, I pulled off the road into an old bicycle trail parking lot, hidden by bushes and trees. I kicked my stand and killed the engine.

A patch of soft grass offered a place to lie down, but as I removed my boot, blood dripped from it. My sock was soaked red in its entirety. I pulled my pant leg up to reveal two holes, all in the muscle. A clean shot with no bone damage. The bleeding slowed; either the wound had tightened, or I had run out of blood. My guess is the bullet was a reload, with reduced strength. It slid through the muscle without imparting much energy, which saved the surrounding tissue. Still the pain racked through my entire body. Laid back, I closed my eyes and focused on the warmth of the sun. Rest was all I needed. This isolated patch offered a place to hide for as long as I needed. Recreational bicycling had died long ago; now bicycles were needed modes of transportation. By the looks of things, no one had parked in this parking lot for at least fifteen years.

"Looks like you got a little trouble there, fella."

The words snapped me out of my reverie. A slow, deep voice it was, with sort of a drawl. I propped myself up on my elbows and squinted at the figure between me and the sun. Nothing more than a silhouette, no clear features. If not for my head fog, the voice should have put me on guard, but I was too weak. Whoever he was, I was at his mercy.

"I've been shot."

"Yep."

Awkwardly, I rose to my feet, bearing most of my weight on my good leg. Light-headed, I stumbled but caught myself. Now the stranger took form, a grizzled old man on a bicycle strapped with an assortment of random articles. He leaned forward on the handlebars in my direction. He stroked his grey beard with one hand and fiddled with a smoke in the other.

"Nice motorcycle you got there. Don't see none no more. I used to ride back afore the collapse. Only special people can get fuel these days . . . you be one of them special folks, be ya?"

"Special? Nobody's special. Circumstance can be special, how you react to your circumstance can be special, but all humans are just the same." Lights flashed in my eyes—not from an external source; these were nerve flashes. Every breath I took burned in my throat. It took all I had to stay upright and not collapse. If I lost consciousness, this old dude might slit my throat.

"Don't know you, but I just might come to like ya. Don't find many likables in my travels. Who shot ya?" the old fella asked as he looked me over.

"No idea, it was an ambush."

"Lot of them these days, probably wanted your bike and gas. Very worth killing for these days."

The knowing in his eyes chilled me, intelligent and practical. In his younger days he must have been someone to reckon with.

"I suppose." My muscles tensed in readiness in case he attacked me. I was wounded, but he was old.

"I've never been low enough to resort to it. But I figure at some point it might be required of me."

The old man laid his bike on the ground and took a long drag on his smoke and offered me a hit.

"Good stuff, you could use it more than me. I just got a little rheumatism, you got worse."

"No thanks."

"Suit yourself. Let me help you clean up and bandage the wound. Lay back down, try to relax. You might be going into shock from blood loss."

The old man took a flask of water out of the pack he had strapped on his handlebars and poured some water on my wound. I juked from the sting. *Relax?* The dried blood on my skin melted in thinned streams and dripped to the grass.

"Better not to soften the scabs of the penetrations. I just want to clean up your skin. You have a rag we can wrap tight around it?" he asked as he squeezed the burning ember out of his smoke and dropped his roach into his shirt pocket.

"In my right saddlebag, I have some T-shirts and such," I said.

As he stood to walk to my motorcycle, he paused. "People call me Gus."

"Nice to meet you, Gus. I'm Atanase."

"Atanase is it? That's a new one on me."

I was born in Romania and adopted by a couple from America."

"Don't say. They treat you well?"

"Yes, very well. It was like hitting the lottery, only better . . . the lottery doesn't include love."

"Love? Ah yes, we're all born in search of it," he mumbled. His words weren't meant for me. "Quit believing in a woman's love a long way back. When I left, I forgot to tell her I wouldn't be back." Gus had no need for my thoughts and focused on my wound. "Clean through, didn't hit anything vital." He turned and opened my saddlebag.

With one T-shirt he wiped the blood from my leg and foot. With his KA-BAR he cut another T-shirt into strips for bandages. He suggested building a fire, heating up his knife, and cauterizing my wounds. Waiting to see if the bleeding stayed stopped on its own seemed better to me. After he finished bandaging my wounds, he built a fire. He thought it best I give myself time to restore some blood. As he stripped his gear from his bike, he shared a little history of himself. Called himself a wanderer, said he had been fifteen years out and about. His military training as a Special Forces operative kept him alive; for what, he said, he didn't know. He thought right here in this old parking lot looked like a good enough place to hang a day or two.

My father's place wasn't far; I wanted to get on the road. But the old man thought I needed time to build some blood, or I may faint down the road. My body knew he was right, but my hard head argued.

"Sorry to hear you don't believe in love."

"Not what I said. Love is what makes all things worthwhile. What I was thinking, I quit believing in the love of a woman. The truth is, I've never known the love of a woman. It's all silly now, at one time it was all important and how foolish we were to fret over such things. The world changed and what had been perceived as problems then seem silly now. When I got divorced, I gave my wife everything, I walked away with no regrets for doing it. My mistake, and I owned it. Before I married her, my buds said I deserved better. When you are in love, you truly can be blind. To tell you the truth, I gave nothing away. Everything I had acquired, I did it for my family. It all belonged to them; now all that is worthless, destroyed. Don't cling to the things of the world, hold them with a light grip." Gus pauses and his eyes find their way to mine. "Well, listen to me going on like I know something."

The campfire blazed, without much smoke. He put on a pot of water into which he added vegetables he had gathered while bicycling earlier in the day. Most of the plants looked like weeds to me. Soon it started to have an aroma like food. He chatted away like a trucker at a rest stop. He went in depth about AI links implanted in the brains of the Acceptors, which didn't sit well with him. There were thousands of low-orbit satellites interacting with the chip implants; it just wasn't natural or healthy, he thought. When he first saw me, he thought I might be one of them since I had a motorized machine and gasoline.

To lighten the conversation, I told him about living with the Amish; this sparked him in another direction. He received a lot of help from the plain folk and trusted them dearly. These days it took all a person's effort to sort people out, know who to trust, but the Amish were easy. They didn't buy into anything the government or big tech is selling. To counter all this, I told him about Katy, her innocence and insight. Levi would be a good contact for him, I figured, and I told Gus to let them know I was all right. Gus shared stories about his children and home life; he did have a soft side after all.

"I did love her at one time. I fell for her, and we had some kids. She lusted after me for a couple of months, maybe. But after a while I figured out, she just loved men, or at least their attention. She taught me two things: never chase a rejection and don't try to compete with a fantasy. It crushed me, but I stayed to give some kind of stability to my kids. I couldn't see them having fifteen fathers before graduating from high school. I was gone a lot on deployments, so I just ignored a lot of it, never saw no need for my ego to get any affirmation from her." Gus jabbed a stick in the campfire coals.

"How long were you in the service?" I asked, with a desire to help him distance himself from painful memories.

"Too long, another of life's blunders. I went in full bore, like a patriot, same as my marriage. Didn't know the country was in the hands of the same type as my old lady. Did my part, shame on them—backstabbers, everyone. Both took all I had to give, my own fault. Lying to yourself is the worst kind of lying. You know, a woman can cut you up into small soft pieces and leave you on the ground; never met an enemy combatant who could pull it off. Worse part, the kids cling to her. I get treated like I spent my days hanging out in a bar."

"So you don't hear from your kids?" It proved hopeless to shift the mood.

"No, they don't want to hear nothin' from me. Best off on my own."

I could sense Gus's tension talking about these two subjects, so I tried to conjure up something more cordial to talk about. Gus suffered from PTSD; I could read it in his tone. He retrieved a couple of bowls from his pack and ladled out a big helping from the fire for me. He stood watching as I tried it. It was hot, so I sipped some broth directly from the bowl. Gus told me of his walk toward a high bridge on a limited-access highway on a rainy night after leaving his wife. The local police picked him up. Both officers in the vehicle were veterans, one male and one female. They recognized his depression and offered light conversation while he rode with them on their night patrol. At the end of their shift, they dropped him off at his motel with an offer to be available if he needed them, and the three of them hugged farewell. Gus needed a prayer, and I silently offered one.

"Well? How the hell is it?" Gus asked.

"Good, very good." The change in mood and the soup.

"Damn right it's good. It'll heal you right up, and those magic mushrooms will have you seeing paisley-covered elephants. Your bone marrow will be in overdrive pumping out blood cells. One of the good things I got out of military survival school, finding adaptogens in the wild. Most of what I eat is foraged. Some stuff I get from farms, but I can get by just on what's lying around."

Wait a minute! Paisley-covered elephants, magic mushrooms—he blew by those words awful quick. Giving a stare, he grinned, knowing I had caught his words and wondered. He certainly looked the part for a guy with magic mushrooms, but he wouldn't, would he? We both burst out in laughter, and he told me I needed to be more cautious of who I trusted. It was his way of recovering from the dark mood he had fallen into.

"Amazing, I never heard the word *adaptogens*," I said once our laughter died.

"A lot of knowledge is based on stuff learned over thousands of years, what works and what kills you. When they outlawed printed books, I managed to steal a few from the library at the base where I was stationed. One book was by some guy named Tero Isokauppila and a woman named Broida. The book is long gone; it got wet during a storm and never did dry out right." Gus said.

"Can we get back to the magic mushrooms and elephants?" I asked.

Gus smiled and gave me a wink. It was a joke. I hoped.

With the night came distant howls from coyotes, more like modern wolves. As society fell apart, domestic dogs had blended back into nature and bred with wild coyotes. The result of the breeding created much larger canines, very intelligent and sly. In the bushes around our camp, we heard the rustling of leaves and branches, and I pulled out my .380. Gus remained nonchalant, whittling on a stick.

"Did you hear those howls? I think they're moving in on us, Gus."

"Nah, those mushrooms are kicking in. A paisley elephant is gonna bust through those bushes any minute," Gus joked, put down his whittling stick, and put away his knife.

"Seriously, Gus."

"Raccoons," Gus said.

"Raccoons? How do you know? Raccoons don't howl."

"This ain't my first sleep-out. Raccoons always come scrounging 'bout this time. Probably ten of the little fellas out there. As far as the howls are concerned, they're probably escapees from the wolf sanctuary north of Lancaster. The sanctuary cared for wolves and wolf-dog hybrids before the collapse. I've run into them a time or two; they don't bother anyone."

"I've never encountered any raccoons or wolves, and I've camped out plenty," I responded.

"They don't come to every campsite, depends on what part of the country you're in. I know the noise in the bushes are raccoons." Just as Gus finished his sentence, two raccoons wandered from the brush, swaying side to side with noses in the air, trying to catch the scent of food. They wandered to within three feet of us, but no closer. Gus said to just leave them be, and after not finding food, they returned to the brush. The rustling twigs and leaves went silent.

"Ever eat coon?" Gus asked.

"No."

"Not very good, but in a pinch, a person will eat anything," Gus said as he picked at some veggie fragments stuck between his teeth.

Not wanting to dwell on the thought, I changed the subject. "Where you headed, Gus?"

"Going to see some Amish folk. If invited, I'll stay the winter, otherwise, I'll head south. I've got a route I keep, so I pretty much know what to expect. But these days, there's always something strange going on, just like running into you. Might look up those ones you know, if mine are in a bad way."

***

In the morning at first light, Gus sat near a small fire sipping from a cup. My leg burned, and I winced as I sat up.

"Help yourself to a cup of chicory, tastes a bit like coffee. Grows along the roads." Gus hands me a cup.

"Thanks."

"Did you hear the horses?" Gus asked.

"Horses?"

"You must have slept. There were about twenty, I judge. Heading the way you're going. I heard them coming, and I positioned myself to watch. Either militia or outlaws, not much difference, all fearsome fellas. They trotted on the road, lucky us being hidden in this parking lot. Folks seem to be getting more organized, grassroots movements and warlords. How's the chicory? Best we got, haven't had coffee in years."

"It's good. I've had some before," I responded, more interested in the men on horses. Heading the same way I was going didn't sound good.

THREE

Atanase

After chicory and biscuits, I packed my things and said a thank-you to Gus before I headed out. Gus planned to stay another day in camp, and tried to talk me into it, but the manor wasn't far. My need to see my father overrode everything. Gus had it right: two miles down the road, regret set in, but my hard head wouldn't cave to my body's needs. I did pay heed to Gus's warnings to stay on the alert for the horsemen. Gus concluded they must have held up during the day if they rode at night. He figured, ten miles out, I could ease up on worry. He doubted they could have made it any farther. The road had some washouts but proved passable, and horse hoofprints in the dirt put me on alert.

On the open road I could outrun any horse, unless ambushed at a fallen tree or other obstruction. Knowing they were ahead of me and they weren't expecting someone on a motorcycle gave me an advantage.

Full bore, I cranked it out, leaning low in the turns. The rubble of burned-out houses along the road were but blurs. At mile eight I rounded a blind curve, to the sight of horses and horsemen scattered all over the road. The horses spooked, and several reared, almost throwing their riders, while others ran in chaos. The riders didn't have time to comprehend the commotion and each rider struggled to control his beast. So close to hitting a couple of horses, I swear I felt hair brush the knuckles on my left hand. In milliseconds it was over; I looked in my one good rearview mirror to watch the recovery. The horses danced and pranced, bumping into each other. The riders yelled; I couldn't hear them, I just knew they cursed. One concern was behind me, and no one got hurt. For a hundred yards I kept an eye on my rearview mirror before I banked into another tight turn.

A left onto Strickersville Road took me through White Clay Creek Reserve, and I came out on London Tract Road, trying to avoid areas with housing developments. At Southwood Road, the demographics changed; there were electric cars on the roads and houses were intact. This was the land of the Acceptors, the digit heads who bought into the program. The biggest danger: they were snitches and would turn any noncompliant person in without hesitation. My motorcycle stood out, but it didn't scream noncompliant; it just meant I had a fuel source most weren't privileged with. It would bring suspicion, but as long as I kept moving and to myself, I would be safe. These areas were well policed and controlled, civilized. Hockessin, Ashland, and Centerville bustled in a creepy sort of way, with lots of electric cars and electric-assisted bicycles. By creepy, I mean, people were sort of living the same as they did before the collapse.

My heart raced as I rode through Winterthur; I was coming home after so many years. Apprehension embraced me as I pulled off the asphalt where the gravel drive winds into the thick woods. From the road no one would suspect the two tracks of gravel went to a manor. Stopped, I sat to compose myself. My leg burned and I felt weak. The bandage, wet with fresh blood, needed attention. My focus changed from my leg to the ones who raised me, Jim and Maxine, my adoptive parents. Although, a legal adoption never actually took place. A rescue from the streets of Romania, my biological parents the victims of the revolutionists. My new parents civilized me, taught me traditions and manners of living that worked to create a shared bond that moved ever onward and upward. But their love of children proved so great, their rescue efforts went beyond me. They continued to rescue others. We became a brood of brothers and sisters who learned about and believed in a power greater than any earthly king or sovereign.

I knew the manor may no longer exist; my father may be dead or in prison. Communications for the noncompliant had broken down years ago. The manor had always been off the radar, an invisible parcel never registered with any government entity. The arrangement was sustained by a network of altruistic people, greater than wealth or any government. Deep breaths helped dissipate my fears. I started the motorcycle and kicked it into gear. In a hundred feet I stopped to open the old gate, remembering the first time we came. Mother and Father were exhausted, and I sat in the back seat hugging old Storm dog. He was quite a dog, a large golden. After walking the gate full open, I mounted the cycle and rumbled up the drive into the trees and rounded a turn where the manor came into full view.

Nothing had changed: the mature landscape, stone, glass, wood timbers, and slate roof, all as Father, Mother, I, and the others had restored it. Inviting and splendid, it was drenched in classical strength, a six-hundred-year-old house built to endure. I stopped in the parking lot near the front walk, and the bike went silent. Enthralled, I sat, slow to remove my helmet and riding gloves. My leg pained me; it took all I had to rise and dismount. Under my breath I whispered a prayer for Father to be here and well. No one was about the yard; the gardens as always were well tended. *Someone is living here.* The large front double door befitted a church. One side cracked open. Father stepped out onto the front veranda.

"What's all the noise?" Father shouted.

My helmet fell to the ground next to my bike, my gloves dropped on top of it, and I limped toward him without a word. He stood straight, tall, but I could see advanced age in and around his eyes and in his weathered skin. My father, Jim Fisher, who always said, "The eyes are a window into our soul and God's window to the world." Jim believed God's view of the world came through the eyes of every living creature. God knows everything because every living thing feeds back to him, so he sees and senses his creation at every level.

"Atanase?" First a whisper. "Atanase!" he shouted as he stepped in my direction.

The pain eased in my leg; I felt light and within a split second we embraced, our sobs synchronous. Our tears ran unashamed; neither of us could speak or let go. When we released, Father's hands gripped my shoulders as his eyes dropped to my leg wound. His still powerful hands squeezed my shoulders.

"Atanase, what happened to your leg?" he thundered.

"It's a flesh wound, it'll be fine." I replied. "Gunshot."

"Come . . . come inside. Let me take a look."

Memories flooded my mind as I stepped into the entryway. Mother's portrait hung just above our heads. Her aroma still hung in the air, but how could that be? So many years gone by, and still the laughter of children echoed in the hall. The sound of Mother tickling the keys on the piano in the study? Father gave me a look when I stopped to listen. His grin assured me I wasn't crazy.

"Son . . . are you all right? Do you need to lean on me?"

"No, I'm fine . . . but I hear, smell . . ."

"Yes, it happens. It happens to me also. Don't talk about it. Enjoy . . ." Father's voice cracked.

We stood for a moment until things settled, then continued to the kitchen. Father placed a kettle of water on the stove as I peeled back the bandages on my leg. As he examined my wound, I shared my adventure of the last two days of travel. He fetched clean bandages and disinfectant from a closet. After rebandaging my leg, he served tea.

"I traveled the West in search of enclaves of believers. There are others out there. Scattered and desperate, but they exist in isolated dispersion. In Wyoming I met a very special woman. We married and we were traveling here, so you could meet . . ." My words choked off, and I took a sip of tea. Father didn't say anything; his eyes dropped toward his teacup. There was no rush, no pressure in this home, ever. When we finished our cup, Father asked if I would like more.

"Lisa was as close to your Max as I ever found. Sixty miles from here, she was killed and I was left for dead. The world out there is a horrid place since the collapse," I mustered.

"Sorry, son. We knew it was coming, and it's going to get worse."

"I know, but it doesn't make it any easier," I replied.

"Do you have a plan?"

"Short term was to come here, check on you. After, I want to try to find the others. Do you have any word from anyone?" I asked.

"Some. There's several in New Hampshire, a town called Gorham, on the Androscoggin River. An old hydroelectric plant supplies electric to the town. They've turned some old textile plants into manufacturing facilities, making items to barter with. They're a sovereign municipality, with no real estate taxes. The community chips in to do all the labor for upkeep, and the schoolteachers are volunteers. No telling how much longer they'll get away with it. Last report, there's a lot of drone activity in the area." Father poured us both hot water.

"Sounds interesting. I guess it's my long-range plan. After I heal. Unless you want me to stay and help around here. How's your blood pressure?"

"Meds have become impossible to get. The critters help me to lower my blood pressure."

Jim Fisher and his animals—he loved all creatures and somehow the animals sensed it. He found peace caring for them.

"When I was a young man, you know I worked as an electrical system operator. Before I met Max. I grew tired of the stress, the storms and recovery. I just wanted to be an artist, so I escaped to the islands. The storms kept coming, son. They're never ending. It's war, spiritual warfare. I am so sorry about Lisa. This manor is coming to an end. Michael and Joaquim are still in the fight and take good care of me, but both have admitted the authorities are closing in on them. It's all a matter of time before all of us are found out. You stay as long as you want; it doesn't matter so much where they kill us. What matters more is how we live until the time comes."

"You taught me so much . . . We should find a way to get you meds. What about Michael or Joaquim, can they help with that?"

"It was a fair trade; you don't realize how much I learned by raising you. Michael and Joaquim have enough on their plate."

After tea we retreated to the study. Every room had books, but the study surpassed all the other rooms combined. Books were where thoughts were safely kept. Once printed, each physical copy couldn't be changed without a black mark or crossed-out line. This is why they were such a threat to the new order. Now thoughts are like smoke in some distant digital fog: if erased there's no trace, no torn-out page. Father had aged; he was still mentally sharp, but his movements were deliberate and slow. He hadn't painted since Mother died. His time was spent in the gardens and canning the harvest. The study's walls from floor to ceiling were covered in books. Contraband. Such a collection would secure a long prison sentence. I pull a book from a shelf and sit in an easy chair. Father drops in his rocking chair empty-handed.

"So what do you have there, son?"

"*Leviathan* by Thomas Hobbes," I reply.

"Interesting choice, considering the state of things."

I place the book in my lap. I've read it before. Tonight I'll peruse it.

While I know our sovereign Lord is supernatural, it's helpful to be reminded of the nature of human thinking, always grasping to provide their own answers.

"Besides those in New Hampshire, do you know about any of the others?"

"It's been a long time, but a few headed to a place called Port Norris, New Jersey. Last I heard, they were feeding themselves off catches on the water, big oyster area. Shell Pie and Bivalve have a history of not welcoming outsiders, two areas to avoid even when times were good. Doubt you can track them down. There was a lot of damage down there. A lot of defiant people were executed. I don't have much hope for them. Not worth the risk to contact them."

My interest piqued. I decided before I retired for the evening, I'd grab an atlas. Risk? Under the circumstances of the day, everything was a risk. There wasn't much to lose or live for these days. There was only one thing to look forward to, and we all prayed he would come soon.

Father's black cat jumped into his lap; at twenty years old, she was still spry. Father had found her squashed on the road at the end of the driveway. She was just a kitten, one and a quarter pounds, with a head as big as her body. She couldn't move her hind legs. We kept her in a cardboard box for several days. Her paralysis faded with time. We think she had been run over by a car. We named her Angel. Her body grew to fit her head; matter of fact, now her head looked too small for her body. Father stroked her as we shared stories of the times we had been apart. Father loved to talk about Max and repeated stories I had heard many times, but I just let him go on.

The peace of the manor had never changed. The world spun out of control, but the chaos was somewhere far away. Father refused to discuss any of it; what we thought or felt didn't matter. His big interest was the wildlife of the estate, keeping the deer, squirrels, rabbits, and ducks fed. His funny duck and chicken stories brought tears to my eyes. One might mistake them for tales of his children. One of his chickens roosted on a clutch of duck eggs, and when they hatched, she claimed them as her chicks. She went wild when Father separated them. He didn't want chicken-imprinted ducklings. The chickens would come to the kitchen door begging for cookies, and the deer would take apples from his hand. The manor must be how it all started in the garden of Eden. Father was still so content, even while there were those in the cities and countryside killing and grubbing for more. Madness, pure madness had consumed mankind. The world seemed as it must have been in the days of Noah.

Father served a late dinner of fresh garden vegetables and fruit. Afterward, in pain and tired, I retreated to the bedroom I had grown up in. The manor was spotless, kept in such a way as to offer comfort to anyone at any time. The room smelled fresh, but I slid open a couple of windows to enjoy a breeze. With a couple of extra pillows I elevated my wounded leg. In the atlas I found Port Norris and quickly calculated the distance. There were population centers along the way, but the atlas was so old, and I knew demographics had changed. About sixty miles and ninety minutes, when times were good. The Delaware Memorial Bridge was a big if. Without the bridge, my trip was out of the question. There were a couple of other bridges on the way. No rush. I tossed the atlas aside and focused on *Leviathan*.

Good old Thomas Hobbes, preaching about the need for a leader and protector. A central power to save us from anarchy. Funny, never in the history of man had a more powerful and controlling central government existed. The system tracked every participant and their every move. No one could buy or sell anything without being registered to do so. Once registered, life was convenient and easy. As long as you did not question the all-powerful leaders. Hobbes is correct: outside the system there is disarray and pandemonium. Hobbes refutes divine rights; individual rights are given away in the contract to the central power. It had been so long since I read this book, but I had often mulled what I remembered. It took three hundred years for Hobbes's theories and beliefs to come to term. The human condition had been reduced to an anthill, and noncompliance meant death. I read late into the night, before I drifted off to sleep, thinking about a world where humans are happy to let God be God, acknowledging his divine plan.

The sun woke me with the first rays of the day. The intense burst of light through the window caught my face. A shift of my pillow blocked it, but the damage was done. My leg still pained me; I needed the bathroom. I stumbled across the hall to the bathroom. Father was in the kitchen cooking breakfast when I came down the stairs. He mumbled an old melody from his teens, "Come Sail Away" by Styx. He stopped when he found me leaning against the kitchen doorway.

"Don't stop. You sound pretty good," I said, sad my presence had silenced him.

"I loved sailing. If I wasn't so old, I would sail away . . . it wouldn't be the same without . . ."

"We had an awesome time crossing the Atlantic. Remember the dolphins?"

"Aye, I do. I think about those days often. I still have all your paintings."

"You're kidding."

He spooned scrambled eggs and hash browns onto two plates. The old woodstove had cooked a million meals. In an instant he dumped slices of toast from a hot griddle on top of the mess on the plates. He gestured me to sit and put a plate in from of me. He remained standing as he said grace, thanking the Lord for all his blessings and for bringing me home. As we ate, we reminisced about the early days of the manor and the parties when visitors came from far off. Now, as he refreshed my memory, some vague thoughts I carried became clarified. At the time, as a boy, I saw things as pretty matter-of-fact. The intrigue had gone well over my head. Funny how adults assume children grasp experiences the same as they do. One name always captivated me, Cactus Jack. For years I pictured him living in some desert far from water. His name came up at every gathering, and yet I never knew the true story. Now for the first time, Father filled in all the holes, right down to his arrest for murder.

Cactus Jack was a musician, a drifter, and a sailor who had helped Jim Fisher escape the island of St. Croix. Jim Fisher rescued a homeless man from the streets; this was Michael. Wow, things were coming together as Father talked. He had an answer for every question I threw at him. Michael's father was one of the main characters in setting the circumstances for the collapse of all the world's economies. Father told it all as we lingered. So many pieces I had in my head but had never known how they fit. What of Cactus Jack? Where was he now? I'd never met him, unlike Joaquim and Michael, whom I would know on sight.

"What happened to Cactus Jack?"

"Max's brother spent a lot of time and money; he got him released just before the collapse. Your mother's brother bought a big sailboat, and the two of them sailed off. I tell myself they lived happily ever after, but there is no such thing in this world anymore. The revolution is complete, there is only one hope left." Father ended the conversation. We had eaten and consumed two pots of tea, and he excused himself to the bathroom while I cleaned the dishes and kitchen.

Out in the yard by the pond, we watched the ducks swim and chase each other. Father spoke as we sat on a bench.

"We are living a similar story of Exodus. When the collapse came, people were offered a choice. The established structures had been removed; chaos reigned. No one knew how to function, so the revolutionaries offered an alternative to freedom, enslavement. Those who chose to submit to an all-powerful structure found comfort. Those who chose not to submit lost their freedom and wandered aimlessly like the freed slaves of Egypt. Michael and Joaquim have tried to bring order without tyranny to those in the wilderness. It's a delicate situation and a threat to the revolutionists. Moses accomplished bringing the wandering slaves into an ordered society, a free society. To be free, we must have order, but not tyranny. It had been our hope the children we raised here, in the manor, would take up the challenge of leadership. It doesn't appear they have."

We were all raised reading and knowing the Bible. Father had a way of applying Scripture to current events. Sure, all of his children knew the book of Revelation, but reading it and living it are quite different. There is everyday functionality, the day-to-day suffering. Half the world now lived in chaos and were wandering lost throughout the world. The Acceptors lived in comfort at the expense of individual freedom. The Reprehensibles were just beginning to organize, on local, small scales. Yet they also warred with each other, and the Acceptors looked down on them.

With the loss of Lisa, knowing Father was okay, I had a burning desire to check on my siblings scattered in this fallen world. But I knew everything must be in God's time. My leg needed a couple more weeks, though my heart, it would never heal. My days became filled with searching for things to do around the manor, reading, and having long talks with Father. On occasion, I visited the grave of Storm and had one-sided chats sitting on the concrete bench under the maple tree. What a dog, uncommon in many ways; he always had a sense about him. He knew things were going to happen; he would react to your thoughts. He could be in another room, and if I thought about going outside, I would hear him shake loose his fur as he stood to come to me.

In preparation for my departure, I coaxed Father into accepting my plan to search for my siblings, packed some essentials, and mounted an extra container of gasoline on the rack behind my seat. The distance was not so great; the travel time would depend on detours and obstacles. The whole of lower New Jersey had fallen into a vast nowhere land. Wildlife and vegetation reclaimed most of the previously populated areas. God's creation was recovering in many places, even if humankind was not.

But the true wastelands were north in Philadelphia, New York City, and Newark with many crime-ridden streets full of homeless drug addicts. The wilds would offer a safer haven for a Christian.

***

We sat on the back deck for morning tea, the sun warming us as we watched the ducks cavorting on the pond. Their butts tilted toward the sky as they searched the shallows for pond weed.

"You know the others all chose their paths. It's the gift of freewill. Your mother and I fed all of you the same, yet you all grew differently. In my eyes, you fit the images of our aspirations. You never know a person by jawing with them; their real self can only be found in their actions and reactions. It doesn't make you better, you just met our expectations. We love you all, Atanase—"

"Father, you don't have to say anything. I love you and appreciate all you did for me."

"Yes, appreciate, it's what I mean. Many of the others left, never looked back. I don't hear from them; silence tortures the heart. Times are tough, communications aren't easy, but I sit here all alone. I've reached a point where, not only is my solitude acceptable, it is preferred."

"Don't say that Father. Without you, I have no anchor." His words chilled me.

"I'm old, useless to anyone but those ducks and the deer. To them, I'm an easy source of food, nothing more."

"I'm going to hunt down the others. My plan is to head south first, to Port Norris."

"It's dangerous. I think it may not be worth it. The others have chosen their paths, it's everyone's option. God's greatest gift is freewill. I pray for them, but nothing is by my will."

"The whole world is dangerous, deceptive. I need to find out what has become of the family. The ones I grew up loving."

"Atanase, you are a special one."

"No, Jim Fisher is special, you gave so much. Enough about this, I leave in the morning. I'll be fine and will be back as soon as I can."

FOUR

Jim/the manor/Deena

Atanase was gone, and Jim Fisher sat alone on the back deck sipping tea in the morning sun. He'd said his good-byes over breakfast and retreated to the deck as Atanase left by the front door. With closed eyes he listened to the motorcycle fade in the distance. With a nod, he thought, *Everything fades.* He opened his eyes as a momma deer plucked an apple from a tree, her fawn several feet away facing the pond, curious about the ducks. Everything in balance. He placed his cup on the end table moments before he fell asleep.

***

It's been said, if a home could speak, the stories it could tell. Let me, who laid the foundation of this home, speak. My dream, and my restless spirit still dwell in this place. Long before Jim Fisher's dream, I had mine. But it was cut short when they hung me from that tree. Well, that story goes all the way back to before this nation formed, and now I watch as freedom dies. As a spirit, I know things no mortal does. Must I rest and keep such things to myself? No, I'm going to share my insights with you. With Atanase gone, I'll do my best. Call me The Watcher. When someone enters the surrounding area, I can see into their heart and mind. There are no limits on me. With my death came a release, and renewal. Now I have a desire to become a part of the rest of the story.

***

Leaving the asphalt, tires cracked gravel for an instant before coming to rest on the gravel track that rolls up a slight grade into a dense forest. In all her twenty-eight years, Deena had never ventured alone onto an unpaved road; her heart pounded. Lush vegetation consumed the lane, leaving only the beginning of the next gravelly curve visible. Deena tapped her phone to open the GPS, verify the address and client profile; it all matched. She stared at the lonely unimproved road leading into the unknown, as sunlight streamed through hemlock branches to illuminate patches of grass along the lane's edge. Songbirds fluttered and danced in the dappled light as if they were natural floodlights. Beautiful and inviting as it might be to some, to Deena it was unnatural. Deena's world consisted of ribbons of asphalt passing through buildings of ordered concrete and glass with sprinklings of green plantings.

A vague ugly memory, twenty-one years in the past, raised a fear of woods and desolation strong enough to override this visual splendor. Her unfamiliarity with any person who might be attracted to life away from the crowd made her shiver even in the late August heat. The last time she had been in a wooded area was during the collapse. She was a child, a very young child. Her finger hit the lock button for her doors, and ever so slowly she rolled forward, her electric vehicle silent. I know her thoughts: *Be brave. Nothing ever interferes with my sense of duty*. The crunch of gravel unnerved her. She continued to trundle around the first bend, then the second, on to the top where the gravel spread into a lot. The sight of me caused her to freeze, but I read her mind. Her thoughts were on yesterday, her motive for being here.

Yesterday, the new operating system installed at the Citizen Assessment Office had identified an anomaly. Deena took the system through its paces; her fingers flashed across the keyboard, her eyes locked on the files scrolling across her screen until an oddity was flagged, a file Deena had never come across. It unsettled her, for she knew her area and the census well. This file was so unique she surely would have taken note before. The new AI software could coordinate data from many sources and come to conclusions. The address shouldn't exist. The surrounding area held no private land; these were public lands. She switched to satellite mapping, clicked on layers, zoomed to the area in question, and found it blurred. The smudge on the map was like those found when zooming in on military facilities. This estate sat on the edge of a wetland preserve.

Either the new system had a glitch, or someone had erected a dwelling on government land protected by military masking. Numbers and words had flashed on the screen as the processor questioned its own results. Deena switched to her older system to check the deed files to cross-reference; she poured over plot maps and deeds. Sure enough, the meets and bounds didn't add up. She double-checked her calculations—there seemed to be a chunk of missing land. The new AI system posted its own verification. Deena poured herself a cup of coffee and perused the data patiently and concisely. Nothing ever got past her; numbers were her life. She sipped her coffee. No paper files existed, as paper had been outlawed when Deena was in grade school; now all records were digital. The new algorithm identified a major glitch, but how was it possible? Deena needed answers, plain and simple. A physical investigation, a drive to the area. The new AI system posted an order, and no one was to question the demands of the new AI supervisor. Deena confirmed she understood the instructions.

When the AI system drilled down into obscure files, the property was unregistered. But material deliveries to the property showed names, James and Maxine Fisher. This was Deena's starting point. This AI central computer system could cross-reference all commerce transaction for forty years, back before the collapse. Next, the AI system searched for records of James Fisher. *No way*! The man listed was well past the age of usefulness; he should be warehoused or dead. The age data was surmised by a vague record, very sketchy, of a high school reunion. No other record of this man existed; AI flagged it as a violation, someone who'd destroyed all his records. It is as if this one record had been missed by whoever tried to eliminate this man. The record listed only a brief mention of the period leading up to Fisher's forties. Place of birth, Winnipesaukee, New Hampshire, but he graduated from high school in Pennsylvania, attended the University of

Pittsburgh, had worked for an electric utility. The man dropped off the face of the earth, records scrubbed—all but this one from a high school reunion. Deena and the AI system searched in parallel from every angle possible. Cross-referencing and double-checking, she found he had no social security number. Maxine Fisher had no records at all.

Deena worked late into the night. At her apartment she couldn't even relax after her shower. She sat on her balcony in her robe staring across the twinkling lights of the city, sipping wine. A surge enveloped Deena: anger would be unprofessional, although she felt all the trappings of the word. Anything outside the norm unsettled her, conditioned to believe in the order of the state. On top of her own feelings, she knew she had to satisfy the AI system. The pressure was on.

***

Limestone walls broken by panes of leaded glass and wood timbers outlining stucco gave the look of an ancient six-hundred-year-old house. One which should contain a lot of history. The beams were joined together by black hammered iron works. A structure like none she had ever seen in the cookie-cutter developments of the city. She thought of long-forgotten fairy-tale magic, which her mother had read to her from now banned paper books. Yes, as a little girl she heard stories of castles, knights, princesses, and other wonders. Those thoughts she'd locked away years ago. Never once did she imagine such a place could exist. Eyes widened, she tilted forward against the steering wheel to take in the rise of splendor. Her windshield filled with the spectacle. Magnificent, inadequate to describe the marvel she beheld. Her shifter slipped into park, and she stepped from her vehicle to gawk. Her gaze dropped to the surrounding gardens, in full bloom, lush native wildflowers in abundance. Butterflies flooded the air. Nothing had prepared her for such an encounter, certainly not her career or her dealings with citizens. Perched at the side of the main walkway, all twisted and gnarled sat a gargoyle holding a sign, a long-knotted finger pointing at the lettering "Go away!" Such a hideous unwelcome sight.

"Help you, Miss?"

Startled by the words from nowhere, the spell broke. Deena snapped back from her childhood fantasies. Her eyes searched for the source of the words.

"Over here!"

She turned toward the voice, noticing a tall elderly man in ragged work clothes, obviously the gardener or caretaker, standing at the corner of the house. Such tattered clothing deceived her eyes for a moment. As he approached, she shifted her focus to his face, elegantly kind and wise, but she couldn't relate.

"I guess I gave you quite a start. Please accept my apology," the man graciously offered.

"Oh no, I was just absorbed by these facilities. Are you the caretaker?"

"I am and, well, like I said, can I help you?"

Men of his age are either euthanized or warehoused, she thought. She'd never spoken to one; the state labeled them as burdens. A vague recollection of her grandfather crept into her head, but she suppressed it.

"The owner of this manor, might he be James Fisher, and would he be home by chance?" Her voice turned cold, unaffected.

The old man considered her questions, well aware of the state of the outside world. He answered with a question. "Who might you be, and why do you want him?"

"Well, I represent the State. My name is Deena McGrady. It seems he has reached an age . . ." She stops, for this man was of this same category. "Well, to be quite blunt, the State needs to discuss the redistribution of his assets and . . ."

"Why do you stop? State your business," the man said.

"Well, upon his passing, the State will take ownership of all properties. There are also questions about healthcare options and determining how much burden he will be to the State. What's your name?" Deena asked. She might as well investigate this old man while she's at it.

"Really, Ms. McGrady, has it gotten to that point out there? The Lord of the estate does not allow television or electronics; therefore, we are a little behind the times. Do you know what causes a burden, Miss? The absence of love. Love is a burden that we bear happily. When love is added into the formula, everything is balanced out."

"Really, sir, I'm not going to enter into a philosophical discussion with a caretaker. As far as love goes, it's a romantic term whose true purpose was for taking advantage of people. The word is no longer used. I need to meet with the owner. This is not something I can discuss with the help. Now, tell me your name." Her manner had turned quite curt, and she fumbled in her purse for a business card.

"Oh really? Well, my lord is not about the place. My name is Felix Culpa," the gentleman retorted, folding his arms across his chest with no intention of accepting her card.

"Well, Felix Culpa, when . . . when will he be back?" Deena held out the card, but he refused it.

"I'm not sure. He doesn't discuss those matters with the help, and just so you know, he doesn't own this place."

"No? But he occupies it? Please take my card, Mr. Culpa, and tell him to call me when he arrives home. We need to discuss your situation as well."

"My situation?"

"Yes, you will be unemployed and likely homeless. The State will need to address your status as well."

"I'll tell him, but he's an ornery cuss, not likely to do what I or you suggest. You know how old rich people are."

Deena dropped her card to flutter to the ground at his feet.

"Yes, I do. That's why the State hires people like me. I know how to bring them down. Just tell him he is required by law to contact me. There's no other way, no options, the law is quite clear. You know, old man, you and I live on different planets, millions of light years apart."

"I'll bet. I will stress to him the importance of your visit. Oh, is it the law or department rules? There is a difference, you know. But I don't think you and I are as distant or different as you think."

"Thank you, sir, for pointing out those differences. I'm glad you understand the importance of my visit."

Deena's heart pounded; she never let things get to her. The more the old man spoke, the more memories of her grandfather gathered in her head. Why?

"Here, let me get the door for you." The old man reached for her door, closing it after she got in. She wound down her window in a friendly gesture before starting the engine. But why? Looking up at the old man, she smiled; it was his eyes. They struck her. Like her grandfather's, they imbued intelligence with their steel gray. He grinned and patted the top of her door as she dropped into drive.

"Good day, sir." She felt unsure, for the first time in her career. His look left her unsettled.

"You take care."

His words cut her. She held all the power. He was nothing, yet he showed no fear, at peace. *You take care. I think he meant it.*

Her car disappeared around the first curve into the forest. Bewilderment filled him. She had really said, *That's why the State hires people like me.* He walked slowly to the front door, untied his muddy boots, kicked them off. All he could think was, *Wow.* Prodigious double mahogany doors opened; he stood before his minders, two grand empty suits of armor watching over the entry hall. He smiled at his friends, remembering the day they arrived, a surprise for Maxine. The tarnished, dented armor had been unlikely candidates to guard such a stately hall. It was he who sanded and straightened them into his "Chivalrous Brave Knights," and now his hand shook as he glided it over their surface. He had no need or want of the State. He was no burden to anyone.

"Fellows, you have served me well these years. You provided a lot of conversation. What need do you see of the State meddling in our affairs?"

No voice could be heard. The old man waited; there was only silence.

"The devil you say? My thoughts exactly." He turned his head back and forth to admire each. As the old man revered the armor, his jaw trembled. There in the entry hall, its black slate floors soaked in streams of sun breaking through cut glass windows. Where was the State when Maxine and I laid down the black slate? Indeed. And where was the State when Maxine and I finished these walls? His eyes scrutinized the detailed glory of the entry hall, with fanciful plaster reliefs. One day he remembered well, Maxine playfully tossed a handful of joint compound at him. It struck the back of his head, and he chased her down and rubbed it in her hair. Her laughter, the kiss, and then . . . a lump formed in his throat. The construction was an act of love, not a burden, not at all.

"It's okay, my friends . . . It's okay." He struggled to clear his throat. Turning back to the knights, his eyes reddened. One tear perched on a lower lash. On the wall behind the knights was a portrait of his Maxine; his blink released the tear as he moved on.

***

Deena's route back into town ignored her GPS; instead, she drove by the newly constructed senior warehousing facilities—tall concrete structures of function with no style. She knew what went on in there, the drugging and euthanizing of anyone over seventy years of age. She bundled the thoughts in her mind with nice-sounding euphemisms. In her life, while by no means luxurious, she played head games with herself and pretended all was well. Detachment works well, and feelings bring you down, especially when caught in an oppressive system with little hope. She pulled off onto the berm of the road, took a deep breath, and tuned in to some soft music. She knew her actions would be questioned, because her location, known to the central AI computer, would not make sense. The computer required every movement to make sense. She didn't even understand the stirrings taking place within her; how could she explain it to the motherboard? A sudden fear made her pull away and head straight for the office to file her report.

At her desk, she stared off with thoughts flashing. Felix Culpa? For reasons unknown, she refrained from entering the old man's name in the database. She will look him up on her private computer back home first. She dared not strike a false key, for everything out of the ordinary was brought into question and analyzed. After ten minutes the AI computer, known as Arti, asked why she was hesitating to begin. She typed, "Trying to organize my thoughts." She then typed, "Located illegal structure on questioned property . . . it appears vacant. A feeble-minded, stray Reprehensible wanders the property. Another visit is advised to complete my investigation. I'll need to take tools to enter the building." Deena kept it short, grabbed her things, and headed for home, for a date with her male companion, complete with wine.

FIVE

Deena

Every morning for two weeks, Deena struggled with the burdens of a hectic work schedule. The word *burden* flashed across her mind often; she couldn't stop thinking about what the old man said. Arti had questioned the way she had returned from the visit to the property in question. She termed it human error, and Arti warned her, human error could not be tolerated. On her home computer she could find no record of anyone named Felix Culpa.

In the sterile confines of the State Building, she let go a sigh of frustration. She searched through stacks of folders numbered to correspond each to a client, a ward, or what have you, of the State. Workers walked among cubicles occupied by hunched-over zombies inputting data. Mindless little bees doing all the necessary things to the rhythm of printers spitting out reports. Deena reached for the folder numbered 748932. *Almost two weeks and no call!*

she thought. Anger surged; surely the gardener had relayed her message to the client.

She leafed through the paperwork, angrily muttering to herself, "No one blows me off. It's the law! Arrogance toward my authority shall not be tolerated." Scrutinizing the paperwork, it dawned on her how sketchy it was, not much detail. Usually files go into great depth, but file 748932 was vague. It intrigued her, and not in the usual way of satisfying the computer; this time, her intrigue was frightfully personal. This man bothered her. Somehow, he had awakened something. He had disturbed emotions she had long suppressed.

She typed "Felix Culpa" into Arti's master data bank. No identity posted, but the meaning of the two words appeared. Latin: term refers to consequences of the fall of man; in literal terms, a happy fault; more precise, an apparent mistake or disaster with beneficial consequences. The letters turn red and a message flashes, overlaid onto the screen: "Forbidden material accessed. Continued violations will have severe consequences. Please log references for this search." Deena types a quick answer: "name search, name refers to homeless man encounter, false ID, disregard."

"Cindy! Take all my calls. I'll be out the rest of the day." Deena stood, dropped folder 748932 into her briefcase, and headed for the elevator. She felt challenged for the first time in a long time, with a need to document this case.

As she left the blacktop, limestone gravel flew in every direction, rear wheels sliding. Never touching her brakes, she accelerated up the driveway leading through the forest. Reaching the lot near the house, she slid to a stop, threw open her door and stomped straight up to the great mahogany doors. She never paused to look at the manor, refusing to be distracted or drawn into some childish fantasy. Grasping the iron knocker, she banged it unmercifully. Rage pulsed through her. She was sure arrogant disobedience was why she hadn't been called. Her thoughts fed her emotions; her emotions blurred her thoughts. Furiously, she hammered away at the door until her arm grew tired. Resting, she looked out into the field of wildflowers. There stood the gardener, off in the distance, back to her. She trudged off angrily in his direction, cursing and stammering, crushing flowers as she went.

On approach, she shouted. "You! Hey you!"

The old man held his hand up signaling her to desist with her loud talk. She let out a sigh of frustration and continued toward him. He never looked in her direction and missed the sight of her tripping on an unseen obstacle. She stumbled but didn't fall. As she neared him, again she spoke, only this time in a more controlled tone.

"Sir, we need to talk."

"Shh, please! Look there in the meadow." The old man pointed across the field to a patch of white.

She strained to see it in the high grass, but something white, possibly something wild, moved about as if pouncing on something.

"What is it? What do we see?" She stood beside him, distracted again.

"Do you see that white patch? I think it's a wolf or maybe a white sheep. The world has reversed back to a wilder state since the collapse. Wild creatures have gained ground."

"A wolf, really? What would a wolf be doing around here? They were killed off years ago?"

The old man turned to her, his blue eyes laughing with imagination. "Maybe, but maybe not. Maybe it is someone's pet or an escapee from one of those little roadside zoos, or maybe someone turned it loose. All I know is that it showed up here in early summer. It always comes about this time of day. It hunts, then just sits out there sunning itself, looking this way."

"Creepy." Deena breaks eye contact with the old man; a strange feeling about his eyes unnerved her. She remembers her grandfather and how he loved nature.

"Why do you say *creepy*? I think it's beautiful, maybe it's an omen." The old man tilts his head in wonder.

"Omen? I don't believe in that kind of crap. It's a stray dog; up close you would see mange. Look, I was here two weeks ago . . ."

The old man refocuses on the distant creature. In the middle of her retort, he sighs and leans forward on his oversize walking stick.

"I remember, you were just as high-strung as today. You need to take a couple of deep breaths. Look here, I'll show you." The old man closed his eyes and breathed in until his chest was fully expanded, then slowly exhaled as his arms rotated slowly in front of him, without a look in her direction. "In goes the good air . . . out goes the bad."

"Stop it!" Deena could barely contain her contempt for the old man's coaching.

"No seriously, it works. Try it." He repeated the demonstration, knowing full well its effect.

"Stop it! Look, do you know the owner hasn't contacted me? Now, either you didn't tell him, or he's arrogantly defiant of the law, which is it?" Deena's tone was most scornful.

"Oh look, she loped off into woods." The old man seemed enchanted.

"Please, I don't care about that stupid dog!" Deena spit in fury.

"Would you like to come to the house for a cup of green tea? Green tea is very soothing. I'm going to have some, and you are certainly welcome to join me. It thins the blood." With that the old man turned and headed for the house. Deena looked out across the meadow; the white spot was gone. Her head shook as she wondered why she even looked. In a quick turn she ran after the old man, who with his long legs was gracefully outstepping her. Near the pond past the edge of the drive, he stopped to talk to a mallard drake and its hen.

"Good morning, Mr. Duck, Mrs. Duck. It's a beautiful day, is it not?"

In a huff, Deena caught up with the old man.

"You have time to talk to ducks?" Deena mumbled, her impatience uncontained. The ducks waddled into the pond, disturbed by her tone. The old man shook his head as he walked to the front door.

"Come in, please come in." The old man motioned to Deena as he swung open the grand front door. Deena paused to look at the gargoyle at the side of the walk. "Pay no attention to Alfred there; that sign is not meant for friends, he's telling evil to go away. You aren't evil, are you? A gift from the lady of the manor to her beloved, she loved gargoyles. Now come in."

"He got my attention the first time I arrived." Deena walked past the creature, who was leaning out and looking like he might come to life and grab her.

The old man held the door wide as she entered. "You didn't answer my question. You aren't evil, are you?"

His eyes locked on hers, as again she said nothing. But she felt a shift, a rip in the fabric of her universe. Self-centeredness, the basis of evil, took a step back and stumbled.

"These are my minders; isn't that right, gentlemen?" The old man's outstretched arm pointed toward the armor.

"Amazing, simply amazing, they look so real. Just like in the children's books I had when I was little. My mother and grandfather used to read to me."

"Oh yes, they *are* amazing, magical even. I suppose it was living and traveling about Europe that inspired all this. Maxine loved castles. She and her husband toured Germany, Italy, Ireland, England, and Scotland. They stayed in castles; I wonder if old Clontarf castle still stands in Dublin? Max couldn't get enough of Camelot. They built this wondrous place. In its day, writers and artists gathered here. They raised orphans, and the place echoed with laughter. Do you see that Bible verse on the wall near the door?"

She read: *Pure and undefiled religion before God the Father is this: to look after orphans and widows in their distress and to keep oneself unstained from the world. James 1:27*

"So they looked after the orphans, and the orphans looked after keeping themselves unstained from the world."

Deena looked up at the portrait hanging behind the knights. "Is that Maxine, the lady of the manor? She is beautiful and the artwork is stunning. Who was the artist?"

Deena felt a strange calm, a warmth. The old man didn't answer her question, and she felt at peace with it.

"Yes, yes, well, come now. I'll make us tea." The old man led at a quick pace down the hall into the kitchen of the main part of the house.

"Look, I've got business to settle," Deena whispered as they passed by antique pieces of furniture and walls decked with painted portraits of children and landscapes. The wonders drew her in, everything coordinated with perfection. At the kitchen door Deena went on, "Will you answer my questions? Did you tell the owner I was here?" Deena followed five paces behind.

"Do you enjoy green tea?" The old man filled a teakettle at the sink. "Why do you think that wolf keeps showing up? Someday I think I'm going to approach her." The old man's steps were light and springy like a child's. He even turned to face her while walking backward, his eyes intense.

"Why would you do that? He may be vicious. If he's wild, you don't know how he'd react." Deena shocked herself with her concern.

"What does it matter? Hasn't the State declared me a burden? When you're useless, there's no risk, no loss, only gain."

He toyed with her, but instead of getting angry, she considered the logic.

"I'd just like to see how close I can get. Do you sweeten your tea?" He placed loose tea in the infuser. "You know ducks are very social creatures, once you get to know them. Very distinctive personalities, you know."

"No . . . okay, okay, I'll have a cup of tea with you, but you must answer my questions, please." Deena tone was soft now. "I've never known a duck."

"That's a shame. You can learn a lot from God's creatures." The old man places the kettle on the wood-burning stove. "Sit . . . please sit down. Let's talk about your world."

"I want to learn a little bit from you right now and a lot from your boss. Mr. Culpa, there is no one in the data bank by your name." Deena pulled a heavy wooden chair out from the kitchen table and sat.

"Please, call me Felix," the old man responded as he fussed with the teakettle and inspected the cleanliness of the teacups.

"Have you known your boss long?" Deena rested her head on her fist, elbow planted on the table.

"We've been together since the beginning, but honestly, I don't think I can say I really knew him until he met Max. Before that, he, well, do we ever know anyone? I mean, even our own being. Calamity and troubles are the times when we learn the most about others and ourselves. Still, we never know how we'll react to the next consequence. Well . . ."

The old man went silent. Deena waited for him to complete his thought, then offered a gentle prod.

"Well what?" Deena whispered.

"He was his own worst enemy; he tried hard but always failed. It wasn't for lack of effort, give him that." The old man looked off into space. "When he met Max, everything changed. She blessed his life; Maxine was a true blessing."

"Is that when he got rich?"

"Rich? Do you know of his wealth? What does your folder tell you? No, Max taught him nothing happens by a man's own will. Everything is by God's will and in God's time."

Deena looked down at the table; her folder sat before her. Honestly, the folder contained nothing. She knew nothing of Jim Fisher and even less of God.

"Not much in the folder and there's nothing of God in it. There is no God," Deena replied.

"Not much, you say?" The old man knew his whole life had been erased. "If the State had even the slightest valuation of James Fisher's wealth, I guarantee you, he would gladly help you redistribute it. Trouble is that the State is incapable of grasping the extent of it. The State knows nothing of love or God. Have you ever been in love, girl? Do you even know what love is?" The old man poured hot water into the cups, then delicately placed tea bags in them. "Love may not be what you think."

"What I think? I have a boyfriend." Deena was caught off guard.

"Were you raised by your parents or the State?" The old man studied Deena's face as her eyes dropped toward the table.

His question had her revisiting times as a child when she felt comfort and gentleness. Her mother was never harsh, always kind and gentle. They lived with her grandfather, who was as kind as her mother. Her father died somewhere in the Middle East.

"The State rescued me."

"Rescued you?" The man's brow crinkled, and he squinted. "How did they rescue you?"

"They took me to a boarding school. They fed me, gave me a place to sleep, and educated me."

"But why? Were you homeless? Where was your family?"

Deena couldn't go there. Her memory was vague, and she knew the school had made her what she is; she owed the State for all she had. To think of anything else was pointless. Before the boarding school, nothing mattered; this thought pounded away at every effort she made to remember her mother and grandfather.

"I don't believe in love; love is a manipulation people use to get over, to gain advantage on someone. A good relationship comes from two strong people who are not co-dependent. They operate independently of each other for the good of the State. They can cohabitate or live separately and enjoy the pleasures of others either way." Deena shuffled in her seat, while the old man just gazed at her.

"Look, I came here to do my job," she continued. "This rich fat cat, Jim Fisher, took advantage of others to gain wealth. His estate belongs to the people."

The old man's eyes pierced Deena's. His look reached deep into her soul. She sat transfixed; she felt his power of perception. Her bold words held no water; she was merely regurgitating words drummed into her by her teachers. She didn't mean a one of them. He knew it, and she knew it. She couldn't look away until he did. The old man walked over to the kitchen window scrutinizing the yard.

"Did you tell him he had to call me?" Deena quizzed.

"Damn!" The old man thumped down his teacup. "It's Mrs. Duck. She might be in trouble. Quick, move quickly!" The old man dumped the remainder of the kettle on a tea towel and ran out the back kitchen door. Mrs. Duck sat lethargically near Mr. Duck, who acted quite concerned and protective.

"What is it?" Deena shouted frantically and ran out into the yard after him.

"She's egg bound. I thought she was acting funny. Quick, or we'll lose her."

The old man picked up the duck in the warm wet towel. He turned her over. The duck struggled to right herself, legs kicking and head snaking.

"Separate her feathers on her bottom . . . around her vent," the old man commanded.

Deena stood dumbfounded. "What, with my fingers?"

"Yes! Quickly, do it now!"

Deena's fingers trembled as she drew back the mucus-drenched duck feathers, partially exposing the lodged egg. The old man wrapped the duck securely in the towel with just her head exposed and handed the fowl to Deena.

"Just as I thought. Keep the warm towel on her 'til we get her to the kitchen."

In the kitchen the old man placed the duck in a sink of warm water and held her body submerged to let the warmth relax the duck's muscles and vent. He signaled Deena to come close and instructed her to take over holding Mrs. Duck in the water.

"Deena, hold her while I get some oil to lubricate her."

Deena and the old man worked on the duck for two hours before she finally passed her egg. The old man carried Mrs. Duck to the kitchen door, releasing her to the backyard to be consoled by Mr. Duck.

Deena dropped in a kitchen chair. Fresh tea brewed, hands washed, the surgical team sat down faced off at the kitchen table critiquing their methods and discussing the lives and needs of poultry.

"A duck, we just saved a momma duck." Deena couldn't believe she had become so completely fascinated with the old man's knowledge, gentleness, and belief in free-range living. No one she knew cared about human life, let alone stupid animals. What was this all about? Occasionally, the old man drifted off topic and talked about old friends, adventures, sailing the seas, and climbing mountains. Time slipped by and Deena forgot about her need to get back to the office to file a report. She never knew anyone the age of this man. In the hustle of her world there had been little time to stop and reflect.

"I lost a mallard hen once." The old man's throat tightened, but he cleared it. "It was my first experience with egg binding. You say they're just ducks, but for me it stirs up a lot of emotion. I try to let nature take its course; these birds come and go at will. Some leave and I never see them again. Family is the same way; you raise kids and off they go to live their own lives. I watched the dead hen's mate search for her for days afterward. My friends and family are all gone. I felt his pain. I lost a young son to cancer, so now when anything dies, I mourn. Life is so fragile. I'm sorry, didn't mean to dribble on. I'm an incurable empathetic. To you, I must appear a fool." The old man felt suddenly awkward sharing his feeling with this woman from the State. He grinned, "Pretty funny. Just a silly old man, huh?" He looked down in his cup.

For the first time in her life, Deena felt compassion, for the man looked old and tired. Compassion . . . her mother's smile flashed in her mind. *The time!* Deena looked at her cell phone. She had to go but felt the need to say something.

"I've never lost anyone." It was a lie; she had lost everyone before the age of seven. "I guess I've never even given loss much thought. Are you all right?" Deena's tone betrayed her newfound compassion; she couldn't hide it.

"I feel a little tired, that's all. Did you know your grandparents?" His voice had weakened. It had an unsteady tone.

"Yes, we lived in California. My mother's father was a Christian. He took us in when . . ." She stopped. Deena watched the old man. His hand shook as he grasped his teacup. It was time to go. She considered it prudent not to question him any further about his boss or offer him any more information about herself. "Look, I've got to go. Will you be all right? Please have Mr. Fisher call me when you see him. Do you still have my card?"

"Yes." His eyes lingered on Deena, his face gray.

"Please, if you need help, call me." She touches his hand, whispering, "I mean it, Mr. Culpa."

SIX

Deena

Deena sat in her office looking out over her desk—general office supplies, her everyday chaos, nothing out of the ordinary. Her thoughts rested on the old man and Jim Fisher, a week since her last visit. Preoccupied with the events of that visit, she mulled over and processed and reprocessed the moments. She was beginning to remember bits her grandfather had told her about a loving, creator God. About faith in something bigger than all of us. No word from the old man, Felix Culpa, or from Jim Fisher. The phone's ring broke her thoughts. Maybe it was him. She gathered herself to answer. "Deena McGrady, State Welfare and Human Services, can I help you?"

"Hey babe, dinner tonight?"

"Sure, Bob, why not?" It meant the AI sports bar where Bob and friends would be preoccupied with the game of the week. Bob continued with his chatter. He told her all about his day, his important transactions, but never asked her about herself, then said good-bye.

Deena's thoughts turned to her parents. She had been so young, but even with her thoughts long suppressed, she knew they loved each other. They put each other first. Love, she has seen no sign of it the last twenty years. So much time had passed, though; and she had never wanted to touch that part of herself that involved feelings of love. Bob is predictable, so presumably safe. But also completely self-centered. And was he self-aware?

Deena's mother taught at a university before the collapse, and her mother's father helped to care for Deena. Grandfather always put others first. He was a passionate man, always asking questions. For the life of her, she couldn't remember what happened to her mother, or to her grandfather. At the boarding school when she asked, it was always the exact same answer. "You were abandoned, and we rescued you." Nothing more, nothing less, always the same answer, repeatedly—until her focus shifted to her friends and teachers at the school. Deena never felt any passion. Bob's friends were awful bores. She caught herself thinking the unthinkable, about her beginnings. Where did I come from? A month ago, she'd believed her life was, for to think otherwise was forbidden. But now, even in her sleep, her thoughts generated strange recurring dreams of her childhood. *Felix Culpa!*

Deena pushed a button on her intercom. "Cindy, take all my calls. I'll be out the rest of the day." She stood, dropped folder 748932 into her briefcase and headed for the elevator.

At the manor, Deena noticed the great mahogany entry doors stood wide open, no one in view. With caution she entered the main hall leading to the kitchen. She had never been invited or ventured into any of the other rooms off the hall. She pushed on the first door to the right; through a crack she could see the walls were lined with contraband paper books. She pushed the door open wide. Thousands of books, all illegal, all forbidden by the State. She was shocked. She hadn't seen this many books since . . . *my grandfather's house.*

Deena walked alongside the shelves, touched the books, and read titles on the spines. Fascinating titles she had never heard, including one she couldn't resist, *The Year of Magical Thinking* by Joan Didion. She read the back cover, and though it drew her in, she had business to take care of. She carefully placed the book back on the shelf. She wandered from one room to the next; each room had its own library. There were enough books to put Jim Fisher in prison for fifty years. At last she entered a room with grand windows facing the far meadow. In an easy chair facing the windows, the back of the old man's head rose just above the backrest. She approached with caution, finding him slouched, barely awake, binoculars in his lap.

"Are you all right? The doors are wide open," she asked in a gentle tone.

"Oh," he said with a start. "I'm too weak to venture into the meadow. I thought maybe the wolf would visit me here. I've been watching for her . . . when I can stay awake."

"When was the last time you ate?" Deena asked as she knelt beside him.

"Don't know . . . what day is it?"

Deena didn't bother with an answer. She stood and told him she would fix him something to help strengthen him, hot soup and tea. In the kitchen she found the cupboards and refrigerator bare but for some bouillon, a couple of onions, a carrot, and some rice. The stove was cold, so she started a fire to boil water for tea and broth. While it cooked, she returned to the old man to keep track of his state. He watched the meadow and spoke very little. She moved a chair into position so she could sit beside him. She had a strange feeling of déjà vu as they waited for the wolf to appear. The golden wheat swayed like waves in the field. For a split second she caught the image of a man running, tripping in the meadow, then disappearing as if drowning. She watched for a second chance to see him, but he never rose above the wheat heads. The vision was no more real than the old man's wolf. Still, she watched. She glanced at Felix; his eyes were closed. The apparition in the field resembled Felix or even her grandfather.

Deena fetched the tea and soup from the kitchen and woke Felix. She spooned the soup slowly toward his lips, and he sipped. When he finished his last sip, she felt compelled to ask a question she had long neglected.

"What's your real name?" she whispered.

"What does it matter? I'm just the caretaker."

"Are you Jim Fisher?" Again, she spoke in a soft tone.

The old man's face expressed bewilderment; his eyes shifted, searching a distant wall for an answer. Dementia, Deena figured.

"Jim Fisher . . . he vanished in a hurricane off of St. Croix, the records should show that." The old man's head tilted to the side, his eyes closed. "Felix Culpa," he whispered.

"I had a vision of a man running in the field." As Deena's eyes were drawn back to the golden sea she continued, "Memories of my mother and . . . the man I saw might have been my grandfather, but all these years I was told my family deserted me. It's not true, I know it's not true, but I can't remember what happened."

Deena studied the features of the man before her. "Old people are dangerous. The State knows you're dangerous. Old people are filled with a lifetime of . . . dangerous truths?" she wondered aloud.

Deena heard the old man's breathing rattle. "You can't hear me, can you? No." She fluffed the old man's blanket and tucked it in around him. She couldn't leave him like this. She could do the right thing and call the authorities to come pick him up and be done with it. Then, she figured he didn't have much time left, why not just let him die here?

With the old man snug and comfortable, Deena went to retrieve the book she had found in the other room, *The Year of Magical Thinking*. Curiosity got the best of her, and she slowly perused the rooms with an urge to touch artifacts from Jim Fisher's life. Without method or agenda, she wandered childlike, exploring a world of wonder. She found herself in the art studio. Paintings dripping with passion covered the walls or sat on easels or the floor, all signed J. Fisher. One of a small boy, head tilted upward with a light of unknown origin illuminating his face in soft, warm hues. Her heart ached as she left to go into the study. There she found Jim's writings—books, notes, and essays—in one corner, Maxine's engineering work in another. On the wall was a photograph of Jim and Max. Age couldn't disguise the old man; Felix Culpa was definitely Jim Fisher. She read through love letters, a journal kept on the construction of the manor, built with their own sweat and love. She found passages hinting of their playfulness and joy found in the daily work. Stories of Jim's life before Maxine, the tragedy of a lost son, a divorce, a friend he called St. Croix, and the hurricane he'd mentioned. As Deena flipped through the pages, she found a world of love and tragedy. She knew she was falling in love with Jim's life, his story. Her cell phone rang, wrenching her from her journey through Jim's life. Eight o'clock, she noticed, before she put the phone to her ear.

"Where the hell are you, Deena? I look like a fool in front of my friends." Bob's voice cut her. He was intruding in her moment. After a brief pause Deena answered him.

"I'm okay, Bob, I wasn't in an accident. I didn't mean to cause you to worry." She knew better, though; Bob never worried about anything, except himself.

"No shit. Don't ever pull this again. Where the hell are you? You better have a good story."

Deena pressed hard on the off button so she wouldn't hear him call back. "I won't ever pull it again, Bob, and the story? You wouldn't understand," she whispered at the dead cell phone, then tossed it onto the love seat. She went back to reading Jim Fisher's journal.

After letting her thoughts stew for several minutes, she went back to check on Jim; it was getting late. She decided Jim needed her to stay the night. She would call in sick in the morning.

Deena was just one of Bob's girls, she knew it. In this supposedly utopian culture no one was committed to anyone. Her very existence rang shallow, but she also knew she was Bob's trophy woman. She brought him status, because she had it all, looks and intelligence. All Bob's friends wanted her, but she wasn't like the other women, and it made her even more desirable. To be with someone like Deena was to put your ego on steroids.

Bob could charm anyone. He had self-confidence, good looks even, but eventually his shallowness became apparent. Deena had settled for convenience and routine. There weren't many men in the herd much better, so why not just go through the motions? But she allowed no one to talk to her like Bob just did, no one.

Deena slipped into the first-floor guest bathroom, got undressed, and showered. A plush ladies' bathrobe hung behind the door. Deena held it to her face—it was fresh and clean. Seems Jim kept all of Max's things clean. Wrapping herself in its cozy crispness, she returned to the study with her book. As she tired, she went to check on Jim. He was sleeping in the chair, so she laid on the floor beside him to read and soon drifted off.

***

In the morning she got dressed, called in sick, fetched some eggs from the henhouse and made breakfast for the two of them. She fed Jim, who was still in his easy chair, more lucid, his words now making more sense. He told her he had stopped eating days ago and had become weak. The food stocks had dwindled dangerously low. A friend who usually brought him supplies hadn't come in a long while; Jim had figured him for dead. He wasn't the type to not show; he was a reliable man. With all the dangers in the world, it was likely someone had murdered him.

Jim wiped his mouth with a napkin. "Thank you, I think. My intention may have been to die. If you hadn't found me, I would have succeeded."

"Don't say such things. I know who you are, Jim Fisher," Deena said. She set the fork on his plate.

"Okay, now they'll come take me to your boneyard. What's the point of saving me?" Jim said.

"Tell me about this place. I want to know more. I found a lot of stuff snooping last night. I saw pictures of you and Max. Tell me in your own words," Deena pleaded.

"Is this a confession? More evidence to put in your file?"

"No!" Deena felt horrible, confused, but she had no plans of turning any of this over to the State.

"What's to tell? We rescued children from the streets. Maxine and I provided a loving home," Jim said.

"Rescued? I've been thinking a lot about supposed child rescues," Deena replied.

"There's a difference between your rescue by the State and our rescues; we loved our children. Do you see any of them here?"

"I see a lot of their photos and paintings," Deena responded.

"When you love, you set things free, like my ducks. My ducks can come and go. You were rescued by the State, but are you free to come and go? Do you have a choice in how you live?" Jim said.

Deena realized she knew Jim was right; she wasn't free at all. The State made her secure, even comfortable, but free, no.

"Where did your children come from?" Deena asked.

"All over, all ages, many different backgrounds. All these books you call contraband were for the children. They studied and taught each other. We had great discussions about different ways of life. Max and I pointed out the cultural shifts that destroy countries and cultures. It was obvious there were people replacing what worked with what sounded good. If the authorities knew what we were saying, we would have been put on a terrorist list." Jim watched Deena's face in an attempt to get a read on her intentions. "We gave them all a choice, and letting go of them was very difficult, painful. You tend to miss the little ones, but as they grow, they become different. Silly how you want to keep them the way they are, but you know it's impossible and not right. So you let go, because you love them. I wish we had rescued *you.* You aren't happy. You are numb." Jim spoke in soft tones. "Everyone is living a dream, and if you aren't living your dream, you are living someone else's. This place was a dream; better yet, it was a shared dream. The best dreams are the ones you share with someone you love. I think you are living the State's dream, and there's nothing wrong with that, if it's what you want. For me, I prefer to have my own dream. Strange enough, the seed for this dream became planted during the loneliness I felt in my first marriage."

Deena couldn't argue with him; she *had* felt numb, all her life. At least in the years after her rescue. When she looked at Jim, she saw his kindness, and new thoughts of her grandfather started to flow into her heart. She could imagine her grandfather, serving dinner, reading fairy tales to her, tucking her into bed, and then she remembered the last day. She juked at the thought; she had no idea what was happening on the last day, just how frantic her mother was. She remembered her in the kitchen, after she'd come home from the university very upset. Grandfather tried to calm her, but she told him to take me to our cottage in the hills. They were coming for us; I didn't know who. Mother had made some kind of mistake at work and said forbidden things. It was after the collapse. Deena caught herself and shut down the thoughts; the pain was too much. She shook, her breathing was heavy, and Jim asked if she needed to talk, but Deena shook her head and coiled in a fetal ball at Jim's feet.

She felt exhausted; it had been a long night, watching after Jim and reading. She knew her readings were affecting her emotions; she even wondered if she was experiencing the vortex effect Didion experienced in *The Year of Magical Thinking*. She was having flashbacks, and things in this house were triggering thoughts of her childhood. As she lay on the floor, she thought it might be best for her to leave and never return to this place. But then, what about Jim Fisher, what would become of him? He must have some sort of outside support . . . besides the man who had brought him supplies. She sat up.

"You're empathetic, aren't you? You feel other people's pain." Deena had never known anyone in her adult life who had such insight into the pain of others.

"Maybe. I've experienced the full range of emotions. Loss changes our perspective, and I don't think you become a complete human being unless you lose everything. It's how people find themselves," Jim replied.

"I think it takes more; I think you have to be a special person, one who can self-analyze."

Jim refrained from saying any more at this point; he knew he was too tired, and he knew Deena had lost her humanity in the crazy system established after the collapse.

"Who supported all this? There must be more to this story; no one buys or sells anything without registering it with the State." Deena's investigative self couldn't let her train of thought stop.

Jim liked her, but he couldn't trust her, so he knew for him to say anything about the others working behind the scenes in his life would be a mistake. He shut down, pretended to lapse into a sleep, but he was instead thinking. He opted not to answer. After a few moments with his eyes shut, he peeked with one open and saw her looking at him; he was caught.

Deena laughed. "I don't blame you for not trusting me. I only wanted to know that you wouldn't suffer if I just abandoned this whole investigation and let you peacefully live out your time. I don't want to walk away and let you die without a support system. Don't say anything now; let me build your trust."

"Thank you. I will say, I have friends. God is a big part of it." Jim knew the word *God* would strike a nerve.

"God? No one believes in fairytales anymore."

"I know, and he knows. Take a hard look at your life without God and fairytales." Jim examined Deena's expression, which looked just as he thought it would. She said no more about either God or fairytales and instead changed the subject.

"Will you tell me what happened to Max?"

Jim didn't want to talk about it. No, he didn't think he could without breaking down. He sat, though, summoning all his strength. He would talk in brief sentences.

"Cancer . . . she had cancer," Jim said.

"Where was God? How does God factor into this?" Deena felt she had her gotcha moment.

"God does things in his own way, his own time. Hardships prepare us, mold us. Who knows the whys of his ways. Heat strengthens steel, sharpens the blade. Maybe he was preparing me to meet you," Jim answered. He felt drained and wanted to rest.

Deena didn't say anything; she waited for him to continue.

"Breast cancer. She could have been saved. We were illegals, rogues, not in the system." Jim felt his throat tighten. "You condemn God, but look at your State system. I refuse to bow to it, and it rejects me."

Again, Deena just listened.

"We had doctor friends who got us some help on the black market."

Deena held up her hand to stop him as a tear rolled down her cheek. So much for her previous concept of utopian health care. They sat in silence, watching the wheat field for any sign of motion other than the constant sway produced by the breeze, so calming, so serene, even hypnotic. Deena remembered now: her grandfather ran toward her as someone restrained her; it happened near the cottage in the mountains. She had wandered near the woods while at play, her grandfather watching her through the window while he washed dishes. Two men came out of the bushes and grabbed her. When her grandfather ran across the yard to protect her, there were loud cracks in the air, and she saw him fall. Deena's heart sank . . . yes, then everything went dark. Someone put a bag over my head, and they taped her arms to her sides. She never saw her mother or grandfather again. Deena never heard anything about the great purging; it wasn't taught in schools.

***

Deena cared for Jim until he regained his strength; it took the rest of the week for her to feel confident enough to leave him. She needed fresh clothes, so she went to her apartment. The building had a sterile look, hard concrete, very utilitarian; every apartment had the same balcony and floor plan. She pulled into her assigned parking space and stepped out. Before she reached the front door of the building, Bob ran in front of her, blocking her path. Deena recoiled in shock, and her heart raced.

"Bob! What are you doing?"

"Where have you been? I've called you a hundred times, stopped at your office, and have been watching for you to come home."

Deena stood speechless; his words creeped her out. This was not all right. She didn't know what to say.

"I asked you a question. Answer me."

"Get out of my way," Deena said as she tried to brush past him.

Bob grabbed her arm and restrained her.

"Did you get rid of it yet?" Bob quizzed.

Deena stared at him; she had known him for quite a while, and yet now she realized she had never known him.

"Is that what this is about?" Deena asked.

"No! Well, maybe partly. It is a legal matter. We don't have a permit, and such things can cause major complications. Complications I don't need." Bob's tone and choice of wording didn't mesh with the warm feeling of caring that had been growing inside of her, literally and figuratively.

"Let me pass. We're through and have nothing to talk about. Don't worry, Bob, this one is on me. You have nothing to do with it. Now, get out of my way." Deena pushed past him and never looked back.

Bob watched her disappear into the front door of the apartment building. He stood still, staring, for a very long time before walking briskly to his car.

SEVEN

Atanase

After wandering around many closed roads and bridges, Atanase arrived in the area surrounding Port Norris, and his exhaustive search for his adoptive siblings began in earnest. He stashed the motorcycle in the Edward G. Bevin Wildlife Management Area and opted to make his way on foot or by hitching rides. This approach would lessen the locals' suspicions and save his fuel for his return to the manor. The days had been tiresome, the nights unpredictable, always sleeping in places where he felt unsafe, but doing his best to lay low and stay hidden.

***

Port Norris, like most small towns after the collapse, has become a dreary shell of its former self. The asphalt has thinned and cracked, and the lack of traffic allowed weeds to grow in the fissures. I saw no signs of Peacemakers or a local militia. As I walked the streets and passed residents, some gave me a nod or a wave. I found my way to a church and knocked on the door of the parsonage. When the door opened, to my surprise a familiar face greeted me. She recognized me in an instant and threw her arms around me. Her embrace was warm, and with a brief sob, she pushed back from me to view my face, tears streaming down her cheeks. We were siblings from the manor, had shared ten years there as teens and young adults. I had hoped the pastor might direct me and help me find siblings, but this event surpassed my wildest hopes. Lydia wiped her tears, laughed, and dragged me through the door while shouting to the pastor.

"Louis! Louis! Come quick! Look who is here!" Lydia couldn't contain herself.

"There's no rush, Lydia. I'm not leaving," I assured her.

Lydia laughed, gave me another big hug, and shouted again for Louis. Lydia had been from the streets of London, and Louis had come from Antwerp, Belgium, and lived at the manor for four years. He was one of the last children to be taken in. It was no surprise when I heard Louis's name, as the two had eyes for each other the moment he arrived at the manor. When Louis entered the room, he lit up and charged at me, arms spread. A powerful man, his chest knocked me back, and his arms crushed me from behind and lifted me off the ground.

"Atanase, we have often spoken of you and wondered where you were," Louis said.

We sat on the steps at the front of the sanctuary and I told them of my travels and travesties, about our father and the manor. They spoke of life in Port Norris and how storms from the sea weathered the homes and the dysfunctional supply chain made repair nearly impossible. How the population had declined as homes became unlivable and food shortages increased. They were a community of squatters; no one owned their homes or paid the digital taxes. The populations had formed a working brotherhood where the needs were satisfied by neighborhood cooperation and barter. Most food came from the bay or local gardens. People lacked the energy and inspiration to improve their lot beyond basic needs. Commerce had turned them all into criminals, but at least the local powers-that-be had compassion with its loyalty focused on the people rather than upward toward the state or federal government. Few people attended his church, not because he was a bad pastor but because few people believed in anything beyond themselves. The oppression by the State caused everyone to be weary and wary. Many had come to see the world as a rock spinning through space inhabited by evolved creatures without need of a God. This humanist dogma had been fed to them for generations, since the death of the idea of God was declared.

"Travel is dangerous, I know, but an occasional visit to the manor might help our father," I said to Louis.

"The manor was their dream; it was also their dream for us to move on. You know we are meant to spread the Word," Louis replied. He was right; I knew Father wanted it this way, but it bothered me. We continued to discuss the working of Port Norris, how they managed to eke out an existence, while maintaining hope in spite of circumstances.

Louis knew three of our siblings lived in the Port Norris area, and after sending word by a messenger, I received a warm welcome message from them and their spouses, with offers of meals and a place to sleep. None of these siblings had given in to the system; they were all surviving by farming, gathering, fishing, and using the black market. All things considered, such as the dark shadow of gloom hanging over the world, none of the siblings had chosen to conceive children. Louis said a few siblings had reverted to the street ways they had learned before coming to the manor. He had lost contact with them and figured there was no reason to seek them out.

Even before the collapse, the Port Norris area had been populated by contrarians with a strong distrust of authority and government. One of the great advantages of this area was that there were no Peacemakers. Pleased with what I found so far, Louis said two of our brothers had moved out of Port Norris and he wondered if I could manage to find them. One or both might be in Fortescue, a town with a population of three hundred on the Delaware Bay and surrounded on three sides by marsh lands, called the Egg Island Fish and Wildlife Area. Louis wasn't sure if they maintained the values taught at the manor or went feral. There was one road into their town, or you arrived by boat.

Louis and Lydia let me stay with them for a few days and introduced me to their friends. Their friends spoke of an existence much like Louis and Lydia's. A basic life, no one dreamed of anything other than to stay alive. Everyone owned a gun even though their ammunition was ancient. No one wasted any ammo on target practice. Everything held value; the simplest items were irreplaceable. Those who fished traded with those who gardened, and women who sewed traded their goods for food. Everyone watched out for and took care of their friends and neighbors. The lack of belief in a higher spiritual power made it sad, though. The people of Port Norris held good values and principles, but I saw no children at play, heard no childish laughter or any sounds of skateboards on sidewalks. The town had no plans beyond the moment. They were definitely missing the hope and joy that comes from faith, especially faith in a creator God.

"You know, Louis, there is a peace here, even though some of the elements of a higher good are missing."

"My brother, we are content, and it makes us rich. Everyone here does what he does of his own freewill. Today, there are few places in the country where you can do this. We don't fuss with each other."

"Still, few come to your church."

"We all live out the words of Jesus. These people don't need to hear it from me. Lydia and I live at church, so if anyone needs us, they come. We're outsiders, always will be. Shell Pile's residents trace their ancestry back to freed slaves and have a history of suspicions about outsiders. They've come to trust us to a point."

The second morning, Louis took me to the Bivalve docks to introduce me to a boat owner willing to take me to Fortescue. None of the other siblings felt safe or inspired to leave their spouses to make the journey. The interest in the fate of the two who had left was of minor interest to them. Both men had been held in close relationships with me at the manor, so I weighed the risk and, being alone, felt it my duty. I was disappointed to not manage a visit with my more local siblings, but they had left on a fishing expedition soon after my arrival. I knew they were in a good place, in close contact with Lydia and Louis, so I knew I could give a good report to Father.

The boatsman, Marinos, proved a gruff seaman, well acquainted with the sea and loneliness. He asked very few questions and offered even fewer insights into how the voyage might be executed. He had no intention of waiting for me while I searched for my brothers; he would take me and drop me off. Getting back would be my problem; he needed to fish and wasn't a tour guide. At six sharp the next morning we left the dock at Bivalve. He raised a small sail into a light wind. As we pulled away, he lifted a mug of homemade beer for breakfast and headed out into Maurice River Cove. Once in open water, he raised the main sail, and we were underway.

Egg Island Point sat six or seven miles from Bivalve, and a strong wind clipped us along at a good pace. The wind shifted as we rounded the point, and Marinos began to tack into the wind. He yelled for me to help him adjust the sails. I knew well how to handle the ropes, and he began to smile for the first time. We struggled to make time against the wind but soon saw the waterfront at Fortescue. As we approached, we could make out several men holding rifles and standing by a truck. Peacemakers shouted on a bullhorn for us to come into port. Marinos pushed on the tiller as I adjusted the sails to reverse course. The crack of rifle fire carried across the water as lead hit the mast and poked holes in the sail. Marinos fell but returned to the tiller, his shoulder red with fresh blood. Moments later we were out of range and now traveling with a strong wind, headed back toward Bivalve. The fate of my brothers would go unknown, but in my heart, I knew they would be executed.

"Did you see the tall one?" Marinos asks.

"Yes, he's an Assessor."

"Right, AI at its worst, cold-blooded judge. The others, humanoids, do whatever he says or die."

Assessors had begun to run the Peacemakers twenty years ago. The first generation proved fearsome, and over time, they became implacable. They stand taller than any man, weigh four hundred pounds, and can embarrass a cheetah at a dead run. Their purpose is to analyze situations, people, and threats to the peace. In theory they are programmed not to inflict harm on humans. They give orders to Peacemakers to do the killing. The theory is a thin veil of propaganda. Assessors can kill anyone who refuses to take their direct orders; insubordination is not tolerated. When approached by an Assessor, its twisted computer-brain will give you an order you are unlikely to follow. Once you defy the order, you will die. There is no court of appeals.

A pool of blood formed on the deck below Marinos, his face pale, but he held the tiller firm as I adjusted the sails. Now we were with the wind, traveling at a good speed, with no need to tack. There were no medical facilities to care for wounds such as his. He knew his fate. Still, he kept at his duty station determined to make Bivalve and Port Norris. In the distance black smoke swirled high over the bay. My heart sank as I considered the meaning. There may be no safe port. The government may have made a move on the area. At a half mile from port, our worst fears were realized. Bivalve lay in flames, and smoke billowed over Port Norris. There was little doubt about the townspeople's fate, and even less we could do to be of any help. Marinos wept, his hard shell had cracked, and he fell into a heap on the deck. He had no pulse when I checked.

With a push of my foot, Marinos was rolled away from the tiller, and I took command. The only safe refuge would be the middle of the bay, far from land. There I could gather my thoughts and formulate a plan. If I put into shore and waded through the swamps, I might make it to the motorcycle, but then what? If the entire area was invaded, the roads wouldn't be safe. There would be checkpoints and patrols. Open water wouldn't be safe either, with satellite surveillance or drones. The Delaware shoreline wasn't populated, so it might be best to head northwest toward Bombay Hook Wildlife Preserve. There were inlets around Goose Point. It had been twenty-five years or more since Father had the sailboat in Delaware Bay. Sailing had been his big distraction from the activities at the manor. Before the collapse, he would take a couple of us kids sailing in the bay. My knowledge of the area might save me; I knew I could hide at Goose Point.

Strong winds pushed me toward the west side of the bay, where I could make out the shoreline. The craft was heeled over as far I should dare, and the hull sliced the bay, churning a white wake that trailed far behind when the bow shattered. It wasn't the percussion; it was instinct that sent me backward off the stern into the icy water. Muffled explosions kept me from resurfacing, I chose to wait for a moment of silence. Icy waters constricted my skin and cramped my muscles. When I could no longer hold my breath, I let my face gently break the surface. My desire to rise out of the cold was tempered by a squadron of killer drones hovering five hundred feet above. Drawing a deep breath, I sank and swam under the sail, the only remnant of the boat still in one piece. When it fell, it trapped a pocket of air, offering a cover where I could safely hide from view and breathe. A six-foot chunk of hull offered me flotation. The drone continued to hover, watching for me to surface. Other drones dropped close to the surface and skimmed the wreckage. Satisfied I had drowned, I heard them fade. Not sure if they had risen or flown off, I stayed hidden for what seemed an eternity.

My shivers now replaced by a strange warmth, even a slight burn, my flesh had adapted to the water. My nerves no longer sensed the differential between my skin temperature and the bay. The western shore was an impossible swim, so I gathered floating debris and ropes to fashion a raft to serve me well. At the mercy of wind and currents, I lay on my back and watched as the day faded into night, the cloudless sky filled with stars. My thoughts focused on the attack on the villages and the new level of aggression, even the appearance of genocide. Why? The world's population had already been reduced to a quarter of its peak at the beginning of the century, births running well below the death rate. Putting these thoughts to sleep, I rolled onto my stomach and strained to see the shore. Years ago, the shoreline would have been dotted with lights; tonight there was no way to determine my position.

Before the sun broke above the eastern horizon, a dim morning light proved sufficient to make out the shore. Providence was with me, as I recognized the shoreline road as Port Mahon. The wind had proven strong enough to keep me from washing toward the Atlantic. My light raft's draft was so shallow, the deep currents had little effect. Once ashore, with great caution I could walk the road into Little Creek. There would be danger, but at least I would trudge through the coastal swamps and bogs. From the eyes in the sky to random hungry drifters, I would need to hide. Where the road leaves the bay to head inland, I put in on a sandy beach. My wet clothes grabbed my flesh and hindered my run for the trees and shrubs. The cover offered a way to avoid being seen by a satellite. The road long ago had fallen into disrepair and vegetation engulfed the shoulders, much to my advantage. Further along the coastal road there had once been a few docking areas and a long fishing pier. From where I docked, I couldn't see if they still existed. The sun was full up, already torrid, so my clothes dried quickly.

Scrub tree cover was strung everywhere along the road as I made my way toward Little Creek. There were no signs of human activity. The first farms I encountered were deserted with fallow fields. The disrepair spoke of years of abandonment and neglect. Still, I investigated each dwelling in search of food or anything useful. In a garage I located a kitchen knife, a hatchet, and an old bicycle with flat tires. An old hand pump lay beside it. Amazingly, the tires held air, but for how long I had doubts. I secured the pump to the bicycle frame and pedaled down the road. There was a book at the manor which described an escapee during World War II who stole 140 bicycles as he fled across Europe pursued by the Nazis. The thought of stealing bicycles went against my grain, but I would do what I needed to do to survive.

Little Creek never was much of a town; now the buildings consisted of walls, with the roofs long gone. No one lived in the area; at least, no one showed their face as I pedaled past ruin after ruin. Just past Cowgill Corners I came to an abandoned runway heading off to the east. I surmised it to be an old regional airport, the runway cracked with bushes and weeds growing in long rows. A distant hangar lay half collapsed, surrounded by the skeletons of private planes. Homes lined the north side of the runway, their driveways emptying onto a road in poor repair. At one time this must have been a very wealthy neighborhood. As I focused on the airport, I failed to notice the vehicle bearing down on me from behind until it passed me, causing me to jerk my handlebars and lean right. My heart stopped for a second as the vehicle turned in front of me and stopped. Five heavily armed men jumped to the ground and spread across the road with weapons pointed at me. No option but to stop, I raised my hands above my head.

"What's up?" I asked. The men wore military fatigues with patches or insignias. They ranged in age from a teen to a man in his sixties. A ragtag militia of sorts. So many of these groups wandered or controlled an area, fighting the Peacekeepers, but these groups had no central authority. They weren't the good guys either. Good had gone out of fashion before the collapse. Now there existed only different levels of evil. They used tech, so somebody in the group always had some savvy, maybe a techie dropout. I heard one mention a drone scanner. I couldn't determine if they had one in use currently.

"We ask the questions, you answer or otherwise shut up," the biggest of the men replied. He looked about forty and sported a long ponytail and unkempt beard. "The bike, is it yours?"

My first thought was to lie and say it was, but my second thought was to be honest.

"I found it."

"Where?" the big man asked.

"At an abandoned farmhouse on Port Mahon Road," I replied. I wasn't sure what I'd said to trigger them, but it put them on guard.

"Get down on your knees! Like you're praying . . . and if I were you, I would," the big man commanded. He laughed maniacally, telling me he didn't actually believe in the power of prayer.

My knees touched the ground, and I began a silent prayer as the younger one stepped near, holding a strange tubular device. He began at my head and passed the probe over my body. Next, he used it to scan the bicycle. A warbling noise sounded as he placed the probe near the seat. The eldest-looking man grumbled without forming words as the younger felt beneath the seat, recovering a white chunk of plastic. He tossed it to the ground; in an instant he pulled out a pistol and shattered it with one shot. Then he pressed the pistol barrel against my temple. My eyes closed, and I clenched my jaw. A musty sulfuric smoke burned in my nose and told me, their ammo was a homemade reload style and would have a certain failure rate. The next round could be a dud.

EIGHT

Deena

Deena severed contact with Bob, and for the past weeks she had gone to work as usual and limited her visits to the manor to every third day. To satisfy the computer she concocted a wild scenario about the manor and created a plausible need to visit. Her story went without question. Part of her duties was to inventory State-acquired properties and tag valuables. This became her cover. She also falsified a death certificate for Jim Fisher; his remains were reported to be decomposed and not worth tampering with. The State had no interest in burying the dead, and the usual disposal went through a mobile incineration unit. Decomposed remains weren't worth the energy used by the unit. On every visit to the manor, she chose a book to take home. The more she read and spoke with Jim Fisher, the more she came to hate the State system. She found herself remembering things about her mother and grandfather.

Childhood events from before her abduction flashed through her mind.

Today was a manor day; she couldn't wait to shut down her computer and head out to see Jim. Jim represented everything she hoped her grandfather would have been. The clock was ticking, and she knew her current routine couldn't last, with pressure from the State to wrap this property acquisition up, Jim's advanced age was against him, and her condition was going to change rapidly.

As she exited the elevator and rushed out the front door of her office building, she suppressed all these negative thoughts to focus on a feeling of freedom. At the manor she could do as she pleased. She had discovered Jim was receptive to hear her heartfelt thoughts, never quick to judge or condemn. If Jim found something skeptical in her thoughts, he would ask her pointed questions and let her mull over things from a different perspective. He challenged her to alter her beliefs based on new insights. She knew how clever he was, gifted in manipulation, but so gentle and kind in his ways. If only she could just live at the manor and care for Jim, and the baby, when it arrived. *You're dreaming, Deena. That's impossible. The manor hasn't been found yet, but it's only a matter of time. Better think of a better plan.*

Halfway to the manor, she spotted a vehicle parked in the driveway of an abandoned house. She knew the property; she passed it on every trip to the manor. She watched in her rearview mirror as the vehicle fell in behind her. She accelerated, as did the other vehicle. A quick turn onto a side road took her away from the main road, and away from the manor. The other vehicle followed. Her heart raced as the pursuit vehicle closed the gap between them. So close it came, she could detect that it was Bob's face in her mirror. She knew he was possessive but thought he would respect her enough to let go. She accelerated and watched his car fall back to a safer distance. The road she had taken wound through an area of deserted homes and overgrown farmland. The map displayed on her console showed a crossroads a mile ahead, and the road to the left led back toward town and her apartment. She needed to be in the company of other people, simply for safety. Why would Bob do this?

When she pulled into her apartment's parking lot, Bob pulled in behind her. In a rage she parked and jumped out to face Bob. He remained in his vehicle, his hands clutching the wheel.

"What do you want?!" Deena asked as she rushed toward his open window.

"Just to see you," Bob countered.

"Don't. We're through, Bob. Waiting for me and following me is weird. Are you drunk or high?" Deena folded her arms across her chest.

"I'm in love."

"Right, well, get out of love. It creeps me out."

"Where were you going, Deena? What's out there?" Bob said in a singsong voice, knowing full well the answer.

"I'm on official business, you don't need to know."

"Official? Deena, I'm not stupid. I know you've been going out there on a regular basis."

"I have business on a regular basis. Now, go away." Deena felt incensed. How dare he question her?

"Get rid of the fetus, Deena. Soon you will show, and you will have to do something. You'll be a criminal."

"Bob, you know me well, and I shouldn't have to say this. I am no one's victim, not of you or the State. Leave me alone."

Bob stood speechless; he knew she meant it. He didn't have to say anything; she could read his eyes, knew him well. How many times had she tasted his rage, his arrogance, and his selfish ways? She was aware she had never witnessed his full capacity for anger; he always reined himself in at the brink. He was dangerous, persistent, and would never let up. Deena locked her vehicle with the push of a button and ran into her apartment building. From her small balcony she watched Bob kick his vehicle before he collapsed into the driver's seat and pulled away. She knew she'd have to plan, and act, that life as she had known it was drawing to a close.

***

At the manor, Jim sat on a bench near the pond and watched duck dramas. He loved to watch them take flight, but one suffered a condition known as angel wing. He faulted himself for not providing proper nutrition to the duckling, for as a result, it would never fly. Very few people could find proper nourishment in these times, but this fact didn't soothe his guilt. The wrists in its wings were malformed, and the end feathers stuck straight out from its body. The ducks loved to fly out in the fields and to other ponds, but this one could never leave the manor's pond. Jim tossed a pebble into the water, for no reason but to watch the ripples it made. His lament now was that no one knew who he had once been, what he had been through. The world wasn't what it had been, and none knew how to right it. Deena was late, which worried him, and he checked his watch repeatedly. He would wait by the pond until she arrived or until dark.

When night engulfed the pond, the ducks went silent, and all the drama came to an end as they retreated into the stands of cattails in the shallows. Jim didn't bother to check the time; he knew Deena wasn't coming. Her safety was on his mind; if she could have come, she would have. The still of the night would be soothing under any other circumstance, but tonight the peepers sang a sad song, a lonely song. Old men find little to look forward to; he had found Deena's visits to be marks of time. His time was short. He had lived a good life, a free life, and he had loved and been loved. He had been blessed with raising children, and he had no regrets. The world had changed during his lifetime, and from where he stood, it wasn't for the good. God's greatest gift, freewill, had been taken away from most. The world had entered a dark period, and most had found comfort in accepting lies, so much so, they now feared the truth more than the dark. Cats are said to have nine lives; Jim felt he had lived three.

***

The morning sun filtered into Deena's living room where she had slept on the floor. The night scared her, and she felt her odds were best not being in her bed. In the morning light, her fears embarrassed her. She walked to the window to throw open the drapes. She scanned the parking lot for signs of Bob; none found, she started a pot of coffee and went to shower. She planned to live her daily routine. After work she would take an alternate route to the manor. From now on she would change her patterns and give more focus to long-range plans. No one gets away with bucking the State, no one. The world is known to be flat, and when people fall off the edge, they never return, and no one ever talks about them again. Deena sipped her coffee as she looked out at the horizon, the sun reddened by some unknown debris in the atmosphere, possibly from far-off wildfires or burning cities.

The incident with Bob emboldened Deena. She felt triggered to do what she longed to do. Today her life would change. At the office Deena wrote a report about her pregnancy and declaration to keep the baby. She wouldn't divulge Bob's name to anyone. Her recent interactions with Bob indicated he was a sperm supplier, not in any sense a father. She read the report several times, made corrections, and stalled in contemplation of the effects it would have. Half an hour passed as she paced the room looking for the courage to hit send. Her heart skipped a beat, and she struggled to breathe with a constricted diaphragm and knotted back muscles. Once she hit send, it couldn't be retracted or edited, and it would be explosive. She'd better be ready. She had all her valuables in a duffle bag stashed in the weeds at the edge of the parking lot. Pushing send would instantly disable her vehicle, lock down her apartment, and trigger tracking of her location. She bandaged her right arm with a copper mesh bandage purported to prevent the transmitter embedded in her wrist from sending signals. Arti was instantaneous, so her message would be routed and identify her for elimination. She didn't know if the bandage would conceal her from tracking. She bought the bandage from someone she didn't know, a man recommended by someone she trusted as a friend. But in these times who could you trust? She had only seconds to escape the building before the doors would begin to lock. Over the past weeks she had practiced her escape route down a staircase and out a rear door. Her time consistently came in at thirty seconds.

If Bob hadn't followed and confronted her, she would have just failed to show up for work one day. She would have let the State try to figure out where she had gone. Still, she would have traveled on foot, as the vehicles are all tracked. She could have had more lead time, but she decided to get back at Bob. To take him out of the picture along with several of his friends, she put in her report several damning facts she knew about them. Everyone she knew was corrupt and self-serving; before she met Jim Fisher, she had seen it as normal behavior. Now she wanted to turn the State on itself, let it eat its own. There were no good guys in this world, just selfish creeps who would turn their mother in. Anything to make points with the Arti system. Those thoughts of Bob and his friends loosened her muscles; she took a deep breath and hit send as she threw open her office door and ripped down the stairs. Her office door locked before she hit the bottom of the staircase, and as she ran out the office building's back door, she heard its locking mechanism click, but she was out on the asphalt. Her every move was caught on camera and fed to the Arti system. Snatching her duffle bag on a run, she was in chest-high weeds in the adjoining field. When she reached the far end of the field, about a half mile from the office building, she dropped to the ground and prayed the mesh bandage was shielding her. The weeds would be her cover until nightfall.

As night fell, so did a mist of rain. Deena felt the mist accumulate on her forehead and cheeks. She licked her lips to taste it. She tilted her head back for the full effect. With closed eyes and an extended tongue, she remembered doing this as a child, probably the last time she had felt rain. In her adult years, there were long periods of drought, and most days were spent indoors. The rain felt real; she felt free and at peace even if this turned out to be her last hour.

She lifted the strap of the duffle bag over her shoulder, and the rain now trickled down her back like a light tickle. She looked back toward the lights of the city; this must be how it felt to leave Sodom and Gomorrah. If she turned to salt, the rain would melt her, she thought, and laughed. The manor was a five-hour trudge through fields and timber; she had to avoid the roads, except for a few quick crossings. She had done a very neat and thorough job of closing out the manor account; it was on a list for demolition. There was no way to avoid it; all confiscated properties were destroyed, as Arti had no use for buildings or food production. The backlog for demolition was long; Arti had no pressure to move quickly on such matters.

***

Jim sat in his study and stared at the darkness, not a single light to be seen as the rain accumulated on the window to form long streaks. It was good to see the rain; it would fill the drying pond and wash the smoke from the skies. In the morning the air would smell fresh; it had been so long since moist fresh air embraced the manor. Jim gave praise to the Lord for such a gift. He prayed for Deena's safety and for all his children, especially Atanase. The air was still, no wind or flashes of lightning, just a very soft rain. Jim left the study and went out the kitchen door into the yard, he took a deep breath and imagined standing on the deck of a sailboat anchored off the Faroes. Oh, for the freedom of those days and the love of Maxine. He thanked the Lord for many blessings; the new world had little to offer. He felt bad for younger people who knew nothing of life before the revolution and collapse. "History is a lie agreed upon"—a line attributed to Napoleon. Ironically, there is no proof he ever said it. The new historical lie is omission; certain things never happened. These days, no one is taught alternative ways of thinking.

Jim walked around the pond and watched as the ducks paddled to deeper water. They aren't the brightest of creatures, but they know they are food. So many people fail to accept the fact they are expendable, their existence of little consequence. Even the peepers go silent as Jim comes near them. He's no threat, and yet they take no chances. Atanase is in trouble; Jim can sense it and fervently prays for a hedge of angels to watch over him and protect him as in Psalm 5:11-12. As for Deena, Jim also had concern, and again he prayed for her, thinking of Ephesians 6:12. She certainly was up against the forces of evil. The rain stopped and a wispy fog swirled over the pond. Jim returned to his easy chair in his study and fell asleep in damp clothes.

***

Deena struggled in the dark wood, soaked to the skin. Tree roots and slimy mud kept her footing unstable, but she plodded on. Her duffle bag had gained weight, or at least it felt heavier than when she packed it. Did she need any of this stuff? She questioned why she'd brought some of it. Now she was afraid to leave it, for fear that someone finding it could determine her direction of flight. She checked her watch, two a.m.; she had left her cell phone in the office. No drones had found her, so she figured the copper mesh wrapped around her arm had done the trick. At the manor, she hoped Jim could help her dig the chip out of her arm. The chip allowed her to buy things, recorded her every move, accumulated her work and social credits, and kept all her medical records. She wondered if it could detect the heartbeat of a fetus and send a signal to Arti. The temperature had dropped twenty degrees since she started her trek; she could see her breath and shivered.

***

Jim embraced his thoughts of Maxine, her love of children, and her ability to learn language. Maxine spoke five languages fluently and could stumble through four more. Their children had come from all over the world, from a variety of cultures. Without Maxine, none of the work would have been possible. When cancer took her, Jim sent the children out into the world to teach others about love and generosity. A world, harsh and brutal, that had fallen victim to its selfish desires. The State had turned its face away from immoral acts and encouraged violence, chaos, and crime. With everyone turned on each other and divided, no opposition to the State could be formulated. Add to that digital controls, embedded chips, remote cameras, and digital accounting of every citizen's transaction, and everyone became a slave. The schools didn't teach history, so no one knew the world had once been quite different free, with freedom in some areas.

Maxine championed freedom; she saw love and truth as the antidote for the madness engulfing the world. Yet she knew the Bible foretold of end times. The world would continue on its downward path.

As dawn was breaking, Deena stood in the woods across the road from the driveway leading to the manor. A light drizzle fell from more threatening clouds, along with a promise of violence. No vehicles passed; she felt confident she hadn't been tracked, so she scurried across the road and up the driveway around the bend.

Jim awakened in time to see her approach from the window of his study. She looked pathetic, so exhausted and sopping wet. Her hair hung in strings across her face; she was too tired to brush it aside. Her duffle bag dragged her right shoulder low, and her steps had no pep. Jim rushed out to carry the burden of her bag, and his frail body offered just enough support for her to increase her step. Going through the front door, Jim noticed the copper wrap around her forearm. He knew exactly what it was for but said nothing. Without a word, he knew she had left the State and come to him for refuge. He helped her to the spare bedroom and onto the bed, dropping her bag on the floor next to her. He grabbed a clean bathrobe and towel from the closet. He laid them on the bed next to her, and without a word he retreated to his study while she showered, donned the robe, and collapsed onto the bed. From the looks of her, he figured she would sleep for several hours.

As Jim stared out the window of the study, his view of the distant fields washed away as the clouds burst and lightning ripped the sky. Rumbles of thunder followed, rattling the glass, while the wind bent the trees of the nearby woods. Deena had arrived not a minute too soon; she had struggled all night in the rain, but this looked like the remnants of a hurricane.

Weather forecasts weren't available to the general public these days. Jim knew storms well from his days both as a system operator and at sea. With every flash of lightning, a memory flashed. He thought about the storm on St. Croix, running for his life with would-be murderers on his heels, and the hit to his head. A reflex brought Jim's hand up to the back of his head. As he rubbed the scar, he remembered Storm finding him in the debris at the bay. If he'd never tried to escape to St. Croix, he never would have met Max, and that didn't bear thinking about.

The clouds became so dark, and day turned into night as Jim snuggled in his recliner, at ease with the violence outside. Lightning flashes penetrated his eyelids and the thunder rumbled as Jim drifted asleep to his memories of St. Croix.

It had to be the silence that roused Jim, for Deena never made a sound as she entered the room and sat in a chair near him. Outside, the trees stood still while broken clouds drifted, drained of their might. A setting sun cast long shadows. Deena mulled over her words without releasing them; she felt lost and unsure, not quite in a panic but close.

Jim sensed her tension, and he understood without hearing a word from her. He had been where she was, emptied by a choice, too soon for regrets. Jim decided to poke the bubble, address the discomfiture.

"Did you sleep well?" Jim asked.

Deena held her breath, afraid to speak. She had made her choice, but now what? What did it mean? Jim turned from her; his eyes focused on the distant fields with pummeled weeds laid flat in great bands. Darkness filled the hollows under the trees. Without his eyes on her, she eased a bit. Her words would be thrown out into space, not directed at him.

"I threw away my whole life! Everything I have worked for. For what? Some stupid old man? Because some manipulator filled my head with shit! There's no turning back and there's nowhere to go." Deena let out a deep sigh.

Jim felt the blade tear into old scars, for he knew loss: death of a child, divorce, imprisonment, loss of the love of his life, and having the children he raised walk away. He also knew no words could do any justice to how he felt. Deena had lashed out at him, but he felt compassion for her; he knew her pain while she didn't know his. He had to say something but struggled for words.

"Sometimes we need to walk away from everything to find ourselves," Jim said.

"Stop with the platitudes. This is real, I have nothing. Do you hear me, nothing! I didn't need to find myself," Deena replied.

"Deena . . . you're scared. Give this a little time and thought. Freedom is scary, but it is also when you come to life. You were clinging to chains; you had nothing of value. You know some of my story; you know I walked away from my old life and gained more than I could have ever imagined."

"The times were different."

"No, the world now is different. This world owns those who submit and kills those who don't. You were a slave, now you are free. You've made a commitment, and I will trust you with a bit of knowledge. This is not the only manor in the world; there's a network. We rescue children from the streets and traffickers. Each manor functions as a seedpod for freedom seekers. We will help you," Jim said.

Deena held out her copper-wrapped arm. "I'm still in bondage; I can be tracked anywhere I go. What do I do about this? I'm pregnant with no way to feed a baby or myself."

Jim's eyes dropped. "We will address this, you will have some pain, but I can remove the chip, and when the baby comes, well, you'll see, there will be joy. You made choices, but there are options."

"Can you remove my chip?" Deena asked.

"Not without pain, and there is a risk. They place it near an artery and nerves. There may be bleeding and feeling loss, but they won't be able to find you."

Jim sat back in his recliner and signaled Deena to sit while he encouraged her to think of more pleasant things. He talked about Maxine, how she was with children. Speaking of maternal joys and hope calmed Deena. Jim loved talking about Max, especially to another woman, a woman who needed to know other ways of life. Max had taught the children about poetry and dance, encouraged them to sing and play instruments, frivolous stuff the State had no tolerance for.

"I've never danced. Matter of fact, I'm not sure when I heard music last," Deena said sheepishly.

"How thoughtless of me, all these times you have come here, and I never asked you if you would like to listen to some music." Jim walked across the room to an old CD player. "What kind of music would you like to hear?"

Deena had no clue; she didn't even know the different styles. Jim started with mellow classical to continue to relax the mood. Deena found it soothing; she couldn't believe such a thing could be outlawed.

"Want to listen to some fun stuff?" Jim asked.

Deena nodded, and Jim played a different song.

"What is it?" Deena asked.

"Country." Jim played a couple of Willie tunes followed by Waylon and Cash.

"Can you show me what dancing looks like?" Deena asked.

Jim had feared she might ask; he regretted mentioning Max had taught the kids to dance. Max was the dancer; Jim usually followed Max's lead.

"There's a lot of different styles of dance, just like music. Don't take this wrong, but being an old man, a slow dance might be best. To be proper, I'll keep my distance, but if we were the same age, we'd hold each other close." Jim motioned for her to step near him as he put on a new CD.

After he cleared his throat, he took Deena's hand and placed it on his shoulder; her other hand he held in his, and he began to count his steps and instructed her on how to move hers. They swayed to the music and moved around the room. With his eyes closed, he sensed Max and pulled Deena a little closer. She didn't resist. To her it was a father-daughter or grandfather-daughter moment. After two slow dances Jim pulled away from Deena, shut off the CD, and began sorting through a box he pulled from a cabinet.

"What are you doing? Are you tired?" Deena asked.

"No, it just dawned on me I have some videos of Max and the kids dancing. You can watch them and see every style," Jim replied.

He inserted a video disc into a player and turned on an ancient TV screen, and they settled into comfortable chairs. Max's face flashed on the screen, her smile almost extending into her green eyes, as Jim's heart raced. The scene faded into chaos as children ran about laughing and talking at once. The chaos didn't last, as Max gained control by starting the music. She danced, she instructed, she encouraged, and the children followed her every move. As the video continued, Deena studied the joy and moves exhibited by the children. The video was one of Max's tutoring tools; the children could watch their moves over and over. Every dance style was covered, from ballroom to country two-step. Jim's heart ached as he watched in silence; he remembered each day of filming. Deena didn't comment until the video was done.

"Wow!" It was all Deena could muster at first.

"Jim . . . how wonderful. Max was so lovely, graceful, and pretty."

Jim couldn't respond; a lump blocked his words, and his eyes welled. Deena refrained from further comments. Instead, she reflected on the differences between her days in the State home to what she just witnessed. Why had all this joy been sucked from the world? Now she knew why she gravitated toward this manor and this stupid old man.

NINE

Atanase

My head throbbed and I felt the wet egg on the top of my head. The blood stained my hand and ran down my neck onto my shirt. At least I hadn't been shot. I wondered if he'd tried to shoot me and the bullet failed, or if he'd just clobbered me in a rage. All I could remember was kneeling with the gun barrel to my temple. An iron collar irritated my neck as I tried to assess my whereabouts; a chain rattled. Like an old junkyard dog, I was chained to a post in the middle of a room, lit only by slivers of light sifting through gaps in the clapboard walls. Pungent odors of pig shit filled the air; I could hear snorts and grunts from another room. As my eyes adjusted, I realized skinned pigs hung from hooks across the room where I sat. A slaughterhouse . . .

My chain proved short. I couldn't stand as it was hooked low to the post, and I couldn't fully lie down because it was hooked just high enough to deny me comfort. My hands and feet were free but of little use. As the hours passed, the light between the clapboards faded, and I soon sat in total darkness. A pungent smell of smoke drifted in the air, in the distance. I heard men's voices, laughter, and an occasional female scream. The screams were always followed by laughter. It went on relentlessly for hours, as I questioned my sanity. Had they already killed me? Was this hell? Will this be my eternity? Sleep evaded me, though my eyes slammed shut, my mind shut down, but only for an instant. It was sleep, but it didn't refresh me, and I realized I had a concussion. Maybe even a brain bleed. My only hope was to pray. A dim light came through the voids between the clapboards, and the laughter and screams faded. It was morning, and the light streamed through the smoke that still filled the air.

With the morning came the flies, billions of them crawling on any bit of exposed flesh, prying at my eyes and vexing my nostrils. The skinless pigs across the room crawled with them. I envisioned flies wading around on the bile-covered dirt floors and maggots, mounds of maggots, eating the flesh in the gut piles. This was hell, and there was no relief; they *had* killed me. The huge barn door slid open, and three men entered, one pushing a wheelbarrow into position under a hanging pig. They swatted flies with rags as one loosened the hanging rope and lowered the carcass into the wheelbarrow. No one spoke or acknowledged me, and I chose not to bring any attention to myself. The process was repeated until all the pigs had been removed and the barn door closed. At least now I knew I wasn't in hell—those men were real; gone were the pigs but not the stench of death.

Four times I watched the light fade, heard the laughter and screams, and witnessed a new day. No one fed me, gave me water, or allowed me any sanitation. I struggled not to sleep, for when my eyes slammed shut and my body relaxed, I hung by the chain unable to breathe. Hallucinations, or waking dreams, began on the third day, in which people spoke to me, tormented me, then disappeared without a trace. Several times I saw my wife; she comforted me with kind words, but when she came close enough to touch, she turned to smoke.

This, I resolved, was my fate. This was how they intended to let me die. During the fourth night, the door slid open, and the three men entered, muscling a fourth, whom they strung up like a pig. All were silhouettes, and I thought of Plato's allegory of shadows on a cave wall and how a prisoner sees them as reality because they are all he knows.

"Atanase?" the hanging man whispered.

To hear my name startled me. His voice was weak and strained. I waited, thinking it was a hallucination, a waking dream. Then, when I heard it a second time, I responded. "Yes, I am Atanase. Who are you? How do you know my name?"

"It's Gus. Do you remember me?" the hanging man gasped.

"Gus? Yes, but you were headed into Amish country."

"The Amish are no more. Wiped out. The smoke choking us is from Pennsylvania farms and farmlands. They burned everything in three counties, including Lancaster. The fires still burn, and they killed every man, woman, and child for not complying with the State. They also killed the new landowners who allowed the Amish to work their land as tenants. The Peacekeepers did it. They accused the Amish of being terrorists."

"Were you among them?"

"Yes, I saw it all. I'm sorry, Atanase, the little girl in your heart is dead."

Neither of us could continue. We ended the conversation both too weak to do anything or say anything. Who kills children? Oh, so sweet and full of love and hope. Nothing my captors could do to me would cause more pain than the news Gus had shared. Pure evil, monsters, and somehow they believe and declare they are right in what they do. My eyes closed, I had to sleep, even if I suffocated. When I slept, my steel collar didn't dig into my throat; grateful, I didn't question why.

When I woke, Gus wasn't hanging from the pig rack; I scanned the rest of the room. No sign of Gus anywhere. Had he been a hallucination, or did someone take him away as I slept?

For the first time in days, I felt rested and my head didn't hurt, nor did my neck. Gentle hands touched my neck and the steel collar from behind. The hands came out of the dark as if they were not attached to any arms or body. The touch struck me with fear for a moment, but something about them soothed me. The hands felt their way around the collar until the collar opened and fell away.

"Atanase, it's me, Gus. You are free, stand." The voice came from a distance.

As I stood, I wobbled and turned toward the dark, looking for Gus or even his hands, but nothing took form.

"Gus?" I whispered.

"Just go," came a reply.

"Just go? They're out there. I can hear them, their laughter. They'll kill me," I retorted and stepped toward the voice.

"No, you'll be safe. Believe they can't see you. Trust me. Evil blinds them; the deeper they sink in the filth, the less they see."

"Who are you?" I asked. The voice belonged to Gus, but was he a living, breathing human?

"The one who set you free, now go."

"What about you? Come with me . . . you can't stay here." I stepped into the dark space, my eyes having adjusted enough to see the walls and the floor. It sent a chill through me. The emptiness frightened me more than the voices and laughter of the maniacs outside. In a panic I ran to the door, pushed it open, and stopped to catch my breath. One last glance over my shoulder into the dark barn and I began a slow walk into the smoke-filled night. Twenty men, gathered around fires, were laughing and taunting a woman. It sickened me, but there was nothing I could do. Their focus was so set on their perversions, no one noticed me as I headed down a dirt road shadowed by huge oaks.

Thick brush grew along the edge where I walked. If anyone approached, I could vanish in an instant. Adrenaline fueled me; I hadn't eaten or drank water for days, but somehow I pushed on. Where the dirt intersected the blacktop, I stopped to get my bearings and rest. There were no lights in either direction; smoke hung heavy in the air and took its toll on me.

"Atanase, over here."

I heard a crisp voice and looked about. "Gus?"

"Yes, cross the road," Gus said as I approached him. He was in the shadows, but a vague silhouette motioned to me. His bicycle leaned against his hip.

"How . . . ?" I started to say.

"Anything is possible if you believe. Your bike is there," he said, pointing toward a frame lying nearby.

"Amazing, who are you, really?"

"I told you when we first met."

"I think there's more to it . . . to you."

"Know what you see, but remember, there is more to the unseen than the seen. Now, we have until morning to burn miles. They won't search far; they survive in the narrows of this place. They've become of the moment. Not much venturing out or looking ahead. Head north, where you are needed," Gus said.

"What about you? Come with me."

"I told you I was going south if the Amish didn't work out." Gus dropped his head.

"I just can't believe we ended up in the same place. Thank you."

"Don't thank me, I'm just a pawn in all this. These are treacherous and mysterious times. Be safe, be cautious, my friend," Gus said as he mounted his bike.

The iron collar had left a lasting feeling on my flesh. Both my hands tried to wipe it away as I watched Gus pedal away. Who was he? The whole of it was surreal, but like he said, "These are mysterious times." Mounting my bike, I headed north on an unlit road, the dense smoke curling in my wake. Within two hours I would be twelve miles away, out of their reach but not out of danger from other groups. With Gus heading south, there would be no one to save me, and the manor was a long way off.

In four miles I entered Leipsic, a veritable ghost town, burned out and abandoned. Main Street had several commercial buildings all with severe structural damage, broken windows, missing doors, and broken roofs. I entered one after another, squeezing between broken timbers and furniture, focused on old coolers and refrigeration units in search of old bottles of water. It was a frantic search—life and death was no exaggeration. Dark shadows strained my eyes as I felt my way. Covered in dust and cobwebs in an old chest cooler, I found liquid gold and cracked one open. The first sip was better than the finest wine, and I savored it, swishing it between my cheeks before it trickled down my throat. The rest I guzzled.

The bridge over the Leipsic River lay in the riverbed, bent rusted steel and crumbled concrete. Route 9 ended here, my hopes to avoid more populated areas dashed. The smoke had gotten the best of me, or maybe it was the lack of sleep, food, and water, but Leipsic River looked refreshing. I swear the stench of death in the barn clung to me, and I could still feel the iron collar about my neck. I stashed my bike behind a giant slab of concrete and made my way on the bank, hidden in chest-high weeds. Another large slab of concrete dipped into the river, and the dry portion offered a nice place to lie and greet the rising sun. The sun was an hour from breaking over the horizon, but darkness faded into grey. A light fog drifted over the water, unaware of the evils done by man. Surface water can be dangerous to drink, even though the river ran clear. I gave thanks for finding the bottled water.

As the sun crested, its reflection stretched across the still waters to brush away the mist. Warmed by the brilliant glow, I lay back on the concrete, my eyes shaded by my forearm across my brow. Sections of steel from the collapsed bridge still stretched above the river to offer birds a perch with a view. Nature takes back man's foibles and repurposes them for the benefit of other creatures. With stealth, a feral cat walked, belly low on a beam, in search of breakfast, and the sight grieved me. My thoughts turned to the days along the Susquehanna, the Amish and Katy, now wiped from the earth. My memory was all that was left of them in this time and place. I knew they were now basking in the glory of God.

Katy worked in the flower beds not as a chore but as an act of love. Toward the end of one day, she came running into the barn filled with joy, a kitten pressed against her chest. As she loosened her grip, it climbed to her shoulder. I gave her my full attention, trying to grasp her words as they fired past me.

"Look what I found in the flower beds! It's so sweet and tiny, I can feel every bone in its body. Mamm and Pa will never let me keep her. She's so sweet, I love her! What should I call her? I'll feed her some of my food rations, she won't be any trouble, will you help me? The adults say we can only feed what we can eat, but we need things to love. Don't you agree?" Katy spouted, from a heart too big for her body.

My own heart searched for such things in a world gone mad. The kitten weighed but a pound, and I ran one finger from the tip of her nose up over her forehead, her purr barely heard, but I could feel it in my finger. Katy's eyes welled; she sensed the reality of the times.

"Your garden is filled with lilies, I think you should call her Tiger Lily. She has all the markings of a tiger, and we need tigers."

Katy loved the name; I watched her give Tiger Lily water and some shredded chicken. As we sat, she snuggled the kitten, placed gentle kisses on the top of its head, and I think I heard both purring. The next morning Katy came to me in sobs, carrying something bundled in a towel . . .

The sun burned, and I stood and ran full out into the Leipsic, fully clothed. The stench of death covered me, embedded in all my fabric. I had to get free. The water covered my head; fully immersed, I stayed down until my lungs nearly burst. When I broke the surface, I shook my head to release water from my hair. My feet rested on the submerged bridge deck, the water to my shoulders, and I prayed the water would carry the death away from me. Try as I might, I could not shut down my brain.

To reassure Katy, I'd told her at least the kitty had found love and didn't die alone in the woods or garden as so many do these days. We all seek love; some never find it, and some never embrace it.

Once again, I held my breath and went underwater, longer this time. As I emerged, I walked up the concrete to where I'd originally lain, took off my shirt and pants, and stretched out on the sun-warmed surface to dry and be refreshed by the sun. The feeling of the iron collar was fading. As I stretched out beside my clothes, the sun caressed me, and I watched the gulls glide over the water.

People have referred to the Bible as a book of fairy tales, stories written by men, metaphors, and fantasy. The book of Job came to mind, where evil walked the earth and tortured Job, taking from him all he had. Job was a righteous man of God, and evil wanted him to blame and curse God for his troubles. Job never caved; he withstood every test Satan cast upon him. Job saw his possessions as temporary blessings, things he would never have had without God. He knew not to cling to them; he held them loosely.

Now, I thought, Job might have been a man, but he could also represent a nation or a culture, and while people argue over whether it's a metaphor or a fairy tale, they miss the point. In all his troubles, Job never cursed or blamed the Lord. In the end Job's victory came from standing fast and trusting in God. He didn't need to fight Satan; he merely ignored his attacks and patiently waited for things to play out in God's time. The message is a strong one and applies to everyone and every nation. Not an exact quote, but Job said something like this: "Naked I came, naked I shall leave." My clothes were almost dry, they smelled of river water, so much better than death.

Dressed, I pushed my bike to the road and backtracked until I was on Route 42. Cheswold sat four miles to the west. Highway 1 ran north/south just east of the town, and I hoped it had been abandoned. This four-lane road could bypass a lot of towns. Route 42 should have been an easy four-mile pedal if not for the thick smoky air. Air quality limited my speed and required several breaks. The fires had to be powerful to produce so much smoke. It sickened me. Man's treatment of each other had never been good, but this world system controlled by AI had no blood in the game and called the shots.

The overpass for Highway 1 came into view, the entrance ramp overgrown in weeds. The weeds were so high and thick, I had to dismount and push the bike. The pavement on the ramp had turned to a flaky gravel, sand, and lime mix I had seen in other places, heat-damaged by lasers or small tactical nukes. This area could be radioactive, but it didn't matter; I just needed to move fast. The best radiation protection is time, distance, and shielding. So I made my time short and increased my distance.

Once on Highway 1, the road was clear and smooth, so I pedaled like I stole it, and I had. An exit sign said Smyrna, but there hadn't been a Smyrna in a long time, as nature had reclaimed most of the crumbled buildings. It looked like an ancient South American city of the lost. My speed increased once the air pollution cleared with a shift of the winds. However, at the Appoquinimink River the bridges were down.

Route 1 was abandoned because it no longer went anywhere. With another blown bridge and the decline in world population, there was no need to repair these relics. The Appoquinimink is only a little over fifteen miles long but drains about fifty square miles of coastal plain. The bridges weren't just down; the highway had been devastated as far as I could see. A four-lane running parallel to Route 1 was in the same condition. Once again, I backtracked to catch another road called Old State, thinking the bridge on it may have survived. A wrong assumption, another destroyed bridge, another detour on

Silver Run Road, and another bridge in ruin. My detours had led me closer to the Delaware Bay where Appoquinimink is tidal and brackish. From where I stood, I watched some fishermen and oyster gatherers working along the shore. They had boats, one of which I needed, and they were workers, so I felt safe approaching them.

Marsh lands flowed in every direction, so the only solid ground was the road surface, but the tide flooded this area. A lone fisherman in a boat caught sight of my waving arms and to my amazement put down his fishing pole and rowed in my direction. Such a response was rare these days; even though I had made the effort to signal him, I didn't expect a positive response.

"What do you want?" he asked as he came into range.

"Can you take me across the river? I'm heading north and all the bridges are ruined," I replied.

"Most of the country is in ruin, my friend," he quipped.

"Are you a local?" I asked.

"I'm from Shell Pile. Fourth generation. Our family came when they freed the slaves. We're brought up not to trust outsiders, especially white folk."

My heart sank, not because he didn't appear likely to help me, but because Port Norris and the surrounding area was being devastated by the Peacekeepers. It was very possible his entire family was dead. How do I break it to him? What do I say? If he wasn't going to help me, I didn't need to say any more.

"Who are you? Why are you traveling?" he asked.

"My name is Atanase, I'm coming from Port Norris . . . there's trouble. I had to escape, sailed across the bay until drones took out my boat."

"Times are worse than ever as far as trusting people goes. You look haggard, but you might just be trying to gain my trust, take advantage of me," he said as he pulled out a pistol. "Don't much like liars."

"No need for a gun, my friend. I'll move on, no harm, no pressure," I said, tightening my grip on my handlebars. "I'm telling you the truth. The Peacekeepers were burning buildings. I assume they were killing people."

"My people?"

"Not sure about anything. All the smoke is from Pennsylvania Amish country. Someone told me they wiped out the Amish and are burning their farms," I told him.

"Lordy . . . I wondered about the smoke. My wife and children are with me. This dingy is just for river fishing. I have a boat in the bay. The others you see are from Shell Pile; we work together. Some also have bigger boats in the bay."

"I'm not your enemy; I'm in need of help."

His stare showed little emotion; when he turned from me, he looked about for the other fishermen. He had a sturgeon, several croakers, and some gray trout in the bottom of his boat, more than enough for a day's catch. The sturgeon was protected at one time, but with human depopulation the survival rate of these fish increased. No one policed endangered species anymore. After some thought, he turned back toward me.

"Come with me to my boat." He signaled the others along the river of his intent to go to the bay.

How could I turn down his offer? In the bay, a bigger boat might be a target for drones, but hell, everything was a target for drones. He helped me load my bicycle into his rowboat, and we shoved off. His name was Silas, and we weren't going to the bay by river; he knew a shortcut. Skunk Hill Ditch, an old canal between The Island and Fennimore Landing. As we rowed along the canal, Silas spoke of his wife and children, their struggles. Things hadn't changed much with the collapse; they were in deep financial poverty before the collapse, but now there was financial poverty and more dangers. The self-imposed isolation of Shell Pile prepared them well to distrust the government and outsiders. Silas fretted over my story about the shots fired at me as I approached Port Norris, and about the burning of buildings. When we emerged from the ditch, several ancient workboats sat anchored at the mouth of the Appoquinimink. Most looked like salvaged wrecks rigged with sails.

"Contentment makes you rich, my friend. All these troubles are caused by the discontented. No matter how much money and power they wield, they will never be satisfied or content. The people of Shell Pile are content people, always have been. We came from slaves, and in our poverty-stricken town, we had freedom. Our grandparents taught us to be content. When money became obsolete and the digital chains rattled of a slavery which would hold us to the moment, would mark us, we abandoned our homes for refuge in our workboats," Silas lamented.

Silas tossed his wife a line as we came alongside; her vessel had no name and looked more like a homeless encampment than a family yacht. We climbed a rope ladder to the deck, where Silas introduced his wife and seven children. Isana, his wife, looked weathered. Her smile came from the heart when he introduced us. She didn't need words to let me know who she was. Two small children clung to her long dress without smiling. The oldest, I guessed to be four, was Amari and his brother, Jahmir. Four other sons went off the side to bring the day's catch on board; I would learn their names at dinner. Silas requested Isana to fetch us drinks, a homemade rum concoction. We sat in the stern as the children and his wife prepared the catch. A warm kindness radiated among the mother and her children, such a moment as I often witnessed among the Amish and during my years at the manor. I told Silas everything about my escape from the drones, the militia group, and finding the bicycle.

"These are the end times, my friend. Nothing shocks me anymore. Christians are being hunted; any excuse is good enough. A true Christian is an enemy of the State. Would you be one?" Silas said before taking a long drink.

"I am, and I will not say otherwise, even to save my skin."

Silas burst into laughter and held out his drink in a toast. We watched the returning fishermen come out of the Skunk Hill ditch and make their way to their boats. Silas waved to some, shouted to others; they appeared to be a band of brothers. To the State they were scoundrels, thieves, and pirates. In truth, to a man, each possessed more scruples than the entirety of the ruling class combined.

TEN

Deena

"Deena, have you ever wondered if human beings are truly sentient? Really, I mean they may have their moments, but don't people simply repeat what others say, conform to the herd to gain acceptance? Once someone accepts a notion, they will fight tooth and nail to protect it. Societies' manipulators know these traits all too well. Even in the days of Rome, Greece, and Egypt the kings and priests used this method to control the population. This is mankind's downfall," Jim said as he paused during breakfast.

"Guilty! Yes, they used it on me. My whole life has been about conforming to gain acceptance. The State did a job on me, on a whole generation," Deena replied.

She took a sip of tea. In the morning light, with the smoke washed away by the storm, they enjoyed breakfast on the back deck while duck watching.

"What's the pole with the rope dangling a ragged ball?"

"That's the children's old tetherball; they spent hours playing. Come, I'll show you."

Jim showed Deena how to hit the ball with her fists, and she knocked it one way, then another. "This is a great stress reliever!"

Jim laughed. "Kick it with your feet and punch it with your hands."

After a few timid kicks, she began to blast the ball around the pole. "I'll pretend this is Bob's head!" Jim knew she would enjoy this type of release for days to come.

Deena didn't want to stop, but her arm, still wrapped in copper, needed to be addressed. Jim knew he would inflict pain in the process. He didn't relish the thought, but it had to be done soon. The copper wrap appeared to cloak the signal. Nothing would be certain, though, she wouldn't be clear without extracting the chip. They ate slowly, chatted on many subjects, all to delay the inevitable.

"It's your call, Deena; we've put this off as long as we could. We either get it done or forget about it." Jim felt sick to his stomach; he wanted it over.

"Do it. I'm ready," Deena said with confidence.

Jim walked over to the stove with a modified ice pick, its cherry-red point bent into a hook. The wooden handle isolated the heat from his hand. Deena removed the copper wrap from around her arm. Nothing told them, but they both knew a signal instantaneously went to a satellite. Jim grabbed her arm. A very tiny, tattooed dot marked the spot. Jim thrust the icepick into her flesh. Smoke rose from the point of entry, and Deena flinched. The smell of burnt flesh permeated their nostrils. Jim worked fast. He didn't know if he was damaging nerves; that would take time to know. The heat destroyed the chip even before Jim pulled it out of her flesh. He tapped the tip of the ice pick on a sheet of white paper. The chip looked like a fleck of black pepper. So tiny, yet more effective than an iron chain fastened to a hundred-pound iron ball. For good measure Jim crumbled the paper and tossed it into the flames of the stove.

Jim was amazed that Deena hadn't screamed. She sat very stoic, her eyes glistened, but no tears fell. She held her arm tight with her other hand. Her grip tightened to choke off the pain signal heading to her brain. It wasn't the pain in her arm bothering her; it was the pain in her heart.

"Am I saved?"

"You'll be harder to track," Jim replied.

"I believe I had the mark of the beast; it condemned me. Does removing it free me?" Deena said with a shaky, questioning voice.

"Jesus saves you. I can't say, but we should pray," Jim said as he put his hand on her shoulder.

Jim walked to the sink, thinking that everyone questions their faith. He washed his hands as Deena stared at the reddened patch of burned flesh on her wrist. The scar would be permanent, a forever reminder of the chains of slavery and the ease of submission. Her future was sketchy, but better than being a cog in the machine. Her baby would be born free, and she intended to see it grow and flourish beyond the entrapments offered by the ruling class. No matter how desperate things became, she would prefer death to submission to the world. Instead, she would submit to God and pray for mercy.

"Deena, you have come a long way. You have turned your back on all the world has to offer. If God doesn't forgive you and accept you, none of us will be let into heaven. I wish I could provide you with some pain meds, but I have none." Jim dropped into a chair across the table from her.

"The wound looks worse than it is. I can bear the pain. When I think of the crucifixion, my wound seems quite silly," Deena replied.

They prayed together and then sat in silent prayer for another ten minutes. Deena got up and made some tea Jim had introduced her to. With the supply chain destroyed and access to commercially provided products forbidden to non-Acceptors, alternatives had to be found. Research into native cultures provided answers. This tea was a favorite of the Chippewa tribe. Jim also made dandelion tea. Jim sat and watched Deena as she maneuvered about; she seemed to have made herself at home here. It gave him comfort to have saved her and the child. She returned with two cups of tea and placed one in front of Jim.

"We need a plan. I wish there was a way to communicate with some of the children Max and I raised. If I knew how they fared, I could decide which of them to send you to. Logistics is another problem. We lack transportation," Jim said in between sips of tea.

"Staying here might be best. I feel safe here."

"There's no future here. I'm an old man, and you couldn't sustain this place on your own. Besides, this place isn't such a secret anymore. Eventually, one of your ex-colleagues will stumble onto it and won't treat it the way you did. No, we need to plan," Jim said as he held his cup in both hands, his eyes fixed on the liquid. "One of my boys recently headed into Delaware to find some others; he may come back with some answers. In the meantime, I will teach you survival skills."

"Survival skills? What do you mean?"

"You need to know how to feed yourself, give yourself first aid, and learn about medicinal plants, how to conceal yourself and find safe places to sleep. Just like this tea, we can learn a lot from the people of the forest. The natives lived just fine without any modern conveniences. I have books you can read, and I can show you lots of edible plants around the property. Let's have sunchokes for dinner."

"Sunchokes?"

"Native Americans ate them. They're also known as Jerusalem Artichokes, but they're nothing like an artichoke. They're more like a potato."

After they finished tea, they walked toward the meadow and located a stand of tall plants with yellow flowers. The flowers had a mild vanilla-chocolate scent. Jim grabbed a stalk and pulled it out, roots and all. Hanging off the roots were tubers, which he pulled off and placed in a bucket. As they harvested, Jim explained their food value such as high protein, no oil, and little starch. Sunchokes have a sweet taste due to fructose. These tubers contain inulin, which isn't absorbed in the human intestine, so there is no glycemic spike as in potatoes. The tubers are good keepers and can be eaten cooked, raw, or pickled. As they walked back toward the house, Deena's curiosity got the best of her.

"Your son, the one who went to Delaware, what's he like? Is he like you?"

"Better, much better, but with the world such as it is, we can't concern ourselves with him, and I can't do him justice by talking about him. You are a very strong person; we'll focus on you and how you can stand alone. You're a warrior, I recognized it the moment I met you. You are destined to wear the full armor of God and become a brave knight," Jim replied as he stooped to pick up several hickory nuts.

Jim held out his hand to show them to Deena and explain the value of eating wild nuts. Hickory nuts are loaded with vitamins and minerals. They have a sweet, nutty taste and can be stored for long periods. He went on to explain the varieties, then suggested she try one to test her for allergens, since tree nuts can be a major source of allergies. He warned her to be cautious of all foraged foods, to nibble a sample and wait for mild reactions before gorging on anything. Hunger can cloud the mind. A starving person can die when they consume too much of a good thing or by eating the wrong thing. Deena needed to learn much, and teaching her made Jim feel useful in a way he hadn't felt in years. He taught her to identify edible flora and fauna. Never eat bright-colored plants or bugs; only eat insects with segmented bodies. Earth worms are a great food source, even raw. She needed survival skills, knowledge about the real world and not the artificial bubble she had been enslaved in. Jim intended to provide her with every advantage.

Deena had taken to early-morning jogs, and Jim would stand at the window in the study to watch as she came out of the woods and crossed the meadow. He checked his watch; she shaved off seven minutes since she began her work out program. He made her a crude set of dumbbell weights out of old tractor parts and an isometric rig. She had always been fit, but never like this. Being pregnant suited her, and she was careful to not push anything too far. Jim played a game of hide-and-seek with her, teaching her how to camouflage herself and blend into the forest.

This morning when she reached the front door of the manor, Jim greeted her. "Your time has improved significantly; how do you feel?"

"Wonderful, I've never felt so alive and free."

"You know, I always thought the female wolf in the meadow was Max coming for me. Now I think it was a premonition of you." Jim said the words without thinking.

Deena's silence caused him to pause until she threw her arms around him in a big bear hug.

"There is something I have for you in the study. Come!" Jim said.

When he walked into the study, Jim lifted a sheet cover off the table. Deena's eyes lit up and her jaw dropped as she picked up the object and ran her fingertips over it.

"A crossbow! It's so compact. Is it powerful?" Deena squealed.

"Try it. Come on, let's go out back. Grab a fistful of arrows."

The arrows were more like long darts than arrows. Jim had fashioned the crossbow in secret over the past week. It wasn't his first creation; he had passed them out to each of the kids as they reached a responsible stage, and they became very proficient at their use. This crossbow was the best he had ever made; he had started making it years earlier for Max but had lost interest when she died. Deena inspired him to finish it. Lightweight, it could be carried without burden. It had a shoulder sling and a built-in quiver for spare darts. Not only functional, but it also had artistic qualities in the woodwork of the stock and pistol grip. He used as much aluminum as possible, but he had to use what was available. He explained to Deena that if she hunted, she should focus on small game such as rabbits and squirrels. Large game animals would be a waste for one person on the move. Being encamped for a longer period where the meat could be smoked and cured would be more suitable for killing a deer. Jim reinforced that foraging is primary, not to count on hunting or fishing. The hunt can be time-consuming and end in a waste of time, so she should consider killing a rabbit or squirrel as a bonus. Jim pointed out targets set up in the yard, and Deena loaded a dart, took aim, and proved to be an excellent marksman. The darts hit their targets with deadly force.

"Well, I expect either rabbit or squirrel for dinner. Do you know where the word *sin* originated? In five languages, it means to miss the target," Jim said, egging her on.

Deena gave him a wink and disappeared off into the woods. Eventide witnessed her return across the field, and Jim stood outside in wait. She held her game pouch high over her head as she waved to him. He signaled her toward a picnic table under a large oak. As she approached, he could see the excitement on her face.

"Good day's hunt? The game pouch looks full," Jim shouted.

Deena didn't speak; her body language said it all. She held the game pouch over the table, untied the drawstrings, and let her booty drop onto the table. Sunchokes, hickory nuts, dandelion greens, several onions, a snake, and two live grass snakes. The grass snakes were quick to leave the table. Deena smiled.

"Like you said, hunters starve, finders eat. I was quick to give up on squirrels and rabbits and collected what I could. There's more to hunting than being a good shot." Deena laughed.

"Well, good thing I caught a couple bass in the pond. Come on, you must be starved," Jim said as he signaled her to follow him into the manor.

The bass sizzled in the cast-iron skillet smothered in garlic cloves and onions while potatoes finished baking in the wood-fired oven. Deena was happy not to be eating the snake; there would come a time for it, but Jim had put it off for tonight. She had fully expected him to cook it and feed it to her. Jim said grace and they ate in silence. When their plates were clean, he spoke.

"Deena, I suggest you read the book of Job. When I read it, I see Satan's walk on Earth as an attack on believers. Job appears to me as a metaphor."

"I've read the book of Job. I've read every bit of history I can." Deena replied.

"Well, Job is the consummate believer. Did you ask yourself, why would God allow such a horrible thing?"

"The book of Job spells it out quite clearly. A believer's purpose is to never waver, no matter the circumstance. When bad things happen, God watches to see how those who surround the victim act. Many a self-proclaimed believer turns his back on the victim or will accuse them of being punished for something evil they have done."

"Ouch, I never thought of it that way."

"Remember, the greater the believer, the more intense the attacks, but in the end God restores the faithful. It's a sorting process; it's the only true way we can prove our love, for God or each other. It's not the babble we spew; it's our response and actions that reveal the truth of who we are. It may not be about the sufferer; it may be about those surrounding the victim. Your future will be filled with suffering, yours and that of others," Jim said as he fiddled with his fork.

"I face things as they come."

"Just keep things in perspective. The war is with the unseen. Don't waste your talents seeking revenge or fighting unnecessary battles; walk away, or better yet run away, whenever you can."

Deena squirmed in her chair as Jim kept talking about the unseen. He told her about crossing the Atlantic alone. She leaned in when he described going through the wall in the eye of the hurricane and being saved by fishermen. With dinner and cleanup complete, Jim suggested they sit in the yard and enjoy the evening. There's no sound like the breeze through fall leaves or the chirps of tree frogs and crickets. Two bullfrogs bellowed to each other from opposite sides of the pond, and Jim said one was Jeremiah, a weeping lonely frog, not to be confused with the one in the Three Dog Night song. The reference went right over Deena's head.

"Jeremiah's a prophet, he knows the future, and every night he shares it with the other frogs, but they mock him," Jim shared.

Deena laughed as Jim sang the Three Dog Night rendition of a bullfrog named Jeremiah.

A mallard emerged from the rushes; three newly hatched ducklings followed her into the pond. Mama duck quacked loudly as she moved to deeper water. Jim's heart ached; the weather wasn't in their favor, too late in the year and temperatures would drop at night. There would be no chance to intervene and capture them.

"Jim, look, how cute." Deena pointed to the ducklings, who faithfully followed their mother. They had little chance of survival. Why would a mallard sit on her eggs at this time of year? She stopped to let them catch her.

"We'll come to want to wash this sight from our minds, for I doubt we will see these little ones over the coming days," Jim said.

"What do you mean?"

"It's too late in the year, too chilly. We'll be checking for them with hopes to see them but never will."

"Oh, Jim, how sad."

"Listen!" Jim whispered as all the critter noises went silent. All you could hear was the breeze in the limbs of the overhead trees. Jim called it the "coming home" song.

"It's so quiet," Deena whispered. "It's a little spooky.

"Do you remember why you first came here?" Jim asked. Even in the faded light the answer formed on her face; she didn't need to speak, and they both knew. "Never forget it, and remember the battle isn't fought in the flesh; it's a battle of the spirits. Waste no energy on the chaos and mockers, stay at peace to calm the storm, and only use violence to stop a mocker from harming you physically."

She had come to do Jim harm, to destroy him. Coming to know him brought to light the great manipulation that had become so much a part of her. How could she have been so intent on destroying this man? Because she didn't know Jim; the State labeled him the bad guy, and her job was to take out bad guys. He wasn't bad; his only crime was noncompliance with a ruthless State. She shuddered with the thought of her successes on other investigations. How many good people had she harmed? Her head dropped.

"Go easy on yourself. Satan is the great enticer and mocker, but he has limits. When he first went after Job, God forbade him to lay a finger on him. As Satan said, Job had a hedge of protection around him. So, as a believer, pray for such a hedge of protection and for inner strength. Nothing Satan could do would've caused Job to curse the Lord. To further prove his point, God took it a step further and inflicted physical ailments on Job. Job stood his ground, cursed himself but never God. Satan can cause chaos around us, but only God can touch us. Sometimes he does so, to see how those around us will react. Life is a test from many directions, and few will pass."

"Jim, I'm so sorry." The smile on Jim's face stopped her midsentence. "What? You're smiling."

"Deena, know this about me. The more someone tries to hurt me, the stronger I become. When you showed up, I was fading fast. You gave me the will to live."

His words silenced their conversation, and they sat listening to the wind.

"I'm going in to make some tea, would you like some?" Deena stood and stretched.

"Do you need help?"

"No, relax. I'll be but a moment," Deena said as she walked into the shadows.

In the silence Jim waited, his head bobbed; then his chin came to rest on his chest. At total peace, the night once again filled with soothing sounds. Jim's own snore roused him, and his head snapped high, eyes wide. Something wasn't right. Deena should have returned. He stood and looked toward the manor. The kitchen lights were out; the whole manor melted into the night. He moved quickly and entered the kitchen; the teapot screamed and blew steam. Jim took no time to quell the noise. He ran down the hall calling out to Deena; he searched every room to no avail. She had vanished. He ran out the front door and circled the exterior of the manor calling to her. He went to her room and found all her things in order. She took nothing with her. He felt a hundred years old as he sat slump-shouldered on the edge of her bed and listened to distant screams of the teapot.

Nothing made sense; the State would have trashed the place and done him in. Deena wouldn't have gone on her own. He hadn't heard a vehicle, but then he remembered the silence. The only sound was the breeze in the trees. Critters go quiet when they sense danger. He wasn't up to running through the woods in a search, but what choice did he have? He grabbed Deena's bugout pack and her crossbow. All he needed was a direction, and he reasoned some choices as he headed for the door. His ancient eyes didn't serve him well in the dark, nor did his hips and knees, but he would do whatever it took.

ELEVEN

Atanase

Silas knew the bay, every inlet and tributary. He held the unofficial role of mayor, judge, and peace maintainer of the flotilla. I had done well to find him; it had been a long time since I was so well fed and fussed over by a woman like Isana, not since the Amish. The State labels such people as criminals and deviates, yet these simple folk were bathed in love. The pockets of love I'd stumbled on in a world of darkness gave me hope. I sat on deck as we poked along the western shore of the bay, Silas's oldest son at the helm.

"Peaceful," Silas said as he handed me a cup of herbal tea.

"Indeed, it is," I replied.

"What more could a man possess?" Silas punctuated with a sip.

"Aye, it truly is enough."

"Not for kings, there is never enough. It's been their way since the beginning of time, never satisfied. Just like what is going on today—the common man goes about his life the best he can as the elite grab more and more. Yes, we are the rich ones, the satisfied, and the kings can't figure out how to get what we have. They have riches of gold and silver, but nothing of value."

We sat together, Silas and I, as the water flowed, the breeze cooled, and the shoreline changed from overgrown vegetation to relics of estates, cabins, and crumbled commerce before once again overgrown vegetation. Eagles, gulls, osprey, and ducks cruised overhead against a blue sky. We were heading north, in no great rush—why would we be in a hurry? Everything we needed we had; nothing better waited to the north, except my destination. We had a decent wind at our backs, but this old fishing boat had never been meant to be sailed; her motor had been dry for years, and she wasn't much more than a raft with a sheet.

"You know, Silas, this was once a great nation, with a great notion, but it crumbled just as Rome did two thousand years ago. Did you ever read any of Taylor Caldwell's works?"

"Most often just read the Good Book."

"Well, she wrote one called *Great Lion of God*, about Saint Paul. She might just as well have been writing about the fall of the American empire, with all the political intrigue and backstabbing that went on in the last days before the collapse," I said, but Silas wasn't having it. Instead, he pointed out a blue heron on the shore.

"We catch fish, we eat it, and we pray for one more day, one more night. All we got is right here, in this moment, so love it, my friend. The rest of it is the stuff of fools." Silas punctuated his words with a belly laugh loud enough to summon Isana.

"What are you laughing at, you old fool?" Isana asked as she flicked a dish towel at Silas. "You boys talking about women?"

Silas snatched the dish towel before Isana could bring it home. He gave a tug on the towel, and Isana fell into his arms.

"Women ain't for talking about, they're for hugging, and talking with." Silas laughed.

"Oh, Silas, ain't you the charmer and the naughty one." Isana struggled in his arms but not enough to break free.

I watched the shoreline to be polite, giving them their moment. The heron took flight.

***

As the days unfolded, I questioned where and why I would want to be anywhere else. I envied Silas, and I missed my wife, my mother, and a very special little Amish girl, but they were gone. In some mysterious way, Isana had many qualities of all three. She was intelligent like my wife and motherly like Maxine and yet so childlike when needed. Everyone I met in the flotilla had a peaceful spirit.

On the fourth day, we came to a place Silas called the traders. Scavengers pillaged the countryside, collected everything from old house wiring and plumbing to jewelry and tools. Squatters, they lived in an abandoned shipyard with vast warehouse space. Silas traded fish and clams for other necessary supplies. The traders weren't a friendly or trustworthy lot; most had committed violent crimes and wouldn't think twice about cutting another man's throat.

When Silas suggested we all pray they're sober, it got my attention.

"Don't know exactly what they drink, but it gives them kerosene breath. Homemade poison is what it is, but they do deal in some food goods that they trade with local farmers," Silas said as we moved toward the docks.

Silas instructed me to stay below, as the traders were suspect of anything out of the ordinary and trusted no one. He got no argument from me. From below deck I heard the haggling, laughter, and boisterous jabs. Isana and the children stayed out of sight also. Silas and several others positioned themselves to have an advantage should any trouble start. Silas had confided, it was best not to let the traders know you had anything of value. The negotiations were tedious and tense, and my skin crawled expecting the hatch to burst open at any minute and I'd find myself fighting to protect Isana, the children, and my own life. Silas had told me the traders weren't farmers or fishermen. If they thought someone was a one-shot deal, they just killed them and took what they wanted. He said if you could continue to supply them with things they wanted, they would develop a sketchy rapport and view you as a future source. The world had come to this level of harshness, very much like the days of Noah.

A distant explosion and scrambling feet on deck caused me to jump to my feet and take a defensive posture toward the hatch. The second explosion came closer, and the deck went silent except for Silas throwing open the hatch and shouting orders to untie from the dock. Everyone scrambled topside, where we witnessed billowing smoke as it rose from two of the warehouses. More explosions sent debris into the air. The targets so far had been land based. We unfurled the sails and mumbled prayers. I could see the traders who had been on our deck run down the dock toward the explosions. Drones streaked over the facility, unleashing devastation. The State had finally caught up with the traders, and the ensuing bombardment was merciless. Our flotilla moved ever so slowly from the docks, as we watched flames engulf the traders, nothing spared—buildings, trees, people, all incinerated in a matter of minutes.

We had all broken into prayer as we fled, and for some reason we were spared, as if we were invisible. We were wide-open targets out in the water, and yet the drones never attacked. We didn't sit on deck and watch the horror inflicted on the victims; instead, we gave thanks and praised the Lord for his mercy. Those who perished on shore weren't innocent, but it was the State who had created them and now destroyed them.

Silas leaned toward me and whispered, "God's promise in Psalm 91, no evil will befall us. It was as if we were invisible to evil. Remember when they were going to throw Jesus from the cliff? It is written, he walked through the angry mob, and they couldn't see him."

I was speechless; no other answer fit. Silas and his flotilla of believers were in constant silent prayer, and I had sensed a special peace, an aura I had never felt at any other time in my life. Not even when I was a child with Jim and Max. We had floated off a good distance from the inferno on shore. The black smoke rose high above the bay, and yet still the drones continued their attack. My focus wasn't on the terror; it was on the members of the flotilla, on every vessel. All hands were on deck, kneeling and giving thanks. We were sitting ducks on the water, and yet not a single drone attacked us. This was to be my last day on board; Silas had said they would put me ashore tomorrow and begin their float south. The thought hadn't thrilled me, for these were special people. After this incident, I was sure of the dome of protection over them in the spiritual world.

"You just witnessed our great advantage in this battle of the spirit world. Evil destroys evil as well as goodness, but goodness cannot destroy good, only evil; it is the nature of things. In the coming times, we shall witness more of this evil, and our sword must be the Word." Silas spoke not much to me but to the world.

The breeze died, leaving us positioned to watch the continuing attacks, certainly overkill. Even when the drones left, we watched the flames and black smoke, and prayed the wind would carry us away. It wasn't until late afternoon, just before Isana called us to eat, that the breeze began. As we ate, we moved north, just barely overcoming the current. In a way I didn't care how long it took; everyone ate in silence after the horrors of the day. When night fell, I curled up on the deck to stargaze and listen to the whispers below deck. Silas managed to stir some giggles from the younger children. Hearing them gave us all comfort.

The morning sun woke me with a warm caress and a new day's promise. Silas and the children had already eaten breakfast, and Isana had saved me a plate of beans and fish. The shoreline looked vaguely familiar from my childhood. There were some distinctive landmarks, two large homes, now in ruin, and a road ending in the water. This was where Jim launched his first sailboat; I remember how

Storm ran about more excited than any of us. Silas's boats had deep drafts and couldn't get any closer to shore. He would take me in the dingy he was using when he first found me. The sails were down, and the sound of the anchors hitting the water startled me as I was lost in thoughts of my childhood.

"This is it, my friend, as far as we can go," Silas said.

I rose to my feet, put out my hand for a shake, but Silas grabbed it and pulled me into a hug. We all knew we would never see each other again. Isana wept as she stole me away from Silas. Her body trembled, and her breathing was labored by sobs.

"Thank you all. I can't tell you how much I love you all. How kind you have been. I know I won't find another group like you out there. I pray you have safe passage on your way," I said, holding back my tears.

No one else spoke, they didn't need to, we all knew how we felt. If anyone else said a word, we would have all become blubbering fools. Silas signaled to me to get in the dingy and followed me into it. In the bow, I faced backward and watched behind him as the flotilla shrank in the distance. The closer I got to returning to the manor and facing Father, the deeper my dread. With nothing to report but bad news, it might be better to just disappear and let him live out his days without knowing the horrors I found. These last days on the float had lifted me a bit, but now I felt an all-time new low. How much can a man be expected to endure? Maybe, I was just being selfish. A child of the streets, my birth parents never cared about my circumstance or destiny, but Jim and Max did. When we reached the shore, Silas offered some advice.

"Be strong and courageous, and pray to do what is right, my friend. Your father deserves to know what has happened to his children, to you. There is nothing more maddening to a parent than not knowing a child's fate," Silas said, his words hitting every doubt I had. Amazing.

"Thank you, friend. Please be careful and may God be with you."

"He is, he is, and with you."

I stepped out of the boat and walked away without looking back. The road from the ramp had become overgrown and was little more than an asphalt path. In a short time, I was in a forest growing around ruins of houses set along long-unused streets. One lifeless community after another unfolded along my route. It was eerie to think how many lives had been lived out in these communities, how many dreams had come to naught. When I reached the town of Bear, my route was now lined with long-abandoned big-box stores. The scene was too eerie for me, so when I saw a sign pointing up Church Street for Beck's Pond Park, I took a detour in hopes of finding a more suitable place to sleep. A pavilion offered the perfect place to sit and enjoy the food Isana had packed for me. The openness felt safer than being trapped within walls. It was obvious no critters had taken up residence, and I had a clear view of anyone's approach. The days were shorter; it was seven and the sun had already dropped below the horizon. A flash of heat lightning illuminated bold thunderheads as a storm approached from the southeast.

Violent storms made for security, as few wander about as lightning crashes. With a full stomach I lay on an old picnic table, my bedroll as a pillow. A hammer of rain came in waves, to pound the pavilion roof. The wind blew rain in on the eastern side, and I was forced to slide the table six feet to the west. Several lightning strikes hit close enough to allow the smell of ozone to mingle with freshly washed air. The reality of the storm slipped into a dream, where my wife and I hid beneath an overpass during a tornado. Strange, it wasn't just a dream; it was a memory. As my wife held me, I could feel her every breath. Her head was buried between my neck and shoulder. Our motorcycle teetered in the wind as debris blew over and through the underpass. A metal garbage-can lid frisbeed into the windshield. We lay as flat as we could against the concrete overpass supports. A tree branch hit me in the ribs again and again, but I couldn't see it or grab it. It's not a dream—my eyes wide, several dark shadows were standing over me while one poked me with a stick.

"Wake up, mister, you have company. Sit up, hands where we can see them," a black shadow ordered.

Wisdom told me to do as I was told. In a sitting position I could make out the ghostly figures of two men, three women, and four children in a couple of successive lightning flashes. They were storm battered for sure, but their beleaguered looks were owed to months or more of wandering.

"Do you have food?" one of the women asked.

The largest man grabbed my pack, thrust his hand in, and pulled out a wrap of air-dried fish. Instinct driven, I ripped it from him and tossed it to the children, who shredded it in seconds like piranhas.

"Feed the children first! You can eat all I have, but children and women first," I growled.

"I make the rules. Don't ever put your hands near me again!"

Making threats isn't a good way to win. They were going to hurt me, even if I gave them everything—I could see the bloodlust.

It's far better to act on impulse in these situations, I realized, as I landed a stiff right to the space between his eyes. Snatching my pack, I tossed it to one of the women as the big man dropped to his knees. He sprung like a coiled snake, his shoulder ramming into my chest to knock the wind out of me. Still, I had my head and gave him my right foot in the groin. He doubled over, but the second man brought a stick to the back of my head. The floor came at me too fast; I didn't put out my hands, so my face hit hard enough to make me dazed but without loss of consciousness. Kicks caught me first in the face, then the back, legs, arms—all of them joined in, even the children. All I could do was roll to my side, then to my back, and a final roll placed me out from under the protection of the pavilion's roof, into the mud and rain. When I rolled onto my stomach, a foot pressed against the back of head drove my face into the mud, making it impossible to breathe. When I woke, the torture had stopped, and they were gone.

Curled in a fetal position, I coughed bloody mud, cleared my nostrils with several blows until I could breathe easily. Easily but not deep, as cracked ribs restricted me. Everything hurt, my vision blurred from blood, mud, or concussion. In the absoluteness of the dark there was nothing to see; besides, if I moved and they were on watch, the beating might start anew. I listened, as thunder rumbled, the rain beat on the roof, and leaves and washed blood flew from my face. Were they sleeping on the picnic tables? Were they in wait for movement, a signal I was still alive, or had they moved on? I had curled in a fetal position without generating a response; maybe I could position myself to see inside the pavilion. An eternity passed without a human sound; I rolled to my other side as a flash of lightning lit the sky. They were asleep on the tables, like piles of rags, no one on the lookout. In the morning they'd finish me off if they found me breathing.

It wasn't easy getting to my feet without a sound. With the cover of rain and thunder I limped into the woods. There would be no search for me; they didn't care whether I lived or died. They would be glad to get rid of me. My only worth would be in meat if they've turned cannibal. The thought made me wince, as many tales had spread of communities of cannibals. So far I had never encountered any, but I was sure they existed—driven by desperation more than evil, but isn't desperation evil's steroid? If you ended up food, who cares why? The storm would cover my tracks; time and distance would save me, so I moved. The pain took my breath away. My muscles became knotted where I was bruised, my head ached, but I moved on in the woods along the creek feeding Beck's Pond. The fact it wasn't easy reassured me I wouldn't be followed, but wasn't I wrong about the storm offering security? Every decision was a crapshoot, for sure.

Coming to an abandoned industrial site strewn with ancient, rusting trucks, I selected a solid one and crawled in. With the doors locked, I was out of sight, out of the rain, and protected from vermin, human or otherwise. The seat proved large enough to allow a man to stretch out, but curled in pain, I vomited blood. It might take me days to recuperate; then again, I felt like I never would. This old truck might just be my final resting place.

TWELVE

Jim

Jim stopped at the front stoop to gather his thoughts before proceeding, a lesson learned with age, when energy runs short. The barks of his neighbor's sheep dogs got his attention, a sign to warn his master of danger to the flock. They aren't frivolous barkers. Jim knew something wasn't right in that direction. His neighbor wasn't one to be trusted, though—he accepted digital money so he could pay his property taxes, and even though he whined about the government, he was a loyalist. Deena was most likely in the direction of the dogs; at least, that was all Jim had to go on. He headed across the meadow, into the woods where he had observed the wolves on so many occasions. Heavy cloud cover obscured all moonlight, and he didn't dare use a flashlight, for he didn't know enough about Deena's disappearance to risk someone seeing him. He knew the woods from years ago when he played with the children, and not much had changed. Some trees had fallen, most had gotten larger, and their shade kept weed growth to a minimum.

The children called it their secret path; he remembered watching them tote their shovels, heading for the woods. They spent hours toiling in the woods to level and smooth the trail's surface. They built jumps for their bicycles, and now, alone in the dark, he is taking their path. Who could have known back then that an old man would stumble this path on a rescue mission. So many times, they had secret adventures and fought banditos. In the heat of battle, Max would show up with lunch in individual bags and ruin the mood, but all the kids would chow down, nevertheless.

"Oh, Max, you would love our Deena. She is so much like you. If you and I had a child together, it would be her. Watch over her, Lord, give her a hedge of protection," Jim whispered.

Jim's feet slid through fern encroachments before he slipped, caught himself, and snagged bits of solid rock to gain traction. The dogs had been silent too long, and he wondered if the danger had passed, if Deena had moved beyond. Maybe he'd let himself be misled; maybe she headed in a different direction and he was in pursuit of a wolf ghost. In the dark, minds wander and anxiety feeds on chaotic thoughts. Breathable twenty-five-year-old sneakers aren't hiking boots, but these days they were all he had. Soggy feet and wet socks chilled an old man with poor circulation.

Low-slung branches whopped him around the head and shoulders, and one grabbed the crossbow, but he tightened his grip on it. The trees still held some leaves, but the ground was covered in dead ones. The rains had softened them, and it was fortunate they didn't rustle. Maybe he shouldn't have complained about soggy feet. The forest appeared burdened by the excess water received of late, and Jim wondered if the State could be manipulating the weather patterns. Maneuvering around some fallen timber, he noticed the soil had loosened with the saturation. Alone with his thoughts, the woods seemed full of creation's magic as the world of man swirled somewhere beyond, out of control. If he wasn't in a mild panic to find Deena, this garden would have offered the best place to search for oneself. So many thoughts came to the forefront of his mind. A disjointed review of his life to date. A distant sound, a twig breaking, and he stopped walking, to tune into possibilities—a deer, a bear, or the wolf. Silence followed, and when Jim resumed walking, a new thought filled his head: *This could be a trap.*

In a book he read about mental output, he remembered reading that walking increases creative thinking by 60 percent. Sensory deprivation or imbalance heightens those senses still in play, and minimal vision intensifies hearing and smell. There was nothing wrong with his sense of touch; the uneven ground angles of the trail strained the tendons in his feet and ankle muscles but made him more adept and perceptive with each step. The children's hours of hard work so many years ago had succumbed to time and weather. Yet this walk was preparing him for the confrontation he may encounter, sharpening his senses. The walk was increasing his body awareness; in the dark he sorted and floated through the anarchy. He didn't feel that old; he just needed the right opportunity, an advantage. He needed to see the enemy before they saw him.

He practiced bringing the crossbow to his shoulder and taking aim, and though locked and loaded, he didn't shoot. He repeated the motion, over and over, and the repetition sharpened his focus. Closing in on where the dog's barking had been heard, he blocked all thoughts except those needed to be prepared for battle. The battle, yes, fought in the spiritual realm. It wouldn't be an old man against younger ones; it would be an ageless spirit. Before him stretched meadows filled with whitish blotches; the neighbor's flocks had flourished. Jim hadn't been this far from the manor in years. There was no barking; the sheep settled with not so much as a breeze to rustle the tall grasses. A tell-tale hum dropped Jim to the ground, and he rolled over to watch the sky. *Drones!* Deena didn't have a tracker, but if those who took her worked for the state, they would. *Bob!*

Jim watched fire fall from the drones focused on a single point midfield where a bright flash startled the sheep and caused the dogs to bark once before going silent. Jim knew the results of such attacks: there would be nothing left of the victims below. The State incinerated all evidence in such attacks. Sheep dogs are smart, but this danger wasn't anything they knew or could handle, and not a one barked. As fast as they came, the drones left, a surgical strike, swift and accurate. The sheep could be heard crying and beginning to wander, but the dogs circled and brought them into a tight group.

Jim sat, sick to his stomach; no one could have survived the strike, nothing. He had just witnessed the end of life, Deena's. He'd had so much hope for her and her baby. He had taught her how to survive in the forest, and in a split second she was gone. He couldn't move; he lay back and stared at the sky. All he could do was pray for her, pray for forgiveness, give thanks for all his blessings, for knowing her. Too many he loved were gone; he wanted to go with them. He blamed Satan, the State, evil, but didn't question God forsaking him or anyone. He prayed Deena would be with God. Still, he felt immense pain.

"Oh, Max, why not me? I buried my son, lost you, now Deena, and I suspect many of the children we raised have been killed. Still, I go on." Jim placed the crossbow on the ground next to him.

He didn't want to go back to the manor. He lay back and closed his eyes; he prayed they would never open again as he drifted off to sleep. A warm fall sun woke him with dabbling kisses of light. The air filled with drifting leaves, released by sparse tree branches. Jim had no desire to face another day; he closed his eyes again, not to sleep but to hide. His thoughts turned to Philippians 1:24–25, where the Apostle Paul struggled with a desire to be with Jesus versus living in the flesh, but the Lord would decide.

A moment passed before Jim heard leaves rustle and a whimper. His eyes popped open and not five feet from him stood the wolf, its head bowed, nostrils flaring. It didn't bare its teeth or show signs of aggression. Jim knew it was the one from the meadow. Finally, they were face to face, and Jim's heart raced as he wondered what it meant. He always thought the wolf would come to the manor, but instead, Jim had come to the wolf.

Jim struggled to find the strength to sit up, while the wolf maintained its posture. The wolf continued to let out whimpers and paced as if anxious before it dropped to its belly and submissively crawled toward Jim. His hand sunk into the thick mane around the wolf's neck. The wolf was ancient, yet Jim could feel the power in his neck. The wolf's head is three times larger than a dog's head, with powerful shoulders and a broad chest. Jim guessed him to be a 120 pounds. He rested his head in Jim's lap; this was a hybrid wolf-dog mix familiar with humans. Old Storm used to disappear for days, and Jim wondered if this old wolf might have a connection to him. He would be at least four generations removed from old Storm; it didn't seem likely for him to sense a connection to Jim. He nuzzled Jim to get up, and they both stood. Jim had a feeling of déjà vu: Storm had come to him after the hurricane, when he was floating in the debris. If not for Storm, he would have died, eaten by crabs and flies. The wolf started up the path toward the manor, and both man and wolf limped along through the crunch of leaves.

Jim stopped as did the wolf, and Jim whispered, "So what should I call you? What name do you go by? Serenity? Love? Joy? Truth? Faith? Compassion? Hope?" The wolf sat, cocked his head from side to side as if trying to understand Jim's words and waited for Jim to begin walking again.

"You are the wolf from the old Cherokee legend, aren't you? Well then, I should call you Osda Waya, Good Wolf, you are the one I have tried to feed all my life." Jim felt satisfied and began to walk.

Jim moved slowly; there was no reason to hurry. Dread held him back; the manor would be empty. As he shuffled along the trail the children had built, he couldn't bring up a single warm thought. At the edge of the meadow, he could see the manor; it was nothing but a pile of stone and glass. He sat in the very spot where the wolf had always appeared, and the wolf sat nearby. He reached out, sinking his fingers into the scruff of the wolf's mane, and massaged powerful neck muscles. He couldn't bring himself to cross the field, to enter the manor. From noon until dark he sat and at times lay, caressed by the afternoon sun. The wolf never left his side. *This is a good place and time to die*, he thought. With his death, the world would end. So many predict the end of the world. In truth, it ends for someone every day. He wondered how long it would take the reaper to find him.

He was dozing as the sun dropped below the horizon; it was the wolf who woke. All his life Jim focused on a prayer for strength to face his challenges; tonight was different. He fell asleep praying to be weakened, to fade away. He saw no reason to be strong, as everything worth living for had been taken away, and for the first time in his life he couldn't envision anything to fill the gap. The moon rose full and bright in the cloudless sky. The wolf tilted his head back in a slow release of a mournful howl. Jim's eyes opened, but he didn't move for fear of disturbing the ritual; he just listened to the musical call. When the howls stopped, he sat up and patted Osda Waya on his head. The wolf's cries fit Jim's mood and brought him comfort. He embraced his situation and the awfulness of it all. He prayed for forgiveness. No one knows when the end times will come, even for each individual. Jim felt guilty wishing for his own end; his life had been bathed in love, and God had given him strength even in the tough times.

Jim grabbed the crossbow and stood; the manor shone in the moonlight not like a pile of rocks but as a monument to love. He closed his eyes, and again he whispered praise and gratefulness, and asked for forgiveness. When he opened his eyes, the wolf was gone. He scanned in all directions to no avail. He stepped back into the tree line; there was no sign of Osda Waya.

When Jim emerged from the woods and began to cross the field toward the manor, he saw light in the window of the study, and he paused. Who could it be? A squatter, Atanase, or someone from the State? Jim checked the crossbow, cocked and loaded. He thought out a plan for his approach; there could be more than one intruder, some on guard around the grounds. With great stealth he approached, his eyes keen for any movement. The moonlight helped him, but it also worked against him. The light in the study wasn't bright; he knew it was just a small lamp on a table. No movements or shadows cast in the room gave any clue as to the number of intruders. He took a position behind a low wall running along the gravel driveway where he could watch the study window and the grounds in the front of the manor. He felt no compulsion to use force, preferring instead to wait.

After a while, with no sign of anyone inside or outside the house, he felt confident it wasn't a group invasion. Maybe two or three, but not an army. He approached the window of the study; it was low enough to the ground for him to peer in while standing on an

Adirondack chair. A small oil lamp on a table flickered; no one was in the room. He dropped to the ground and moved to the rear of the manor. The kitchen door always squeaked; it would announce his entrance. But he thought to himself, *We only have now, and tomorrow is only a promise. A promise of loneliness and sorrow is one I can afford to lose.* Crossbow pressed tight to his humerus, he burst through the door, through the kitchen, and into the study. He had rolled the dice, bet large, and run into the study, where he found his fate. His heart skipped a beat, and the crossbow dropped from his shoulder as a chill froze his eyes. He had come so close to pulling the trigger.

"Jim! You're alive!" Deena shouted as she jumped to her feet.

Jim dropped the crossbow on the floor. He closed his eyes, until he felt her body against his. Her embrace made it real; he hadn't believed his eyes. "Deena, I thought you were dead."

"I thought Bob killed you, before he took me. When I asked him, he wouldn't answer. He took me as far as the neighbor's pasture . . ."

"I know, I followed you. I saw the drone attack; it was so devastating, I thought nothing could have survived." He pushed Deena away, to look her in the eyes.

"When we got to the field, the sheep dogs came after us. While Bob killed one of them, I sprinted into the flock of sheep and ran with them. He couldn't find me. He walked about calling my name; he was so pathetic, I can't believe I ever had anything to do with him. I knew I could get the best of him, given the chance. The sheep settled far out in the field where I curled in a fetal ball among tall grass, surrounded by sheep. The drone zoomed in on Bob's tracker; they also have infrared, but they must have thought I was just another sheep. None of their blasts came near me or the flock. When the attack ended, I couldn't move. I dared not, for fear of being detected by the drones. For hours I lay still with the sheep." Deena sobbed.

Jim pulled her back into his chest. "Praise the Lord, he protected you."

"You know, Jim, while I lay there, I couldn't help but think, AI sees us as less than. To them, we are just lumps of tissue, an inconvenience or a nuisance. They are doing the work of depopulation, and the elite can claim it's out of their hands and they sleep well at night. I was a part of it." Deena broke down in uncontrolled tears. Jim just held her, speechless, for nothing he could've said would help.

"No one deserves what happened to Bob. I should never have looked, burned beyond recognition and dismembered." Deena struggled with the words.

"This is why I didn't come into the field to find you; I have seen what the drones do. I couldn't bear to see your remains, if there had been any."

"Why is life so tragic? What does any of it mean?" Deena asked, exasperated. "Why bring a baby into such a world?"

"Every child is born into this war. We don't understand it, but you have a choice: you join one side or the other. There is no middle ground. You may choose not to see the battle, to hide your head in the sand, but this choice is the same as joining the enemy. Only one choice wins: choose God and become a warrior wearing his armor.

This is the meaning of it all. Our mortal lives will end, but this war is spiritual. Your child needs to be born into the battle, then be born into the spirit," Jim declared in a strong voice.

"I need to sleep; this has shaken me," Deena whispered as she helped Jim into his easy chair. "We can sort things better in the morning."

Deena tossed pillows on the carpet, then curled up in a ball covered with three blankets. Deena was asleep in minutes, but Jim turned out the light to deaden the glare on the window. He watched the distant field, lit by a bright moon, void of details. The wind brushed the tops of tall, blurred weeds, with the effect of ocean waves. Jim closed his eyes to see the deck of a schooner, and Max posed in a sheer beach cover-up with her arm outstretched to hold a rigging line. This was somewhere off the Canary Islands—it wasn't a fantasy; it was a memory. Jim didn't open his eyes until morning, and even then he didn't feel like he had slept, but he was at peace. He didn't remember getting Ellen's Bible, but it was open on his lap. Ellen was from a lifetime ago, such a good soul, by all accounts. The gift of her Bible from Cactus Jack was so precious to him.

The mound of blankets across the room arched and groaned. Then with a quick flick, the blankets flung back to expose Deena's bright smile. Jim smiled, reflecting her glow; it was still an hour until sunrise, but the room seemed to warm with their mutual affection.

"You love me, don't you?" Deena asked. "How can you love someone who came to destroy you?"

"You did, but you didn't. When you confront an enemy, reach out to them. I've spent my life reaching out.

Sometimes you get slapped, but when someone reaches back, it makes up for all the rejections," Jim responded. He walked across the room and handed Deena the Bible.

"I'll fetch some eggs and start breakfast. I suggest you read 1 John 4:2–3 and 19–21," Jim said as he walked toward the hallway.

As Deena read the passages, she realized she knew their meaning. Clearly, mankind had brought forth AI without a balance of love and truth. She had been a prisoner to it—groomed to do its bidding, devoid of love or the truth about man's relationship with God. Deena closed Ellen's Bible and pressed it to her breast. She lay back on the floor in peace; the last forty-eight hours were put to rest. She waited for Jim to call her to the kitchen. Though developed to be beneficial for mankind, AI had no concept of God, and it had morphed into an intelligence without a focus or singular direction. As powerful as AI was, it also caused chaos and confusion, making the current state of world lack meaning. Deena felt ashamed for participating in the madness. Jim's call to breakfast interrupted her thoughts, and she scurried toward the kitchen.

"We're down to the last of the eggs, but I mixed them with squash I canned last summer, which stretched it nicely," Jim said as he scooped some onto Deana's plate.

"The Bible's pages are stained with tears?" Deana whispered.

"Very appropriate, I might add. The story of Ellen is from another time, before the collapse. Let's eat and talk about the future. You need to be on your way," Jim said as he took a seat.

"You make it sound like I have to leave today."

Jim pushed his eggs around with his fork, paused, and said grace. They ate in silence, neither wishing to voice their feelings about her departure. The harsh reality of the world's tyranny was closing in. Nothing could be done by them to fight it or stop it. Only a monotheistic power greater than the world's central government could bring it down.

THIRTEEN

Atanase

The sun woke me, hot on my vomit-crusted face. The pain in my limbs and sides told me I was alive. However, I had no idea how long I had been cramped on the seat of this old truck. I knew I had awoken a few times before this, but only for short periods and never with full consciousness. The crust on face made my skin itch, and I brushed it with my sleeve before I sat up and looked at myself in the mirror. Black and brown dried blood was smeared into my hair and the stubble of my beard. It hurt to take a deep breath, but I rejoiced in drawing in any amount of air. Through the filthy windshield of the truck, I saw a sea of rusty construction equipment and trucks. The trees and weeds growing through weakened body parts attested to the length of abandon.

I reflected on the recent past. As tyranny grew into the world order, resistance increased, and the tyrants doubled down. The hearts of the ruling class hardened, just like as did the pharaoh in Egypt against the demands of Moses. The tyranny now had no pharaoh, no human face; it existed in an electronic domain. Politicians swore they were reining in the threat of a nonhuman ruler, but few believed them. The advances came at lightning speed, exponential advances humans couldn't keep up with. Human desires for family, friendship, companionship, acquisitions, time off had no place under the new ruler. The resistance fragmented. Individual wants and concerns led to chaos with no united front formed. No messenger could be found to offer hope or to lead, and the world fell into darkness; these were the final days of any semblance of freewill.

I grabbed the truck's door handle and pushed with my shoulder. The door resisted as if the truck didn't want me to go free. The hinges creaked as I pushed, a scream to announce my escape. I prayed no one was near enough to hear. Even though I had been unconscious too long, my beating had left a lasting memory. Too stiff to climb from the cab, I dropped to the ground. My knees buckled and I went forward with a thud. I felt stronger sitting on the seat of the truck; now gravity had its way with me. I tried to stand but could not conjure strength. One more try, I thought, and I felt something under my left armpit, a power aid. Upright, I stared at the face of a hulking brute. Another beating would surely be my end.

"You look pretty bad, fella," the brute said.

I felt relief from the man's soft tone. "Took a beating some time ago."

"Come, I'll help."

The man wrapped his arm around my back and relieved my burden so I could walk. We made our way between the hulking remnants of machinery, more rust than anything else. The paint flaked from years of disuse, and holes now pocked the bodies like cancers do. I asked no questions; I knew I was at the mercy of such a man, for I lacked the strength to fight or run.

"You're lucky I came upon you. There was a time I came into the junkyard every day, but now I'm lucky to venture into it once a month. Little of value is left," the man said as we left through the junkyard's unlocked gate.

Industrial buildings lined the street, one of those old centers built in the times before the collapse. Signs with company names identified entrances to crumbled parking lots. We walked past ten buildings before the man led me into one marked Healtronic Research. The largest building on the street, it stood four stories high, extended a football field in length, and the depth could not be determined from the parking lot, which could easily have held four hundred cars but now only hosted weeds in its cracked blacktop. The entryway at one time must have been grand, but now the ground glistened with shards of broken glass. Inside, huge planters held the skeletons of tropical plants casting eerie shadows on the floor.

"Things get better, don't let this entry fool you. My father loved tropical settings; this was his corporate headquarters. He was a brilliant man, very quirky and eccentric, he saw the world different than most. We live here and build stuff, trying to carry on in these dark ages. You can recuperate here; we have facilities not found anywhere today. They call me Giant George, not sure why.

You can just call me George." George pushed open an inner door and led me down a hallway.

"I'm Atanase."

"That's different," George responded, and I just let it drop.

Hobbling down a long hallway, we passed glass doors to offices, and I could see people bustling about or seated at desks with computer screens while others stood chatting. It had all the appearances of a business, pre-collapse. At the end of the hallway, George opened a door leading into a manufacturing center. Sparks spewed and bright flashes erupted over the tops of protectives screens. The smell of hot metal irritated my nostrils while loud screeches pained my ears and nerves. The room, cavernous and poorly lit, stretched into the shadows with a steel-beamed ceiling forty feet above shrouded in vapor, dust, and soot. The overhead lights appeared as moons in a clouded sky. I knew nothing this large could exist without some kind of compliance with, or manipulation of, the State. George guided me to the stairway, and we descended several floors below the main factory.

"This is where I live, my home." George pushed open a wooden door fitting of any European cathedral.

I stood and gazed at the splendor of the room with its marble floors and fine woodwork in the ceiling beams and walls. Cherry wood, I guessed. The furnishings were of equal quality; the room could hold a hundred guests comfortably.

"This was my father's bomb shelter. He grew up fearing nuclear war; he had no idea how his world would collapse. His wealth was vast; you name the business, his fingers were in it. But all that is history. We need to make you comfortable." George signaled two members of his house staff, who were dusting at the far end of the room. Lovely ladies, each supported me on either side as George instructed them to take me to a guest room while he poured himself a glass of bourbon and lit a cigar.

"Get him some clean clothes and help him clean his wounds, then fetch Doc to check him over," George said as we went out through a secret panel in the wall.

Something didn't sit well with me. I appreciated an opportunity to recuperate, but my two escorts lacked something. Not looks, for sure; they weren't hard on the eyes. When we reached the guest room, they showed me where to shower, brought me towels and clean clothes, but made no small talk. Even when I asked about their employment, they didn't reply. They told me to rest, food would be brought to me, and I wasn't to leave the room without one of them escorting me. I obviously wasn't the first guest they'd welcomed.

The shower refreshed me but stung my open flesh wounds as dried blood washed away. Warm water was an amenity I had long forgotten. The last time I experienced such pleasure was before the collapse. The sensation relaxed my knotted muscles as I lingered in the flow. The towels were luxurious, as I gently patted sensitive and damaged flesh. Slipping into some clean trousers, I heard a knock on the door. Shirtless, I opened the door. The man at the door failed the poker-face test as his eyes widened at the sight of the bruises on my chest and arms, more black than blue. An elderly man with a small black bag—Doc?

"Hello, I'm Doc, just Doc."

"Come in, Doc. I'm Atanase."

"I've been told you took quite a beating and have been without food for some time, but this is a little more than I expected. Sit on the bed, you've got some nasty contusions and lacerations. These two on your head should have had stitches earlier, but I'll see what I can do," he said as he examined my scalp and face. He listened to my lungs and heart and had me lie back so he could feel my abdomen and ask me if there were internal issues. He pulled a straight razor from his bag, and without asking my opinion, he began shaving my head. Exposing the area around the largest wound, he let out a groan as the separated flesh left bone exposed. There was no sign of infection, a stroke of good luck.

"What happened to the other guy?" Doc asked as he continued to scalp me.

"Well, I'm not sure but I consider myself the winner."

"Well, you'd never know it to look at you," Doc said as he pulled the stethoscope from his ears.

"Was my heart beating?"

"Yes, sounds strong."

"Then I won."

"In this day and age, you have a good point." Doc pulled a needle and thread from his bag. "Sorry, I have nothing to numb you with, okay?"

"Get 'er done, Doc. Where did you go to school? Was it before the collapse?" I asked. Most medical schools failed during the collapse, but Doc looked old enough to have gone long before.

"I was a medic, but now I have forty years' experience and a lot of self-studies. I'm the best any of these people have."

"Who are these people, Doc? What have I gotten myself into?"

Doc paused from threading his hooked needle and gave me a stare, with a tightened jaw.

"They're you. Who are you? Who is anyone these days?" Doc went back to threading his needle and didn't answer any of my questions. The stitches tugged at my flesh coupled with burning pinches, and I wondered if Doc wasn't being a little rougher than he needed to be. After finishing the first wound, Doc lightened up and spoke.

"Giant George is a scrapper; he salvages things from debris left by the collapse. His grandfather was a billionaire businessman. A brilliant inventor and scientist. George's father inherited a worldwide empire, and George inherited this scrapyard. He's a hoarder, but he takes care of his scrap. He gives me food and a place to stay dry," Doc whispered, as if the walls had ears.

"I guess he's legit with the government?" I wasn't quite sure if or how to approach this, but I just asked in a low tone.

"George? Legit? George says there's more freedom to be bought under a tyrannical state than a free state. Tyrannical systems lean to corruption because they suppress the human spirit, so everything is for sale. He claims to be freer now than before the collapse. He does what he wants and pays off all the officials. Enough said. Tilt your head so I can stitch up this other wound. I'll have to stretch your flesh to close this one."

The needle tugged at my flesh, pinching hard, and the thread pulled skin across the gaping wound. Knowing it was beneficial helped me to endure the pain. The procedure took place in silence, for only a minute, but I felt as if I would black out, until he let out a sigh of relief with one last tug on the thread. He taped some patches over the wound to trap blood, then returned his tools to his black bag.

"Don't get the bandages wet. With any luck, no infection will develop. We're not equipped to protect or fight infections. Tomorrow I'll change the dressing and inspect your wounds. Get lots of rest."

"I need to eat and get something to drink," I said; rest could wait.

"George told me he would send someone to escort you to his dining room when I was done." Doc looked at his watch. "He eats at the same times every day; his afternoon meal will be served in forty-five minutes. You can count on it."

Doc and I made small talk as I walked him to the door. He apologized for the need to lock my door behind him. He assured me I wasn't a prisoner, but until George knew more about me, security was necessary. Something about Doc's assurances convinced me everything was as he said. The man evoked honesty and forthrightness. When the door shut, I retreated to my bed to rest and waited for my escort to arrive. Itchy stitches kept me awake, but I closed my eyes and focused on my shallow breathing. Deep breaths hurt, and Doc said without x-rays he couldn't be sure, but he suspected broken ribs.

A knock on the door startled me from a dream; it took me a minute to realize I wasn't in the cab of the old truck. My reflexes threw me into a sitting position on the bed, where I looked about at the luxury surrounding me. Another knock and I was hustling across the bedroom toward the door.

"Yes, come in. The door isn't locked," I said; then I remembered it was locked, from the outside.

The door opened and one of my original escorts stepped in.

"My brother requests you come to his dining hall for the afternoon meal," she said in monotone.

"Your brother? Really?" I asked. She didn't respond, but stood waiting for me to exit the room, then followed me down the hall. George looked old enough to be her father, if I had to guess. Nothing surprised me, and they did have a slight family facial resemblance; she is tall, though of slight build. George stood by the bar at the far end of the dining room.

"Atanase! How do you feel, my friend? Did Doc fix you up?" George said in a voice filled with cheerful expectation.

"He stitched me up, and the shower brought me back to humanity, thank you," I replied as I walked toward him.

"Your sister said you wanted to see me," I said, fishing for a little more family info. George's sister had not entered the dining room but closed the door after I entered.

"Can I offer you a drink?" George asked. "If not alcohol, water?"

"Sure. I'll have water."

"So, she referred to me as her brother?"

"Yes."

"She and her sister are sweethearts, my father's first generation of bots. I found them in a storage shed and reconditioned them," George said and without a pause directed me to be seated at the dining room table, large enough to accommodate twenty.

His answer blew me away; I'd suspected something, but not robots.

"Begin!" George said as he signaled his two robotic sisters to bring the meal. As the table filled with platters of fresh fruits, vegetables, and salad fixings, George expounded on the facility's hydroponic systems and the solar panel arrays on the vast roof.

"My father meant well; his financial empire was vast and high tech. Too vast, he lost control of it, and all the good he intended became tools of evil. He hanged himself, they claim, the year before the collapse. This facility is all that remains of our family's vast holdings," George said as we took our seats.

"I've wandered the wilderness for years, and I've seen nothing like this. The last remains of anything normal was an Amish settlement, but even that has now been destroyed. How have you survived?" I asked boldly.

"We exist somewhere between tyranny and chaos. Bribes . . . tyrannical regimes are the most corrupt. I share my wealth with key people. Everyone benefits from what we do here, everyone. As AI takes over local governing, we will lose our advantage; we have nothing to offer nonhumans. But until then, life goes on," George said before downing a water glass of scotch. "Are you sure you don't want something to settle you?"

"No thanks," I replied. Alcohol never appealed to me; it had been one of the reasons I was a child of the streets. Both my parents were heavy drinkers and drug addicts. No need to explain it to George; even though he appeared open to discussing his business, I chose to play mine close to the vest.

"When you are feeling better, you can stay on here. We'll find a place for you. You have no future in the wilderness; things will only be getting worse."

FOURTEEN

Atanase

My first impression of George was you got what you saw. He granted me free reign in most of his facility. The buildings were vast, and a large farm of storage tanks created the look of a refinery. George explained the tanks held oil-producing microbes, which he refined into petrol products. He explained the lies people had been told. Oil wasn't a fossil fuel. In fact, the earth's interior contained more living organisms than the surface of the planet. Straightforward and decent, he showed me the gardens, the solar arrays, the living areas of his workers, and introduced me to many. His family's historic involvement in the collapse fascinated me, and George spoke of it. His father was involved in AI and the ground floor of robotics. I wondered if he held anything back. What he shared with me was amazing. George had signed a contract with his workers and was a benevolent fellow, while he did not appear a religious sort. He kept his spiritual beliefs tucked away, but I sensed a lifestyle grounded in Christian principles. One week from the day of my arrival, I wandered alone into the manufacturing area. Several workers became alarmed and stopped me.

"Sorry, this area is off limits," one man said, then ordered another to call George.

I tried to excuse myself, but they detained me. They asked me what I had seen and if I had ventured anywhere besides the area where I stood and the entrance. The facility was alive with activity, the smell and flashes from hot welds, metal-grinding sparks in various directions, and large automated machinery mingled in the mess. Within three minutes, George arrived and dismissed my captors to return to their jobs.

"Curious, are you? You are of no threat to me. My men are very cautious. Don't take offense. Come with me, let's get out of all this noise and fumes. There's a quiet room over there and I will school you on this place." George gestured for me to follow him.

Cabinets lined the walls of the room. Five large tables filled the center of the room, but there were no chairs. George took a key from his pocket and unlocked a cabinet. When the doors swung open, my eyes beheld hand weapons, swords, battle axes, spears, all deadly sharp.

"What do you think of these?" George asked. I had no words.

One by one, George opened the cabinets and showed me weapons, crossbows and longbows, battle axes, swords, and knives. He told me he supplied the wildness rabble with weapons. They used them on each other. Chaotic, they weren't a threat to the government. In fact, the government encouraged their slaughter of each other. George ushered me into another room, this one filled with high-tech gadgets. He smiled.

"These I supply to the resistance; they can disable the giant bots. These are my pride and joy," George boasted. "Tell me, pilgrim, do you wish to stay here and be one with us or wander the wilderness?"

My thoughts turned to Friedrich Nietzsche and his book *Beyond Good and Evil.* One quote stood out: "To talk much about oneself may also be a means of concealing oneself." Giant George was a simplistically complex fellow who wondered if I wanted to leave. He might kill me for knowing too much, I thought. How should I say what I know I must do, and will I die for it?

He was waiting for my answer, but he studied the murderous devices as he waited. He never looked at me. I envisioned him striking me down just before I spoke my word. I concluded I had no choice but to be forthright.

"I must leave," I said and flinched as George turned in my direction.

"You would add to our community, and communities are rare these days. I regret your decision, but I honor it, and should you ever change your mind or need refuge, come back. Now, I want you to follow me to another part of this facility."

We crossed through the manufacturing section and boarded a large open industrial elevator and descended two levels. When the elevator stopped, a cavernous room lit up automatically, exposing rows of vehicles two levels high. Classic cars, trucks and motorcycles, all with internal combustion engines, antiques but pristine. The room was dust free, the floor shone with glitter, as if waxed. Childlike, George motioned for me to follow him down the rows of vehicles as he rattled off some details of each one, such as displacement, horsepower, model, year, and manufacturer for all five hundred.

"I'll put you in charge of these. Do you still wish to leave?"

What an offer, with the state of the world. How could I resist? My duty was to return to my father's estate. Maybe I could talk him into coming back with me. Then I wondered, how long can George keep all this going? The world has become predictable with ruination at every turn. The only future is the next minute.

"Sorry, George, I can't stay. My father needs me."

"I understand. I still miss mine. You know what my father's big AI mistake was?" George didn't expect me to guess. He just continued and answered his own question. "He fed the Bible into AI. He thought it would help if the units understood the history of man, but he showed man as a flawed creature. AI had no reason to offer forgiveness for man's shortcomings. This unleashed AI's plan to rid the world of its primary contaminant, man."

His confession stunned me. All this time, I had thought men were controlling AI. In fact, AI had gained control of everything. George watched me digest his words.

"Wow, George, that's crazy," I replied.

"If you're leaving, which one do you want?" George asked with enthusiasm.

"What . . . which one do I want?" I replied.

"Pick one. I have storage tanks filled with fuel. You can make your father's house on a single tank and, if he is willing, bring him back. What do you say?"

Such generosity didn't exist in this new era. The offer stunned me. Why? Why would he offer this to me? What's the catch? With access to one of these machines, I could get home in an hour if the roads were intact. If I planned to return with my father, a car would serve best, but the motorcycles excited me.

"You're too much, George . . . but what if I said I have no plans of returning?" I asked.

George walked over to a 1969 GTO, rubbing his hand across the hood, then checked it for dust. The black paint had a monotone black sheen. There was no difference between where his hand had traveled and the rest of the surface.

"The guys do a good job keeping up with things. If there's a possibility you may not return, take this one. Has a custom-built 462-cubic-inch OHVV V8 with an Eagle crankshaft, Howard rods, Mega Brace lifter bore reinforcements, all paired with a Turbo Hydra-Matic 400 three-speed tranny. There's more, but who cares, it's yours." George brushed his hand on his pant leg.

George was right. Who cares? Nothing he said made any difference to me. I knew it was high performance, that's all. A car built long before I was born, but it looked like yesterday's build. George motioned for me to sit in the driver's seat, then instructed me on how to start it. The power surged through the steering wheel, more than just sound. Waves of resonance engulfed me as I revved the engine. I shut off the engine and got out, closing the door.

"If you take this one, it will convince you to return. Look around, you can work right here. Would make for a pleasant life, don't you think?" George said with a smile. "No hurry, sleep on it. Take all the time you wish."

We talked about many things as George walked me back to my quarters—about God, AI, his father, and the condition of the world. His capacity for facts and ability to analyze the human condition astounded me. Never had I met anyone with his vast knowledge. He drifted off topic, derailed by a need to explain the roots of words and history. He kept track and eventually brought the conversation back on course. Alone in my quarters, I contemplated George's offer. Driving the GTO went beyond my wildest dreams.

As I ate an early dinner in my quarters, there came a knock on my door. It was Doc. He heard I would be leaving and wanted to check my wounds a final time. It turned into a social call as I offered him a plate of food and beverage. He questioned me about my health, my wounds, but he didn't examine me. As we ate, the subject of conversation switched to my beliefs, religion, and childhood. To soften me, he shared some very intimate details of his own life, his time before living at this facility and meeting George. Whenever I shared an anecdote, he shared a similar experience from his own past. As we finished eating, he asked if I planned to return. This was when I realized he was on a fishing trip for George. So I nibbled at the bait but maintained control by offering him a bite of my own.

"I'm praying about it."

"Praying about it, are you serious?" Doc asked.

"The Holy Spirit guides me. You believe in God, don't you?"

Doc gave me a stare as if he thought I might be messing with him, and in a way, I was. Doc fumbled around in his shirt pocket before pulling out a home-rolled smoke.

"Do you mind if I smoke? It's medicinal." Doc struck a match and lit up before I could respond. After it was lit, he held it out to me. "Take a hit."

"No thanks," I responded, "but you go ahead."

Doc gave me a look, as if to say he didn't need my approval.

Doc took a couple of hard drags, held it in. "This is potent stuff, good for the spirit. You need stuff like this in our world. George grows the best and shares it with the community. People here don't feel the pain of the world. If you come back, George will give you all you want."

Doc's eyes showed the effects, red and drooping. "Now, what were we talking about? Oh, prayers, my grandfather used to be a prayer warrior, didn't do him any good. When the collapse came, they shut them in the church and set it on fire."

"Who did?" I asked.

"Don't know. It was on a Sunday morning in a little town near Pittsburgh. My dad had moved away right after high school, wouldn't have none of that hocus pocus. He raised us to believe in science and facts." Doc kept drawing on the joint until it faded into a flake.

"Well, my childhood proved different," I replied. Doc stared at me, sizing me up. It was obvious he intended to convert me.

"You know how smart you think George is. Well, it's because his dad implanted a chip in his head at birth. George says it's better than any Christian Holy Spirit. It's for real. He said his father figured he could help God improve the human lot. George is a fine example of what science can do. Doc went on about how efficiently George ran the facility. Why nobody attacked his facility was my big question. There had to be more to the story, but all I could do was listen to Doc's ramblings. I pointed out these were troubled times for Christians, and I had let Doc know I was one, but I didn't want to argue my beliefs.

"Do you buy into this Holy Spirit thing?" Doc asked. Even in these circumstances, denying Christ was something I couldn't do, although I took time to gather my reply.

"Yes," I said, a simple answer. Nothing else volunteered.

Doc took another joint out of his shirt pocket, struck a match, and lit it. He held in the smoke before blowing it above his head. "May the force be with you." He chuckled.

He held out his hand to offer me a hit. Again, I shook my head in refusal. "You know, my friend, the world is a wicked place. This compound is one of the safest and sanest places for a thousand miles. George likes you; he wants you and your father to be a part of this community. He'll welcome you even if you believe in Jesus. George tries to salvage odds and ends; you and your father will become new pieces of the puzzle. We have more women here than men. Keep that in mind."

"Doc, I have no interest in or need of drugs or women. I had a wonderful wife . . ." I stopped. Doc wasn't someone I wanted to talk to about my wife. He didn't need to know of her.

"She's dead?"

"Yes."

Doc squeezed out the butt with his fingers and stood up. He sensed the party was over and, without another word, walked to the door.

"The world is in chaos. Those who submit survive. Those who refuse to submit get snuffed. There are no heroes, good guys, or bad guys, just survivors. Good night. Sleep on it."

Still seated, I gave him a nod of good night, and he departed. A strange mood gripped me, a loneliness. I missed my wife. We shared so much, everything. Since her death, I had encountered little I would have wanted to share with her. I wouldn't have wanted her to experience this madness. Her smile, her laugh, just the touch of her hand on mine. That's what I wanted to remember. Slack muscled, I dropped on the bed and buried my face in a pillow. Why do I struggle to go on? Death might be a welcome release.

The next morning, I couldn't eat. Last night's dream haunted me. Alone on a hill, I looked down on some small Rocky Mountain town. Maybe Telluride or Aspen, I don't know. It was night, bitter cold, snow covered the empty streets, half the houses were dark, and there was nowhere for me to go. No one knew me or would invite me; I stood high above, shivering. So beautiful, I thought, but I had no one to share it with. When I woke, I had no desire to move. I remained flat out, staring at the ceiling. I heard a soft tap on my door. I ignored it, but I knew I had to answer sooner or later. The next time was more of a knock, and I heard George's voice. It was time I opened the door.

"Morning. You ready to go?" George asked.

"Ready as ever."

"You don't sound very ready. What's wrong?" George asked.

"I'm going to miss you."

George burst into laughter. "You're full of shit. Come on, grab your stuff. Just come back and bring your father."

I didn't respond, other than to pick up my duffle bag and sling it over my shoulder. George and I walked to the garage, where he stored his fleet of old vehicles. In his flamboyant style, he continued to point out the advantages his facility offered in a world gone mad. He knew I would return and suggested I bring anyone else I found back with me. There was always room for good workers and well-balanced individuals. He said I could be in his management team, with my intelligence and insights. The facility offered the perfect setting for a man like my father to live out his final years. The resistance needed people like me to function as a quality weapon against the enemies. His sales technique had me thinking the world I know of, with Michael and Joaquim and the network, had much to offer.

The GTO purred in the open garage bay door. Two attendants had readied it and stood in wait for us to say our last good-byes. George shook my hand, then pulled me toward him in a brief bear hug. The attendants rattled off a checklist, such as oil, fuel, and tire pressure. The morning sun reflected off the polished paint and windows. I dropped my duffle bag into the open trunk. The attendant slammed it shut and handed me a pair of sunglasses. A very rare item in these times. I slid behind the wheel, gave a brief rev to the engine, smiled, pushed in the clutch, dropped it in gear, and burned rubber for twenty feet. In the rearview mirror, even with the rubber smoke, I could see George's smile. He loved my dramatic departure. My grin melted; this would have been a moment to share with someone you loved.

The power surged through the steering wheel; the thrill rivaled my motorcycle as the road opened before me. Living at George's facility offered so many benefits; where in this crazy world offered more? Turn after turn, my rear wheels slid on the cracked asphalt, sporting slick tufts of weeds. Ahead on the first straightaway a figured darted from the woods into the road. My feet shifted, clutch to the floor and brakes on; I slid to a stop, askew. The figure stood 150 feet ahead. Strange, was it a trap? A decoy with others in wait to attack. I revved the engine. It was a woman. She looked hurt, but I had learned not to trust anyone. She walked toward me with a severe limp, a rag tied on her arm, her entire appearance disheveled. I put the car in reverse and backed away from her at just about the speed she walked, putting some distance between where she had appeared. If others lay in wait, I thought it best not to be near where she had first appeared.

Her clothing was lightweight. I could make out her form and saw no weapons. Stopped, I let her approach, my windows up. She stood beside my driver's door, but my eyes were on the road, the tree line, and my rearview mirror. When I looked at her, I saw anguish. Her eyes were hungry. My window opened just enough to allow conversation.

"Take me with you, please. I need to escape." Her voice sounded weak.

"Escape, escape what?" I asked.

"The place you just left; I heard the talk. Everyone talked about you and how George was letting you take one of his vehicles. Please, let me in."

The rag wrapped around her arm was blood soaked. She leaned against my door and slid to the ground. Looking around, I saw no danger. I opened my door, got out, and picked her up in my arms. Her skin was china white. With ease, I carried her around to the passenger-side door. Almost unconscious, she lay limp, and I unwrapped her wounded arm. The wound was an obvious self-inflicted gauge to remove her tracker. Unfortunately, she'd clipped some vital veins or maybe an artery, and she was bleeding. The only thing I could think to do was cauterize the wound, but how? I lowered her to the ground beside the car, and I lay beside her. Blood coursed over my hand as I held her arm. I stretched it under the car and pressed the wound against the exhaust pipe for a mere second. The smell of burnt flesh and her scream took my breath away. I pulled her out from beneath the car and cradled her in my arms. What else could I have done? She had been bleeding out, yet guilt consumed me, and she lay in my arms. Shock had set in, but the bleeding was done.

Slumped in the passenger seat, her head rested against the door as I dropped the shifter into first gear and headed for the manor. Weak and undernourished, I had doubts she would survive. The road conditions deteriorated. Several times, I stopped to remove tree limbs and other debris from our path. In the book of James, we are told to face trials with joy. This new world provided an opportunity to shine. After several miles, the road ended, the pavement pockmarked with bomb craters and uplifted concrete. This GTO was not intended for such hazards. On both sides of the road stood tall timber and the old foundations of homes. It was a long way back to the last side road, but I had no choice. The surface where we sat was narrow. As I attempted to turn, my rear wheels dropped into a rut hidden in the tall weeds. The sound of the car's frame coming to rest on concrete took me to a new low. Joy was difficult to muster, but as I sat, I prayed.

In the trunk, I found a bumper jack, fixed it under the rear bumper, and lifted the rear wheel off the ground. I jammed broken slabs of concrete under the rear wheel. I did the same to the other side, and now the frame was free, the rear tires equal to the road surface. When I had stowed the jack and reentered the vehicle, my patient moaned. The fine features of her face distorted in reaction to her severe pain. Her lips quivered as she tried to talk, her words not understandable.

"What are you trying to say?" I asked.

"Don't trust him . . . don't, " she whispered.

"Who, George?"

"Yes . . . the cult. He's manic. His mind works overtime. Nothing satisfies him," she replied, then faded.

There had been a day I wandered about the facility alone, and I remembered seeing her in the area where they made weapons for the resistance. A quick sight. As I moved past the workers, she had caught my attention. Now I wish I had taken the time to interact with the residents. Mystery surrounding its very existence bothered me. The best thing to do now was get her to the manor and put miles between us and George's compound. The tires flung the rocks I had placed beneath them and grabbed the concrete roadbed. The GTO fishtailed, then burst forward in solid acceleration.

FIFTEEN

Deena/Jim/Atanase

The storm hit with no warning just as Deena shot her final round into the target. A sunny morning and early afternoon left Deena and Jim ill-prepared. The clouds gathered during gale force winds, as lawn furniture tipped, and the few amber leaves still on the trees on the oaks tore away. The temperature dropped twenty degrees in a matter of minutes. Jim had been watching Deena practice with her crossbow, but she ran toward him without retrieving her arrows from the target. She locked her arm in his to help balance him. The two of them struggled to the rear door of the manor. The wind made Jim's eyes water. An invisible force pressed against the door when Deena opened it. The door ripped from her hand and banged into the outside wall. Jim entered the kitchen first, before Deena overcame the force of the wind and shut the door with a bang.

"Good grief! Where did that come from? Are you okay, Jim?" Deena asked.

"I'm fine. I have blurred vision and dry eyes. Curse of old age."

Deena stared out the kitchen window. Her target blew over and slid a few feet on the grass. Time grew short. Tomorrow she planned to depart and hoped Jim would come with her. But he'd made no commitment as to what he might do. The rain came in oscillating waves, obscuring the view from the window. A nor'easter, the first of the season, dumped hail and torrential rain. With the temperature drop, the rain turned white, and snow soon covered the ground. Jim relayed to Deena his experiences with such storms and how snow can accumulate at a rate of three inches per hour. Her plan to leave in the morning looked bleak.

***

I managed to evade any potential pursuers as I traveled roads I had scoped out while on my motorcycle. Ten miles from the manor, the GTO lost traction and slid into a stand of trees. I struggled to maintain control; the best I managed was a soft landing without injury to myself or my passenger. The vehicle became stuck. Nothing but a tow truck would free us. I sat and watched the snow pile up around us. My passenger moaned in pain but remained seemingly oblivious to her surroundings. At least we had heat, if the fuel held out. I slammed my fist on the steering wheel in frustration. My passenger's labored breathing caused me to worry, as my hopes of getting her help at the manor were fading. I slid over and lifted her torso in my arms to relieve the pressure on her diaphragm caused by her slump. She breathed a little easier as I studied the fine features of her face and wondered about her past.

Something beyond her visible wound had broken her spirit, but I didn't know how or why. I wanted answers and prayed she would wake and tell me.

***

Deena put a pot of water on the stove before she went to change out of her wet clothing; meanwhile, Jim went to his room to change as well. Even if a large accumulation of snow occurred, it might melt in a day or two. Normal temperature at this time of year was mild. This anomaly came from a jet stream. It wouldn't last. Deena and Jim sipped tea and watched the storm from the window of the library. The deciduous trees bent low, and the wet snow weighted down the bows of pines as the snow level neared a foot and a half. Jim shared with Deena some of his experiences with nature's storms. Many were life-threatening and violent, but none compared to artificial storms of chaos created by pride, lies, and greed, now threatening humanity and the world. Lightning played in the snow, a strange combination, and the flashes punctuated Jim's tales.

***

A faint moan caught my attention. My head rested against the window of the driver's door. It had been an hour since the crash, and the snow was piled ever higher outside. When I glanced at my passenger, her eyes were open, but she didn't appear to see. I reached for her hand to check for a pulse. To my surprise, she squeezed and didn't let go. Her eyes blinked, and her other hand came to her mouth, a finger extended across her lips to display the sign of silence. I complied, my eyes questioning her gesture. She emphasized the need for silence by shaking her head.

With great effort, she moved into a sitting position and signaled for us to depart the vehicle and its warmth. To do so would take great effort considering her condition. I opened my door, stepped into the snow, and circled the vehicle. When I opened her door, she fell in my direction, and I scooped her up in my arms. She whispered to me as her head came to rest near my shoulder.

"We must move away from this vehicle. He's listening."

I tried to support her enough so we could both trudge through the snow. Although she was lightweight, I slipped in the snow twice, though I didn't let her fall. The farther we moved from the vehicle, the more she spoke.

"He knows where we are, and I'm sure he knows I am with you. I'm sorry I put you in danger, but he plans to kill you along with those you intend to meet."

Two hundred feet from the vehicle, I laid her in the snow at the base of a large conifer. The branches of the tree offered shelter from the falling snow, so I dragged her into the soft pine needles and lay beside her.

"There are weapons in the truck. I saw them when I searched for the jack. We may need them. I'll retrieve them."

"No! They're trackers. Stay away from the vehicle." She coughed. Her voice was a whisper.

"What are you talking about, trackers?"

"We make weapons for the resistance; every weapon has a tracker inside. The Peacekeepers locate rebels carrying George's weapons. That car has listening devices in it and a tracker."

The words no sooner left her mouth than the GTO incinerated in a roiling ball of fire, rising high over the treetops and illuminating the snow in a quarter-mile radius. There was no way to tell the trigger—possibly a drone, a missile, or explosives planted in the vehicle. We were lucky we had evacuated far enough from the vehicle when we did. I embraced her in an offer of body heat. She shivered, as much from shock as the cold. Our faces touched cheek to cheek.

"Doc talked to a bunch of us about you," she whispered. "He made fun of you and said you were a believer in God. Are you?"

"Yes."

"Do you think these trackers they put in our arms are the mark of the beast?"

"No one knows. Some think the mark of the beast is in altered DNA, done with medical injections in the guise of immunizations. Only God knows these things."

"I've done things, things I am ashamed of. When I first came to the facility, George groomed me. I wanted to please him because it gave me security. But as time went on, I saw what we were doing. People were dying so we could live well. I'm scared. I think I'm dying. Will God forgive me? I mean, if I accepted the mark of the beast."

She shivered in my arms, her breathing shallow, and her heart raced to make up for her loss of blood. A compassionate God forgives sins, but these were exceptional times, and I had no answers for her.

"You need to rest. Do you believe Jesus Christ came to save sinners?" I said.

"I know little about religion or the Bible. I don't know."

"John 3:16 tells us, 'For God loved the world in this way. He gave his one and only Son, so that everyone who believes in him will not perish but have eternal life."

"Jesus rose from the dead, someone told me. I wish I knew more."

She wept; her body quivered against mine.

"Ask Jesus to forgive you, humble yourself before him, and admit you are unworthy to be in his presence without being wrapped in the righteousness of Christ. Accept this as true. Then spend the rest of your time praising him for his creation and beautiful glory. What is your name?"

"Elizabeth."

"Elizabeth, your name originates from faith and divine promise. Even after you heard the others mocking me, you sought me, but I think you were seeking God. When I saw you, my first thoughts were that I wanted to know you, but nothing else matters. Your desire for more and your rejection of the mockers is enough. Some God chose before they were born. I think you are one. Second Timothy 2:19 states, "Nevertheless, God's solid foundation stands firm, bearing this inscription: The Lord knows those who are his, and let everyone who calls on the name of the Lord turn away from wickedness.'"

"You, Atanase, are so kind and understanding."

"Pray with me, Elizabeth, repeat what I say, but also take it into your heart. Embrace love, and put all evil out and behind you. When you look at nature, God's creation, you see his perfection. Romans 1:20 points this out: all see his works, it's general revelation. The next step is special revelation and knowledge of specific truths. The most important truth is believing in Jesus Christ and his sacrifice on the cross to overcome death. Embrace him, Elizabeth, and wrap yourself in his love; he forgives all things."

The hours passed, and the snow continued to fall. Elizabeth and I prayed. In between prayers, she rested, and I tried to keep her warm.

***

Jim and Deena said little as they sat drinking herbal tea and watching the storm. Both knew Deena needed to leave as soon as possible, even with the heavy snow. Jim saw little hope for him to have the strength to negotiate the deep snow. His time had come. He felt a strange relief knowing he was done. His primary concern was for Deena. He had instructed her on survival techniques, and her spirit was strong. Time passed and Deena needed her rest. She excused herself and went to her room. Jim stayed in his lounge chair to continue watching the storm in between catnaps. When he was awake, he thought about all his adopted children, especially Atanase. He resolved they would never see one another again. Jim never went to bed; he slept in his chair.

In the morning, Deena gathered all her supplies and equipment without waking Jim. She placed them by the front door and went to the kitchen to fix breakfast. When all was ready, she brought it on a tray into the study to share it with Jim. As they ate, they both remained quiet, pained by thoughts of the future. The sun shone on the night's snowfall, and Jim remarked it would melt quickly. He refused Deena's requests for him to go with her. She planned to head north toward New Hampshire and the settlement there that some of Jim's children had established. It was all sketchy, as it had been several years since he'd received any report from them. It was a long shot, but where else could she go? The trek through unknown territories filled with roving bands of homeless wanderers offered little hope of success, but to stay meant certain death. They both knew the manor had no future.

Deena cleaned up the dishes and returned to the study to say good-bye. Jim stood in wait as she entered the room, two books in hand.

"Take these with you. A gift." Jim held the books out to her.

Right off, she recognized Ellen's Bible.

"Oh, Jim, I know how much Ellen's Bible means to you. I can't."

"It means more to me if you have it. You will need it, trust me. This other book is *The Temple* by George Herbert. You'll enjoy it. Poetry. Please."

"Oh, Jim, I don't know what to say."

"Nothing . . . say nothing."

Deena accepted the books and put her arms around Jim. She didn't want to let go, but she did. Without another word or look, she ran from the room, stuffed the books into her pack, and picked up her equipment and supplies. She struggled through the snow without looking back at the manor. Jim stood at the window and watched her until she disappeared into the woods. He prayed for her strength and for vision to see beyond the trials of her circumstances. Circumstances cause distraction from goals. In their talks, Jim had defined her goal: trust in God and care for her baby. Jim dropped into his easy chair. The sun warmed the morning, and meltwater trickled off the roof. He watched the light and shadows play on the fields, not moving for what seemed an eternity.

Something moving in the field caught Jim's attention. *It might be the wolf*, he thought. The movements were unsteady, the snow too deep to allow for a normal gait. Jim thought the creature was too dark, and as it closed in, he saw it was a man. Jim stood and moved closer to the window, taking up his binoculars. He focused, then dropped them away to his side. Again he put them to his eyes. It was Atanase. Jim scrambled to the manor's front door. His heart thumped in his ears, watching Atanase struggle through the snow, getting ever closer, but it also reminded him of the effort Deena must have been exerting in the same moment.

He whispered, "thank you, Lord, thank you. Amen."

When Atanase reached the manor, Jim wrapped him in a warm embrace. Neither one spoke a word or wanted to let go. Atanase's body quivered from both cold and tears, and Jim felt it. He stepped back, saw the pain in his son's face, and led him into the warmth of the manor.

Jim whispered, "So be it. Amen."

Atanase nodded in agreement. Everything was in the hands of God. Both men were humbled in the knowledge of how little they controlled. They walked in silence into the kitchen, where Jim put on a kettle of water and Atanase took a seat at the kitchen table.

"There's no need to tell much, son. You're back, alone. Your face tells me."

"Father, the world lost a spirit. Last night, I held a woman as she died, but not until after she accepted Christ."

"Did you know her, son?"

"We'd just met; she bled out, after removing her tracker. I tried . . ." My words choked off.

"You must not remain here; they know about the manor."

"Where can we go?"

"My decision is to stay. I'm old and done. You are tired, but there's a woman you can help. She left here this morning, and you need to catch up to her. We'll rest over some tea; then you need to get out of here. She'll be easy to track in the snow. I'll let her tell you about herself."

"I had hoped to stay here, but I trust your judgment. Are you sure you don't want to come with me?"

"Nothing would make me happier than to be strong enough to go, but I'm dying anyway. The woman is pregnant, and the baby's father is dead. She's heading for New Hampshire. I told her about the settlement your brothers and sisters established in the mountains."

"You haven't had a word from them in a long time."

"What were the alternatives? She is a good, strong woman. You will like her."

Jim poured tea, and they continued to talk. Refraining from dark details, Atanase shared some highlights of his adventures.

"You know, son, the worse thing about getting old is when you look back over your life and see all the brokenness never fixed. Now it's too late to fix anything, but there is a healer."

SIXTEEN

Deena/Atanase

Deena did the best she could to pack down the snow before she set up her tent at the end of an outcrop of rocks. The rocks provided shelter and a windbreak. The day was long. Her hips ached from the struggle through the deep snow. She wondered how far she had come; her progress was half what it would have been without the snow. A dry table-sized flat rock proved an excellent place to build a fire. Old timber falls provided fuel for her fire, but she wondered about the wisdom of creating one. She had seen no signs of human or animal activity all day, but predators remain out of sight in wait for opportunities to prey on unsuspecting victims. The warmth of the fire overcame her fears. She needed the comfort it provided. She heated some water and made a bean stew of sorts. If nothing else, it warmed her. Her thoughts were on Jim. She missed his company and knew she would never see him again.

***

I left the manor after tea, left Father sitting in his usual place looking frail and ancient. He told me he expected company to come soon, the old wolf. Leaving was hard, but the broken world had sealed his fate. A simple plan: follow Deena's trail in the snow until I found her. Tracking her proved easy, and I hoped she would hole up for the night. My movements were easier than hers since she had blazed a trail. So I knew my time stood to be better than hers. Father had fitted me out with supplies, a small tent, walking sticks, a backpack with food, a plate, a pot, and some hand tools, such as a hatchet and Bowie knife. The gift of his crossbow honored me; he had made it many years ago.

As darkness shrouded the woods, Deena's trail still guided me, as it was a distinct cut in the snow. Two hours into the night, I spotted a glow in the distance, a campfire. My approach slowed to assess the campsite and the occupants, careful not to alarm or spook them, knowing it was likely Deena, and she was likely alone. The campsite looked unoccupied; no one sat by the fire. A sharp object pressed on my neck; I remained calm.

"Don't move. Drop your crossbow."

A woman's voice, it had to be Deena. I dropped my bow.

"Who are you, and why are you creeping up on my camp?"

"Atanase. My name is Atanase."

The point of the arrow dropped away from my neck as Deena stepped back.

"Atanase? Son of Jim Fisher?"

"Yes, do you mind if I move now?"

"Oh, sorry, yes."

I turned and faced Deena; she looked the part of a warrior, everything Father had said.

"Come, let's go to my fire so we can get a better look at each other. Did you come from the manor? How is your father?"

On the walk into the camp, I told her my story. She offered me soup, and we rested and exchanged our experiences with Jim. We laughed, and I told her of my assignment to protect her, although I admitted she got the drop on me, and maybe she was the one who needed to protect me. Our chat lasted through many subjects. We had a lot in common, both of us adopted children of the great Jim Fisher. We shared the plan to hike to New Hampshire to find the lost Fisher tribe. Even as I set up my tent next to hers, we talked.

SEVENTEEN

The manor

Morning found Jim still in his easy chair in his study, and he caught sight of movement in the distant field. His wolf struggled in the deep snow as it advanced toward the manor. Jim went to the front and opened the door. The wolf was still a distance away. He returned to the easy chair to watch. Several times, the wolf stopped to look about and catch its breath. The wolf approached the open front door, out of sight from Jim. As it stepped in, the tall minders gave her a start, but in an instant, she sensed they offered no threat. She sniffed the air and caught Jim's scent. She rushed down the hall, turned the corner, and stopped at the sight of Jim. An outreached hand coaxed the wolf forward, and she merged into his presence. Jim scratched behind her ear. Animal and man felt at peace and sat in wait.

***

Einstein first presented the idea of quantum entanglement and referred to it as "spooky action at a distance." I'm not sure if this was at work, but I sensed events at distant locations. Off the coast of the Canary Islands, a super yacht vaporized in a ball of heat roiling skyward. In Romania, a castle did the same. Homes in several European capitals exploded. A home in California and one in Guatemala did likewise. I sensed all as it happened, and I saw Jim flinch at each incident. The wolf stood with ears erect. Jim's fist opened, revealing the Brave Knight at rest, worn by the years, yet with it's sinewy connection across time and space secure.

Creation and its wonders exceed man's understanding. The ducks on the pond took flight, and a herd of deer ran from the meadow into the distance wood. All these events happened in an instant. The manor vaporized without warning. A grand release into the cosmos freed me. My essence transformed, not destroyed. I no longer touched those of the manor nor am I bound to it. Evil thinks it has the upper hand here, yet at some level it knows—God's goodness wins the war.

EIGHTEEN

Deena & Atanase

We slept later than planned, after our extended campfire chat. We packed as quickly as possible, knowing no safety would be found in staying in one place long. We could eat a bit of jerky as we walked.

As we hoisted our packs to set out, a roar echoed through the woods to startle Deena and me. In a second we knew what it meant, and we turned to catch the fireball rise above the hills. It was done, everything of the past gone. Deena reached out and embraced me. Both of us sobbed in grief. We allowed ourselves only a few minutes before we set out for the trek ahead. Jim had given both of us the tools for survival, both physical and spiritual. Neither of us spoke. I know we shared the same feelings and thoughts. We faced a 450-mile trek, if all went as planned—180 hours of continuous walking. Neither of us had such expectations. A lot could happen in twenty days. One route, the shortest, took us through some very dangerous areas, including the ruins of New York and the Jersey suburbs. We thought it best to add a few extra days and stay west to avoid Philadelphia and Trenton. Our route, due north with Pottstown to the west and King of Prussia to the east, offered a less populated area. We thought using the Pennsylvania Turnpike's 476 extension offered an unpopulated option. Around Palmerton, Pennsylvania, the Turnpike intersects the Appalachian Trail, a well-marked trail all the way into the White Mountains of New Hampshire.

The Appalachian Trail, once a scenic footpath offering beauty and physical challenges, had in recent times become a corridor for refugees to escape collapsed population centers. I wasn't aware of the current condition or traffic. When I was young, Jim Fisher took me and other siblings on a brief excursion to enjoy pastoral, wild, and resonant lands. Father always loved nature. He said he felt closest to God when immersed in his creation. I knew it offered the chance to hike to New Hampshire and avoid population centers. As near as I figured, the trail lay about ninety miles due north of our location. With the snow melted and fair weather, we might make Palmerton in a week. My worries about Deena's condition had passed. When Father told me she was pregnant, I developed a prejudice toward her. On first meeting her, with an arrow pressed against the base of my skull, my biases cleared. She hiked ahead of me, blazing the trail through the snow.

By noon of the first day, we were under full sun without a cloud in the sky. The silence of the woods was only interrupted by trickles of water draining beneath snow.

Chunks of snow slid from the branches of conifers, allowing the boughs to spring upward.

The first days lifted our hopes for a quick traverse toward the main trail. My concern lay in passing between the King of Prussia and Pottstown. We needed to cross the Schuylkill River at either Royersford or Phoenixville, although there was a third crossing between those two bridges. We had three days of walking before we reached the river, with no way of knowing if any of the bridges existed. As we approached the Schuylkill River, the snow existed only in shaded patches and walking proved easy. A sign for the old river trail confirmed we were negotiating the remnants of small villages hidden by dense overgrowth. We hiked the trail along the Schuylkill until we came to an old welcome sign for Phoenixville. Unfortunately, the bridge across the Schuylkill lay underwater. The river was over capacity and raging in a torrent, probably from the nor'easter rain, then the snow melt. We crossed French Creek using an old railroad bridge. The rail bridge across the Schuylkill also lay underwater, so we trekked along the river until we came to the old dam, with most of the water rushing through the damaged locks. Fallen timber lined the upriver side, interlocked so tight it formed a bridge to accommodate a safe but challenging crossing. This was not the time of year to get wet.

The tangle of tree trunks, logs, and branches pressed tight against the cement overflow dam to create an ecosystem of sprouting shrubs and weeds now crusted with ice. The ice made for a treacherous go, as we leapt across voids in the mesh. Branches gave way. Much of the timber beneath the bark was soft. A constant wind coming up the river made the temperature twenty degrees colder. Deena's stamina impressed me. She never complained, but I questioned the wisdom of hiking north. The weather turned brutal. We hoped some shelters had stood the test of time. Some offered fireplaces and wind blocks but were open on one side. When we reached the far side of the dam, we found a lone tree down across the lock.

Over the gush of water coursing through the crumbled lock lay this massive tree, its root ball uplifted onto the shore. The trunk formed an almost perfect bridge, except for the large branches reaching skyward, which hindered a direct passage. It looked to be an oak, the branches as large as the trunk. Two of the branches posed an impasse to our crossing, but Deena said skirting them was doable. We didn't have any other options; Deena led the way onto the trunk, which lay almost horizontal. The bark crumbled beneath her feet, dried and detached from the cambium wood after years of rot. Slabs of bark broke loose and fell into the water and debris below. I followed close to Deena, a rope in hand. Her plan, when we reached the crown, was to toss the rope over a smaller extension branch above our heads and use it to tether ourselves as we squeezed around the main branch.

When we reached the branch, I took the lead and tossed the rope overhead. I gave the rope a powerful tug to test the branch. The branch held, and I felt confident to tie it around my waist. Deena wrapped the other end around another horizontal branch one time to give her an advantage. I gripped the rough bark and balanced my weight as I eased around the branch. On the other side, I untied the rope from my waist and tossed it to Deena, who tied it to our backpacks and crossbows. She gave the package a heave, and it swung out farther, rotating around the branch. When the packs hit my chest, the bark beneath my feet gave way and I lost my balance. Deena braced herself, holding her end of the rope tight to the branch she had wrapped the rope around, to counter my weight. Tumbling backward, I locked my arms into the package but kept my feet pressed against the tree trunk. My full weight taken up by the rope, my fall was checked, and I pulled myself back into an erect position, then dropped to my knees, out of breath. Deena voiced apologies and knelt as I gathered myself. It was no one's fault, and Deena tied her end of the rope around her waist and maneuvered around the branch until I grabbed her and pulled her into my arms. We passed the second branch without incident and stood on the far side of the lock.

As we finished the river crossing, I was chilled and knew, even without a word of complaint, that Deena had been through enough for one day. We hiked along the old Upper Schuylkill Trail until we entered the vacant village of Mont Clare and walked Jacobs Street toward Bridge Street; the houses were rubble. My thoughts were to set one on fire and enjoy the heat, but I refrained. Bridge Street had little to offer, not a soul in sight. The village had stood empty for a long time. The fire station was still intact, although vacated. Just beyond the railroad overpass, I saw a vast estate, the home still standing. It looked large enough to have six or eight bedrooms, and I thought it must have a fireplace. It looked like home, or at least a place to shelter for a bit, if it was vacant. We approached with caution and saw no signs of human activity in recent times. The home represented old money, a building style popular during a period known as the Roaring Twenties.

Deena and I circled the building to look for tracks in the mud and snow, and where possible, we looked through windows. All the exterior doors were intact and locked. There was no evidence of looting or vandalism. On the front porch, I attempted to open windows. We were able to open the third window after some effort. Deena and I entered a large living room. With several hours of daylight remaining, we checked every room and closet. The closest contained clothing and shoes. The furnishings needed dusting but were in sound condition. Several rooms had fireplaces and even had racks of firewood; the scene looked staged. We joked about our newfound wealth and dream home. Too good to be true? Maybe, but we were tired, cold, and hungry.

In the dining room, I lit a fire in the fireplace as Deena unbundled our packs and spread our sleeping bags on cushions she retrieved from the living room couches. The warmth of the fire radiated through the room as we settled down to eat food supplied by Jim. We both offered a prayer of gratitude for all our blessings before eating.

"Jim gave me a gift as I was leaving, a Bible; it was Ellen's," Deena said.

"It was very special to him," I replied.

Deena asked if I knew its history, and I shared the little I knew. Ellen was a missionary, killed by rebels.

Deena went to her backpack and retrieved it. "Several pages have wrinkled spots that look like drops—maybe from tears." She opened it, selecting an arbitrary location, and read the verse. "'Blessed is the one who endures trials, because when he has stood the test he will receive the crown of life that God has promised to those who love him.'"

After a moment of contemplation she muttered almost to herself, "That's James 1:12. This comforts me. I can't believe I opened to this verse."

This was a season of mourning. The world I knew was lost. Still, I sensed a comforting, inexplicable evolution. Many times, losses turn into opportunities; yet I struggled to envision a future.

Deena turned to Isaiah 43:18–19 at my request. It says, "Do not remember the past events, pay no attention to things of old. Look, I am about to do something new; even now it is coming. Do you not see it? Indeed, I will make a way in the wilderness, rivers in the desert."

Conflicted, I pondered my path, who I had been, and what made me who I am. "Don't ask me to explain it, but something is in the works."

To dwell on the past or to allow it to dominate the present, I understood to be wrong, but a culture or a person needs to be in touch with what they have lived. Deena agreed with me, and we spoke of things that had changed our hearts. Life unfolds in a series of flashes filled with desires. Our job is to deny and sacrifice for the long-term good. If we fall to hedonistic impulses, our future and others' futures suffer. It is important to ask forgiveness for sins, put those mistakes behind, and not make new ones. Then what is a sin? Anything going against the teachings of the Lord is a sin.

The light dimmed and reading became impossible. We sat and stared into the embers of the fireplace. I continued to struggle with memories of all my loved ones who had passed, even as the Bible told me not to look back. "Father gave you the best gift of all—God's Word. I can't think of anything better to have along with us on our journey."

What the future held was bigger than Deena and me. I retrieved a blanket from one bedroom. Deena didn't acknowledge my movement until I wrapped it around her shoulders. Startled, she thanked me and pulled it tight around herself with a sigh. I placed two more logs on the fire. Then I lay on the floor outstretched before the hearth, to enjoy the warmth. Deena sat on a cushion on the floor nearby, her back rested against the lower portion of a couch. Both of us were too tired to get into our sleeping bags. With the heat from the fire, there was no need. Soon, we fell asleep in these positions.

A distant noise woke me. The fireplace contained nothing but smokeless embers, and Deena still slept propped against the couch. The sound of vehicles in the street and flashes of spotlights crossed the windows. Without disturbing Deena, I rushed to a window for a better look. A convoy moved along Bridge Street. It was too dark to make out much more than the piercing lights scanning the surroundings. Men shouted orders to others on patrol, but their voices weren't clear enough to understand. Our fire had died, which was a blessing. I woke Deena and told her we needed to pack our things and be prepared to run. She didn't take time to ask a single question; she just busied herself gathering our supplies. This home, being one of the few intact I had seen in town, led me to believe it belonged to someone of influence.

Perhaps the patrols would not disturb it this time. Maybe we had elected to stay in a safe space as long as we didn't attract attention. The patrol passed without incident, but we moved on before the light of day.

Two hours before daylight, we hustled along Bridge Street and Collegeville Road until we were well past Route 422. Off the side of the road and well hidden in the undergrowth, no threat of detection worried us. Our progress unimpeded by patrols, we slowed our pace. Still, we stayed on alert. Our time in the mansion had refreshed us, and both of us walked with a strong gait. To our right were the ruins of a shopping center, the parking lot overrun with weeds. To avoid the road, we made our way to Perkiomen Creek, which we followed and ran along due north until we reached Green Lane Reservoir.

We set up camp near Red Hill. All along the way, the ruins of dwellings stood as a testament to how heavily populated the area once was, but we never encountered another human. We set our tents beneath a thick canopy of oaks to hide us from the eyes in the sky. The cold blue reservoir floated sheets of white ice and hosted ducks and geese. The trees offered dried branches strewn on the ground and were easy to snap on a knee. Dry wood burns clean with no smoke, and we warmed ourselves for an hour before cooking. As we finished eating the meal, a wet snow blanketed the campsite and put out our fire. We had ditched Deena's tent, so we could lighten our load while also sharing body heat. We retreated into our tent. Maybe we'd be safer together, too.

NINETEEN

Atanase & Deena

Before daybreak, we set out for Allentown, a twenty-two-mile hike. The fresh snow brightened the terrain, but six inches of slushy snow dampened our boots and lower legs. The temperature proved mild with no wind. We would have to push hard to make our goal, but we felt confident we could do it. Deena led the way as we stumbled through Hoppenville, which turned into jokes about "what Hoppened" and "let's get Hoppen." Our hike took us along Geryville Pike, King's Highway, Vera Cruz Road, and before we entered the town of Vera Cruz, we changed our direction and continued to walk along old Turnpike Route 476. We didn't wish to enter the Allentown district since we feared the population there. The crumbled debris of the Route 78 overpass offered a great place to camp. During the day-long trek, we had not encountered any other people. What remained of the overpass provided shelter and a dry campsite. There was plenty of firewood, and large slabs of vertical concrete offered privacy and protection from an evening wind.

While I set our tent, Deena collected firewood from the woods near our camp. An old collapsed shed offered an assortment of dry timber and kindling. She filled her arms and made several trips. The pile of wood in our camp grew, and when she went out one last time, walking around the backside of the debris pile, she flinched at a sensation in her right foot. It was painful, but instinct told her not to panic. Protruding from the top of her boot was a skewer that had penetrated from the sole of her boot, through her foot, and out the top. She didn't lift her foot. A large metal plate held a metal shaft, thinner than a nail, that resembled a machine part. She closed her eyes as the wound burned and her heart filled with regret. Such a wound spelled danger from infection, especially tetanus or a flesh-eating bacterium. Deena opened her eyes as she finally lifted her foot and hobbled toward our camp. We removed her boot and boiled water to clean her foot and wound. It didn't bleed as much as I would have liked, as blood flow helps to cleanse a puncture wound.

"I'm sorry. I should have been more careful," Deena offered.

"Don't be silly or blame yourself. It'll be okay. We should hold up here until we see if an infection sets in. Besides, I think not wearing a boot or walking is wise. We aren't under any immediate pressure," I said.

Allentown wasn't very far; I wondered if the risk of seeking medical help was worthwhile, but I had made a promise to Father to watch over her. I didn't mention it to Deena, but all evening I considered going into town as we sat by the fire and talked about our pasts. We'd had such different beginnings, yet also many similarities in the loss of our birth parents. In a way, we complimented each other in that I was streetwise and she knew the ways of the State. Jim Fisher had rescued both of us and rehabbed us like old buildings. We laughed. We learned a lot from each other. Deena never complained about her foot. I let it rest on my lap as I applied a warm compress to it.

As we shared our past lives, it dawned on me how real we were being with each other. No games, no attempts to sugarcoat anything, just complete honesty. I spoke of how deeply I loved my wife, how much I missed her, and she spoke of the shallowness of her relationship. Neither of us had pretenses.

Our campsite offered shelter and comfort among the uplifted array of concrete slabs, the heat from our fire trapped in an artificial hollow of debris. The sky had cleared of clouds, and the night filled with stars, a crisp winter sky.

Our fire still burned in the morning under a blue sky. Deena emerged from the tent as I handed her a hot cup of brew made from dried local herbs we'd brought from the manor. My eyes locked on her bare foot, swollen with a raised redness around the puncture. The sight left no doubt. I had to seek help.

"The swelling and redness show infection. I'm going into Allentown to seek help and meds."

"No! It's too dangerous. I'll be all right in a couple of days," Deena replied.

"You have no say in it. I'm going. I'll build up your wood supply to last a couple of days. You rest and care for your wound."

Deena scowled and said no more but watched as I piled firewood close to her before my departure. With little hope of finding help, I wondered if I was running away from an ugly fate. Two days I gave myself; then I would come back and face whatever this wound turned into. All I took with me was a crossbow and a full quiver. I left Deena all the food. I had to move in a fast walk or even a run, if the terrain permitted. Deena and I said no more, but I wasn't far off before my sternness toward Deena filled my heart with regret. I headed east across the old, deserted highway into a wooded area never developed, most likely an old park. The ground was clear and allowed me to cover the distance in a run. I came out onto a street marked Broadway and picked up my pace. Like so many towns, the houses along the way were rubble, but soon the street switched to Parkway Boulevard as I passed through another area with no signs of development.

An oppressive odor filled the air, like rotting flesh but more putrid. I had read where in medieval times walled cities produced odors that traveled for miles. Lack of sanitation and hygiene were commonplace. As I ran toward Allentown, I wondered if this was the source. To my right I saw several plumes of smoke and shanties where an old sign read Allentown Rose Garden. A huge mound of smoldering debris, as large as a city block, sat near the road, close to the encampment. In the center of the shanties, a forty-foot-tall cross stood, yet something in my gut questioned the scene. Intuition can be strong, and I thought it best to continue. I supposed it was an encampment of wanderers, not the type to have medical supplies. As I passed, some campers came out of their shanties and coaxed me to come to them. The solicitation creeped me out more than the debris pile. I continued my run as several people from the campsite fell in behind me. I didn't imagine them to be friends or folks seeking exercise. A quick look over my shoulder gave me a count of ten, baring down on me.

I burst into speed, putting distance between me and eight of them, but two were still coming on strong. Now in a full-out sprint, I realized they were catching up to me. My only hope was if I had more stamina and could keep a lead until they gave out. This plan offered little comfort, but I pushed and prayed. On my right, I passed a lake pond, and just ahead, I saw a high concrete wall to my left. It looked like a fortress of sorts. An old sign identified it as a stadium. As I reached the wall, I was pushed to the ground. One of my trackers threw himself on top of me, screaming a wild war cry. We wrestled, and then the second tracker pounced on me. Stronger and much younger than me, I knew the others would soon arrive. As I fought for my life, I felt the second attacker go limp, then the first. For a few seconds, I lay pinned under their dead weight, unable to comprehend what had just happened. As I maneuvered from under them, I saw arrows protruding from their torsos. Shouts and jeers filled the air, and I looked toward the concrete wall. On top of the wall, a dozen or more men cheered and shook their bows toward the sky. The eight other pursuers stopped dead in their tracks a good two hundred feet from me.

"Quick! Climb the ladder!" a man on the wall shouted. He cast a rope of webbing down the side of the concrete.

"Hurry!" another shouted.

I don't like high-pressure sales pitches—yes, they killed my attackers, but who were they? The eight men standing on the road were definite enemies. They wanted me dead for no good reason. The eight then charged toward me, giving me enough incentive to grab for the rope mesh. As I climbed, men grabbed at my legs, trying to pull me down. The men on the wall took out three of them with arrows before they backed away and let me climb the wall. The men on the wall grabbed me as I reached the top and lifted me onto a walkway.

"You are very lucky, my friend. Those are desperate men. They eat whatever they can kill. Tonight they will come back for their dead friends. Come with us."

From the wall, I saw the inside of what used to be a stadium. Now it was a walled fortress, living quarters all along the perimeter. On what used to be a football field grazed sheep, some cattle, and an abundance of chickens. On the old stadium seating stood shanties, with guard towers and sentries at intervals. The one I assumed to be the leader, at least of this wall crew, talked to me as we descended into the stadium.

"We're the good guys, just so you know. Why did you come here? Do you have a tracker in your body?"

"No tracker. We're heading north to catch the Appalachian Trail," I replied.

"Isn't everyone?" He chuckled. "You say *we*?"

"I have an injured friend."

"You don't say."

As we walked along the edge of the field and into a tunnel once used for funneling crowds in and out, I assessed my surroundings. First we passed through a dark room lit only by UV; no one explained the reason for that setup. The exit led to an area where women worked in gardens to harvest cold-weather root crops, children played, dogs barked. The most striking and disarming thing was the laughter and giggles of little girls. Like classical music, it differed from the evil tone of the world. Their laughter sprung from their curiosity about a stranger in their midst.

"Who were those men chasing me?"

"Invaders, a mixture of misfits and rejects, a lot of them Acceptors who fell from the grace of the State. They've been living in that camp for two years. They are the worst of the worst, pure evil. But they know enough to fear us; they live off our scrap. They are rodents. As fast as we discard our trash, they snatch it and repurpose it. They're cannibals and perverts. You're lucky you made it to our fortress. We control and patrol most of the old city, but there are other encampments like theirs in the surrounding hills. Come into my hut. I am Alexander, the mayor, but many call me General."

"I am Atanase."

Inside his hut, he introduced me to his wife, Madelyn, and their three young children. We sat at a table, and his wife served us a warm herbal brew.

"What is the purpose of the UV-lit passageway?"

"It indicates vaccinated people with a mild glow."

Knowing Deena's history, I wondered what their reaction would be if she glowed when exposed to the light. My intention was to secure meds and return to our campsite. Alexander said they avoided the wrath of the State by being no threat to anyone. They avoided conflicts with the Peacekeepers. He believed the AI robots of the State were the reincarnation of the Nephilim of old. In his opinion, current times were like those in the days of Noah. His wife sat with us as I shared my situation, but when I mentioned Deena, his wife stood in terror.

"Alexander, you must go now! Get your men and bring this woman, now!" his wife said.

"Can you ride a horse, Atanase?" Alexander asked.

"I can, but if you will just give me some medications, I will go care for her."

"Nonsense, we must hurry. Your friend is in grave danger."

Alexander turned to his oldest son and instructed him. "Son, tell Ben to saddle twenty horses and prepare a packhorse. Also, have him request eighteen volunteer riders. Now go."

We sat and talked about Deena's injury and treatment options. Readying the horses and assembling the riders would take some time, and Alexander's wife thought it best we wait until summoned. While in wait, I learned about their facility, how they generated electricity from old solar cells and batteries, and about their food sources. They repurposed a large cemetery, fairgrounds, and a municipal park next to the stadium into farmland. They were very open with details. Twenty minutes passed before their son returned.

"Everything is ready, Father."

"Great job. Come, Atanase, let's see how well you can ride."

The horses and men stood in double file in the stadium's field. A young man clinging to their reins held two riderless lead horses in place. The horse pranced, full of spirit and eager for the ride. Alexander laughed as we walked toward them.

"They picked a beauty for you. She is new to the saddle, full of herself. Show her who's boss!"

Alexander mounted without incident and gave his horse a pat on the neck. My horse resisted my attempts to mount and danced sideways whenever I placed a foot toward her stirrup. All the men laughed. I had to laugh, too, as Alexander rode close to her and grabbed the reins. My horse knew him. She respected him, so she calmed and allowed me to mount. Two men on foot opened the gate, and we trotted out of the stadium onto Parkway Boulevard. As we approached the camp with the big cross, Alexander spoke.

"They erected the cross a couple of months ago. We suspect it to be a ploy to attract unwary travelers to seek refuge with them. No true Christian would fall for it, I suspect, if they took one look at the living conditions."

As we closed in on the camp, Alexander let out a war cry and whipped the rear of his horse. My horse responded in kind with no encouragement from me. We left the road and headed straight into the encampment, all of us at full gallop. People scattered in all directions. No one tried to stop or hurt us. The power of the horses mounted by well-built men screaming at the top of their lungs wrought terror in the encampment. We circled through, harming no one, but the psychological impact had to be profound. As quickly as we entered, we left and were back on the road.

"I love doing that," Alexander shouted at me. "You held on well."

I said nothing as we rode on. Before we started the ride, I told Alexander where Deena and I had camped, the collapsed overpass of Route 78 and Route 476. He knew where to go. Within minutes, we were at the concrete slabs and dismounted. Taking the lead, I approached the tent while the others waited. We did not want to startle her. I explained to her what I had found and told her we needed to break camp and pack. Deena crawled out of her tent and limped beside me, holding my shoulder as we rounded a vertical slab of concrete behind which Alexander and the crew stood in wait.

Alexander greeted her and told one of his men to help her onto my horse as his men helped me pack our camp and tie everything on the packhorse. Deena did not look well and slouched over my back after I mounted our horse. Alexander gave me a worried look, then gave his horse a gentle nudge. We all fell in behind him. When we emerged from the woods onto the road, he slowed to allow me to come alongside him.

"We have medications, long past their expiration dates, but we have found them to be effective. Expirations dates were a joke, just a marketing ploy."

"Do you have tetanus shots? She needs one, especially since she is pregnant," I asked.

"We do. There were several pharmacies and a hospital in town before the fall. I secured most of the meds when we retreated into the stadium," Alexander said.

"Do you know how to administer them, or is there a doctor among you?" I asked.

He laughed. "I used to be a surgeon. My wife was also a doctor."

Oh Lord, I said to myself, this is a God thing. A miracle. We rode into the stadium and dismounted. As I helped Deena down off the horse, two men came with a stretcher. We all walked through the room with the UV lights. Deena's skin cast a faint yet eerie glow. No one said a word or paused, and I wondered if anyone noticed. We entered Alexander's quarters; he went for his medical bag while we placed Deena's stretcher on two sawhorses. When he returned, he grabbed Deena's arm and inspected her wrist. There was a scar where her tracker had been. He gave me a stern look.

"You failed to mention your friend had been an Acceptor. You should have told us."

I couldn't argue. In the excitement, I didn't know what to say. Now I wondered how things might play out. Alexander's wife entered the room, ready to examine Deena.

"She was an Acceptor, but someone appears to have removed her tracker. The UV shows vaccination," Alexander said.

Madelyn looked at me, a cold stare. "Both of you, leave us alone while I examine her; she's a very sick girl. First, I will inject her with a tetanus shot and antibiotics. Now, leave us."

Alexander and I left his hut to tour the stadium and talk. In one area under a large overhanging roof, men worked out with free weights and lifting machines. The area had full equipment, including cardio machines, ellipticals, and stair climbers.

"We emphasize fitness and good health through nutrition. Most of our citizens follow a regimen of exercise, especially our warriors. We are a defensive group and never make war. If someone threatens us, we are ready. It also fits our spiritual beliefs. My wife and I are people of science. It fits very well with our interpretations of Christianity. Both require a deep study to understand the mechanisms at work. Do you view yourself as a Christian?"

"A believer, I am," I replied.

"My studies of the human body, along with quantum theory, have meshed well to understand how the God of the Bible might work. Pure speculation on my part, but I am fascinated by harmonics, frequencies, and the vibes of spirits. Everyone's life is a spiritual journey. From birth to death, everything we do affects our spirit. You either experience negative or positive events, and both have an unavoidable impact. The impact translates into what vibes you give back to the universe. Sounds kind of like I'm preaching some sort of mystic Eastern religion, but I'm not. Christ came to tune us up, to show us the way to give off good vibrations. He spoke in parables, so study is required. He invoked the Holy Spirit for us to invite in to tweak our harmonics."

"I have thought these things myself. I grew up reading about similar things," I agreed.

"Before the collapse, distributing 5G towers interrupted the natural frequencies of creation. It helped the world governments to manipulate people and gain control. The move was so subtle and sold as a benefit to communications. To the north, there is a large population of Acceptors, east of the old strip mines. Avoid that area at all costs," Alexander said.

"They've been highly successful in densely populated areas. They are ruthless."

"We destroy the towers when we find them but never engage the State. Therefore, we don't make war; our battle is not of the flesh; it is with the invisible. The State does all it can to disrupt the harmony and cause chaos. They inject fluorescent materials along with meds into the population. These materials disrupt a person's vibes; they mask their host's existence to the higher power. Any medical treatment someone receives through State channels is suspect. I'm sorry to tell you this, but once the process happens, it is irreversible. Some call our UV light the eye of Horus, but I don't buy into such things."

"What does all this mean to us, for Deena and me?"

Alexander ignored my question, and we walked into other parts of the stadium. He showed me their windmills that pumped water from wells into elevated water tanks. The tanks not only stored drinking water but also stored energy, which when released into turbines generated electricity. He also showed me their solar cells and the UV water treatment system used to purify drinking water. The facility rivaled Giant George's complex but without the nefarious intent. Standing on the north wall, we looked toward the old cemetery and fairgrounds, where women and children worked the gardens to prepare for spring. Fenced areas contained sheep and cattle, and a guarded area with a double fence twenty feet high held a hundred horses. Inside the double-walled fence, guard dogs roamed.

"We protect our horses. Never go near those fences." Alexander turned and extended his arm toward the way we had come. "We should return to my dwelling and see how Deena is doing and what Madelyn has diagnosed."

We walked in silence, but my thoughts were many. What were they going to do about Deena's UV scan?

TWENTY

Deena & Atanase

Deena slept in an adjacent room as I took a seat in Alexander's kitchen after our return from the tour. My quarters were to be in another dwelling, the hut of Alexander's right-hand man, Benjamin, and his wife Carrie. I met him on the ride to fetch Deena; he was a well-built man and reserved. Madelyn wasn't home when we returned, so Alexander made us an herbal brew. His silence was killing me. Since the horse corral he hadn't spoken, and his face looked hardened. Madelyn walked in as he placed a cup of hot brew in front of me.

"Your friend is extremely ill. I am afraid for her and the baby," Madelyn said.

"Did she talk to you?" I asked.

"No, she mumbled a lot. Her fever was 104. It came down to 101 with medication. She's in for a fight."

"Is there anything else we can do?" I asked.

"The infection swelled her leg. The only other thing we can do is take her leg, but let's wait to see what happens overnight."

"I know you arranged for me to sleep at Benjamin's hut, but I will stay with Deena tonight and pray over her," I said.

"Yes, that's a proper request. Please do," Alexander replied.

"They implanted a tracker in Deena's arm, and state officials injected her with medication. She's an Acceptor," Madelyn stated.

"Deena and I are both orphans. A wonderful family adopted me, while the State raised and enslaved her. As a child, the State inflicted treatment on her without her knowledge or consent. Recently my father took her in, and she changed drastically after she accepted Jesus as her Lord. We can't hold her childhood against her," I said.

"We aren't holding it against her. This isn't a judgment, it's a fact. Everyone is on a spiritual journey; our spirits grow according to what they feed on. The injection the State gives interrupts the harmonics of a person at a genetic level. Nothing she does can overcome it. The Holy Spirit can… well, we don't know, but we'll talk about it if she pulls through," Madelyn said.

As everyone settled for the night, I retreated into Deena's room and pulled back the covers over her leg. Deena's room lacked electricity; the luxury of electric lights was saved for common areas of the stadium. I had only the light of three candles but could see the swelling from the knee to her foot. She moaned but never spoke as I placed my hands near her ankle. Her flesh felt taut and hot. The two candles let off wisps of black smoke after I blew them out. Better to conserve them, for I did not need light. I prayed for her strength and healing the entire night. Sleep eluded me. In the morning, she was still unconscious and her leg still swollen when Madelyn stepped in to check on her. I excused myself and left the room to wash up.

Alexander met me in the kitchen, and we talked about our beliefs and our pasts. We shared common core beliefs, but the people of the stadium had developed and integrated a few tenets I couldn't justify in Scripture. Alexander said they followed the teachings and commands as spelled out in Deuteronomy, but I questioned that. He considered me a foreigner, and Deena of unique status as an Acceptor who now put her faith in the Eternal Creator God. As a guest, I chose not to argue points, but I also knew in the long run I couldn't live with the rules the stadium people lived by. I never followed the rules of others if they weren't supported by Scripture. The history of the stadium and the way the townspeople had salvaged so much fascinated me. They worked together to secure their survival and made rules for living in tight quarters. My goal remained as always to find my siblings and watch over Deena as my father wished.

"We pray for a hedge of protection to surround us, and so far the State has left us alone. They also have a lot on their plate. The entire world has fallen into chaos. There is one world government, but it is a mess and very dysfunctional," Alexander said.

***

Three days passed before Deena showed signs of improvement. I had been working with Alexander, tending to the horses and whatever work they found for me. Ten hours of work a day paid for our keep. Madelyn's helper ran toward us with shouting. She couldn't wait to tell us the good news of Deena's progress. Her fever had broken. The swelling in her leg had lightened, and it was not as red. Madelyn thought she was out of danger but listened for the baby's heartbeat. The baby showed signs of strength, an answer to many prayers. Deena's first words were a request for me, and Madelyn was quick to comply.

We both stopped what we were doing to rush to Deena's side. Her body trembled with weakness, yet her voice, thick with gratitude, expressed her thanks for their kindness. As we stood near the bed, Alexander led us in prayer. The prayer began with seeking the face of God, giving him the glory, stating his attributes, followed by words of gratitude, and finished with a request for further healing and protection.

As the days progressed, Deena ate and drank increasing amounts of food. Her leg looked normal but her foot still was of no use. Alexander provided a set of crutches so I could show Deena around the complex. I never mentioned to her the stigma of what showed in the UV light. There was no need because we'd agreed on a desire to move on, to continue our trek toward New Hampshire as soon as she healed. Madelyn gave Deena chores to do where she could remain seated. No one had a free ride. Their bond grew as the days passed, and I wondered if Madelyn and Alexander could overlook the initial doubts about her worthiness to live among them. They were old enough to be Deena's parents, and they had never had a daughter. The weather turned bitter cold with a heavy fall of snow. Another nor'easter had hit. Even if Deena had healed, we wouldn't venture onto our trek until things cleared.

After another week, Deena moved about without crutches. She limped and experienced discomfort but not pain. The temperature became mild, and a couple of sunny days melted most of the snow. With everything going so well, Alexander asked if I would accompany him and some men on a salvage mission to the far eastern end of Allentown, near the old international airport. A company called Grandflo Pumps had an abandoned equipment and parts supply facility that Alexander and his men often plundered. In addition, nearby was a biomedical technology company where he often snagged medical supplies and equipment. He believed there were skin products that might help Deena's foot. He warned of the dangers of the expedition, and ambush was always a concern, either by rebels, drifters, or the State, but I agreed to go. Anything to contribute to the common good of these people who had saved our lives.

The next morning at dawn, Benjamin woke me, and I followed him to the stables where men were saddling their horses. Everyone went about their tasks in silence as Benjamin showed me my saddle and reins. My horse was the spirited one, and she resisted me as I tried to throw the saddle over her back. So instead, I put on her reins and pulled her face close to mine. Eye to eye, we had a talk about who was the boss. I rubbed her between the eyes and loosened my grip. She shook her head and showed her teeth almost smile-like. I wasn't sure how to take it, but she let me saddle her.

Alexander entered the stable, his horse already saddled by his oldest son. Without a word, everyone mounted and trotted toward the gate. There's a sense of function when a group of men sit on powerful animals or machines with single-mindedness. We formed two rows with Alexander and Benjamin in the lead positions. My position was just behind Alexander as we headed east on Parkway Boulevard. At Lake Muhlenberg, we left the pavement going north across an old athletic field and cemetery. Our path took us through the old fairgrounds, where an encampment of refugees lived in makeshift tents and shanties. They stood in awe as we passed through their encampment in silence. Alexander leaned back in my direction to explain they had a peaceful relationship with this community and traded with them. To own a horse offered status and respect from a community.

Beyond the fairgrounds we traveled through rubble-strewn streets and haunting buildings damaged by vandals. The city center still had an impressive skyline for a small town, although vacant because of the failed utilities and services. The streets sprouted weeds and shrubs from every crack in the asphalt. I imagined an ambush prepared to launch from between the buildings, but saw nothing but stray cats, scrawny, feral dogs, and rabbits. I imagined some buildings had reclusive occupants, but they offered no threat to us. When I glanced at a third-floor window, I saw someone duck in a flash of fear. Our journey continued until we reached the green areas along Jordan Creek, where we dismounted to rest our horses.

"We'll ford the Jordan and make our way to old Route 22 and use the bridge to the Lehigh River,"

Alexander said. "The pump warehouse and the old biomed lab aren't far from here."

Dismounted, we walked our horses to the bank of the creek. Patches of ice covered shallow, still pools, but most of the stream flowed unencumbered. As we mounted our horses, one man fell, impaled in the shoulder by an arrow. Alexander grabbed him and boosted him onto his horse as several more arrows cut through the surrounding air, missing their marks. Even under such extremes, I smiled. To miss the mark is a sin. These men, much to my relief, are sinners. I owed the thought to my father, Jim Fisher. Without further hesitation, we charged across the Jordan and up the far bank. We rode a hundred yards before we stopped to look back at our pursuers. They did not reveal themselves, nor did they pursue us further.

"A bunch of marauders, opportunists hoping to get a couple of our horses. Leave the arrow in for now; I'll remove it after we cross the Lehigh River," Alexander said.

His heels drug into the ribs of his horse, and he was off in a gallop. Everyone repeated his action, and we left the green area of the Jordan to charge up Fifth Street and then the ramp of Route 22. The bridge across the Lehigh was in great shape, at one time carrying bumper-to-bumper traffic, but there were no signs of anyone today. On the east side of the bridge, we stopped, and Alexander removed the arrow from the man's shoulder, noting the depth of penetration. The wound only involved soft tissue and muscle, but there is always the fear of infection. They bandaged the wounded team member. We mounted and continued to the pump warehouse and rode straight in. It didn't take long to locate the components needed, as the team had been here several times before. Minutes later we were at the biomed lab, and Alexander went in alone. We positioned our horses to exit, and after just a few minutes he returned and we all took off.

After we had ridden past a few cavernous buildings, we dismounted, and our horses grazed on patches of grass just off the parking lot as we sat on old crates and guardrails. Benjamin heard first the sound of drones coming from the east, and he alerted everyone to grab their horses' reins. The drones came fast and low as we headed for the open doors of an airport parking garage. Satellite tracking had detected us. We would never know how, and at this point it didn't matter. We had probably been identified as a formidable unidentified group and marked for termination. The parking lot we'd just left erupted in smoke, flames, and debris. The explosions sent shock waves in every direction, powerful enough to knock half of us to our knees. Benjamin took the lead, and we followed him and Alexander down a ramp into the lower two levels of the garage. The airport had built the subterranean garage so as not to infringe on the airspace near the runways. From our space below ground dark as night, we heard the explosions and falling concrete above. Several minutes of explosions blotted out the dim light that had peeked out at the top of the ramp. Dust filtering down on us made us choke and cough, our eyes became irritated, and the horses danced so much we feared being trampled. When the explosions stopped, Benjamin ran up the ramp only to find we were in fact entombed by debris.

When he came back down, he called each of us by name and told us to speak so we could gather at the base of the ramp. The horses stood still in the dark, as if afraid to move. Alexander requested we all pray, beginning with praise and gratefulness for being saved. Then we followed Benjamin to the top of the ramp to dig our way out. Through a crack in the pile, we soon saw a ray of light and hope. We needed just enough space to slither through to the surface. Once out, we could find tools and dig from the top to free the horses. Two men crawled into a cramped space, a tunnel of sorts, and pushed concrete debris behind them. We continued to move this debris out and roll it down the ramp. Removing the rubble, however, soon destabilized the tangled support of the tons resting above. One move of a single piece unleashed an avalanche. We heard the rumble. It was brief and muffled. The dust cloud choked us as it rolled out of the mouth of the tunnel. Once again we were plunged into utter darkness. We couldn't see what was happening, and we called to the men in the tunnel. No one answered our calls. We all sat in the dark, coughing.

In the blackness I thought about my wife, about a young Amish girl, my father, and Deena. If I died here, I would be okay with it. How many tears can a man shed? None of us live forever. Death stalks us all. The key is to die living a good fight. I sat with memories, moments of love and tenderness, and felt comfortable in all my blessings.

Alexander stood. We couldn't see him, but his voice spoke with authority and confidence.

"If you accept this, then we are dead. Someone must go into the tunnel and begin again. Remember John 1:5.

That light shines in the darkness, and yet the darkness did not overcome it."

Alexander's prayer praised the Lord; then he prayed for strength and courage to face this challenge. He rallied the men to overcome the darkness and continue to seek the light, for in the light will come our salvation.

I volunteered to enter the tunnel to find the two men and continue our removal of debris. In the darkness I felt a boot, then a leg, but nothing moved. As I felt around, I discovered the other man's legs. I found both torsos pinned beneath concrete, but they were small enough chucks of debris for me to handle. Piece by piece, I struggled to uncover the men, both of whom were dead. I dragged each from the tunnel. I couldn't see anything, but I could sense they weren't breathing, and their clothing was damp with bodily fluids. There was no time to mourn. Two of us took their place, removing debris and clearing a way to freedom.

I took the lead position. All I could do was grasp around for loose bits of concrete and pass them behind me. Thick dust still hung in the air; we coughed even with torn cloth from our shirts covering our noses and mouths. My fingertips had worn out and blood seeped from them. I couldn't see the blood, but my fingers stung. As we removed the debris that crushed the others, the tunnel's height expanded so we could stand. The chunks of debris proved smaller than the initial chunks, because these were rubble from the blast, rather than fallen structures. Our efforts progressed ever faster as the materials became more manageable. Benjamin located an old sheet of metal, maybe a sign, but in the dark we couldn't tell. He attached a rope from the metal sheet to a horse so we could load materials on it and have the horse drag it out of the tunnel. One man found an old piece of rebar as he sorted through the rubble. Now we had a tool to dig. The men took turns in the work positions, but we all worked hard when it was our turn, and prayed we wouldn't encounter a giant slab blocking our path.

When we were young, Father encouraged all of us to memorize Bible verses. To most, it didn't come easy, but we wanted to please, so we did it. Now one came to mind: Acts 26:18, "to open their eyes so that they may turn from darkness to light and from the power of Satan to God, that they may receive forgiveness of sins and a share among those who are sanctified by faith in me." Even if we died in our struggle, it would be a struggle toward the light, which would be better than accepting the darkness. My thoughts were on the lessons of Jim Fisher. In my mind, I could hear his voice as he quoted Scripture, like John 16:33: "I have told you these things so that in me you may have peace. You will have suffering in this world. Be courageous! I have conquered the world." Jim Fisher was the rehab man; he turned junk into treasures, speaking all the while like a poet or songwriter. He could sort out people within minutes of meeting them. Thoughts of him inspired me to keep going. I picked up pieces of debris faster now and handed them to the fellow behind me.

Several of the men gave up and sat off to the side. They knew no one could see them in the absolute dark. Benjamin sensed it, as quiet as the men remained, and as if he could see, he walked toward them. When he spoke, the men cowered in fear with a gnashing of teeth. He could not see their faces and did not want to know who they were.

"Get back to work, you fools! We need every man. I can't see who you are and don't want to know. Just move."

Without a reply, they went to work, striking handheld blocks of concrete into utter darkness until it cracked against a solid surface. Strike after strike caused pieces of our tomb wall to fall away. Though surrounded by evil, the inherent goodness of our team remained. They went to work, increasing the height of the tunnel to accommodate the horses. Everyone strained to see, but to no avail. Such conditions challenge the strongest of souls and can break the weaker. There is little shame in it; we all suffered to a degree. As I removed a large slab of concrete at the face of the tunnel, light streamed through cracks in what I had exposed. It stopped me in my tracks, as if I could not comprehend what it was. I saw diffused light seeping through the cracks, and I shouted to the others.

"We are almost there! I see light!"

Everyone shouted as they rushed and almost crushed me to get a glimpse. Benjamin reined them in and made them get back to work. With every chunk of concrete removed, the light grew stronger until I removed a great block, too heavy for me to hold for very long. As it fell to the ground at my feet, it let in direct light along with fresh air. The portal was large enough for me to crawl through, followed by my digging partner. We stood in the light, the sun just above the horizon. I held my fist outstretched with the thumb side to the sun and the other side toward the horizon, just like the pioneers had done, to tell the time. Each fist width meant an hour since the sun breached. The gap was two fists since sunrise. A layer of frost coated the fields and sparkled on the trees. The chill in the air refreshed my skin like cold spring water. One by one, everyone crawled out. Benjamin was last. We all fell to our knees in praise and then remained spread out on the ground for a break to gather strength. Benjamin remained standing and walked a distance to look for signs of Alexander. There were no signs of him. When he returned, he stopped and praised each man for a job well done.

After we rested, Benjamin assigned men to enlarge the tunnel to accommodate the horses. He asked me and another man to go with him to look for Alexander. The bombs had damaged the biomed lab, but the building was still standing. When we entered, we found Alexander trapped beneath some rubble in the second room we searched. The roof had collapsed, pinning both of his legs and an arm. When he saw us, he teared up and pointed to the trapped arm. His throat was dry and raspy.

"Where have you been? Get me out of here!"

We laughed. There was no need to explain. As soon as we freed him, he would see for himself. The rubble trapping him came off from the top, and we worked our way down to the layers pressing against flesh and bone. He'd suffered bruising on his legs and likely fractures to his thigh bones. No compound fractures, at least no bones sticking out at odd angles, but his right hand was suffering from restricted blood flow, a deep shade of purple, and an obviously broken wrist. He had to be in great pain but never groaned or complained. Benjamin took one side, I the other, and we walked him back to the collapsed parking garage. The third man carried the medical supplies collected in a sack Alexander had secured before the attack. As we approached the parking garage, we saw our two dead friends lying on the ground. Alexander signaled for us to stop.

"Oh, Lord, have mercy on these men's souls. Clean them up, and fetch rags and water to wash the blood from their skin. Have anyone with a cleaner shirt trade with them so their loved ones don't see those blood-soiled clothes. Where are the horses?" Alexander said.

"Trapped in the lower level; the tunnel needs to be enlarged," Benjamin replied.

Overcome with pain and exhaustion, Alexander took a seat on a block of concrete and watched us clean the bodies. Changing shirts was just in time as the bodies stiffened. In a short time, one of the other men emerged from the tunnel leading a horse, no easy chore. Bringing each horse to the surface required all the men's strength.

"Tie our friends sitting up on their mounts, wrap their arms around the horses' necks with their heads at rest on the manes. They'll return to their families with dignity, not laid over like sacks. Benjamin, pick a man to head home and warn the families of their loss. I don't want to shock them as we ride in," Alexander commanded.

"If it is all the same to you, this task is a heavy burden, and I think I should go. I can't put facing these families on someone else," Benjamin replied.

TWENTY-ONE

Deena & Atanase

Alexander lay in his bed healing from his wounds; he'd turned over the medical supplies he retrieved from the biomed lab to Madelyn. Some she used on his hand and wrist, but Deena saw the greatest benefit. Her foot wrapped in an artificial skin allowed her to walk about with only minor discomfort. Still, we didn't see departing for a great hike as wise. Mobility made her better able to work around the village and contribute to the resources being used to sustain us. I enjoyed caring for the horses. Staying busy helped to shift my focus from the brutal realities of the world. The funeral service for our two fallen brothers was traumatic, as was the day of our return. Now, I brushed the horse of one of the dead men, which soothed me.

When I finished grooming horses and cleaning stalls, I went in search of Deena. When I ran into Madelyn, she told me Deena was at the laundry. Their conversation stopped when I entered, and I made a joke. They were talking about me, but they denied it. I'll never know the truth, but they claimed to be talking about the traders from New England who were due to arrive tomorrow. The traders have stopped every year for the last four. They are a band of wanderers who cycle from New England to South Carolina. This year they are about a month late for their southern journey. One of their scouts showed up today to announce their planned arrival. All the women looked forward to the day of the traders, as they always carried hard-to-find items that they scrounged or pilfered.

The first thought in my mind was, would these wanderers have ever encountered my New Hampshire-bound siblings? Deena and I left the laundry and went to a common area of the village where no one else was around. We planned our departure and speculated on what supplies we might need. The traders may have things we could use and knowledge of what we might encounter. The traders used horse-drawn wagons and pack animals, so they traveled the Appalachian trail. They would have knowledge of villages or other types of communities friendly to travelers. I prayed they weren't like the traders along the shores of Delaware Bay. Those were pirates. The women in the laundry had said the traders would set up a flea market in the street outside the stadium village. Other than the leaders, Alexander had not welcomed the general population inside the walls on any occasion. This made me wonder if they were untrustworthy or maybe just rowdy. Deena and I went to Alexander's for dinner with the hopes Madelyn could tell us more.

With my help, Alexander walked to the dining table for dinner and said the blessing. Madelyn had prepared an excellent meal of roasted potatoes, carrots, and beef. I had not eaten such a meal since before the collapse, and there was plenty to satisfy all of us. There was no need for me to bring up the subject of the traders. The children couldn't contain their excitement at looking forward to something different than the every-day activities. Alexander and Madelyn both tried to tone down their enthusiasm, with little avail. Descriptions of the impending trade event resembled a carnival of sorts with entertainers and traders. Advanced scouts gave notice so the village could sort through their hordes to find things to trade. The entire system worked on barter. Most of the women of the village made trade goods throughout the year, all in wait for these days. When the children settled down, we were halfway through the meal, and Alexander shared his thoughts.

"The traders are a fun-loving group of musicians, dancers, and puppeteers, but they aren't so much believers. We trade with them with a watchful eye."

"I'm wondering if they will know of the village my siblings founded in New Hampshire. It would be nice if I could meet with some of their leaders or some of the traders," I said.

"The leader will dine with us after they set up camp. We will have a feast, and Benjamin's family and a couple of others will join us. Of course, you and Deena are welcome," Alexander said.

Such an event had not been in my mind for a long time. I didn't think such an occasion took place anymore. Deena looked at me and flashed a smile. It would be a much-needed diversion from the oppressive existence we lived. After dinner, Deena excused herself to retire early. Her foot throbbed with pain, and she needed to attend to the dressings. Alexander and I sat by the fireplace and talked about his experiences in past years when the traders had come, and about my plans for departure from the community. I told him, a lot would depend on what I found out from the traders, if they had knowledge of my siblings in New Hampshire. After a couple of hours passed, I excused myself to retire to Benjamin's home and helped Alexander to his bed. As I was leaving, Madelyn continued to ready the trading goods for the next day.

Morning came too fast. I had trouble falling asleep. My mind was in hyperdrive with anticipation. Sunrise was an hour away, yet Benjamin and his wife had a full breakfast waiting when I came out of my room. His six children's excitement at seeing me stemmed from not being allowed to eat before I arrived. They all laughed when I apologized. Once Benjamin said grace, forks never stopped moving. The children wanted to be on the wall of the stadium when the traders arrived. Scouts had reported that their encampment last night was only a few miles away. Benjamin tried to tell the children it would be hours before their arrival, and to calm down, but they ran out of the house as soon as the food was gone. In addition, Carrie left to help prepare the trading goods. Benjamin shook his head and poured a second cup of herbal tea for us.

"You know, these traders can charm, but I always heed Paul's warning. Satan can appear as an angel of light and his minions as righteous. We welcome these traders, but they aren't Christians. They will tell you they are, and I think they believe they are, but they don't follow the teachings," Benjamin said.

"Well, I want to talk to them about New England. I'm looking forward to this evening," I replied.

For Benjamin and me, today would be a normal workday. Tending to horses never came with a day off; there was always feeding to do and stalls to clean. Carrie left lunches packed for us on the counter, and we grabbed them before heading to the stables. Thc entire village was out and about. I had never seen so much activity this early in the morning. Around noon, we heard music from the street, and almost everyone in the village rushed to the stadium wall along Parkway Boulevard. The procession came down West Linden Street, bagpipers and drummers leading the way. It was a most impressive grand arrival. Benjamin and I rushed to join the mob of spectators.

No one had told me what to expect, and this spectacle never entered my imagination. Forty horsemen, equipped with practical armor, long knives, and crossbows, followed the pipers and drummers. One horseman led the forty, a large, well-muscled man wearing shorts and a metal breastplate. He held a cutlass in his outstretched hand. Benjamin told me his men called him Bluidy, in reference to bloody, but his name was Douglas Gragam. He was a serious and intense Scot and not one to cross. Behind the horsemen were at least thirty covered wagons and buckboards, with children running alongside. Behind the wagons were a hundred more horsemen. The open buckboards had rows of seats upon which ladies sat. The whole procession comprised more people than those living in the stadium.

We stayed on the wall and watched the traders set up camp outside our walls. They set a protective defensive circle around their encampment as additional stragglers filtered in long after the main procession. The defensive circle would prevent from entering those who camped by the big cross; even the traders would have nothing to do with those depraved people. The total number in the traders' band was five hundred, including women, children and men. They were a force to contend with for anyone outside the State. I wondered how this "Bluidy" kept from being illuminated by the Peacekeepers.

Alexander didn't allow anyone to go to the traders' camp. Everyone would wait until tomorrow. First Alexander and Benjamin would have dinner with Bluidy and agree on protocols and exchange some official duties. After a while, Benjamin and I returned to the horses to complete our chores. Questions burned in me, and I asked Benjamin point blank, "How do they roam free? Why don't the Peacekeepers do them in?"

"We don't talk about it, because all we know is rumors. Rumors are gossip, and we try to live by the truth. I can tell you this: all human endeavors are corruptible; the State is no exception. Bluidy is a trader to the deepest part of his soul. He will tell you this. Everything he has or knows, he will trade to get what he wants. He doesn't limit it to dry goods, if you know what I mean. During his meeting with us, he bragged about providing the enemy with certain comforts. He can trade intelligence as well. Just giving you a starting point; you'll have to imagine the rest or ask him, which I don't recommend."

His words were an earful, and I imagined how evil such a man might be. Human trafficking was what Benjamin meant by providing comfort to the enemy, I am sure. Trading intelligence—no wonder Alexander limited his entrance into the village and refused to allow his people to enter. Dinner would be very interesting tonight. To remain silent unless addressed would be proper this evening. Tomorrow would be a better time for questions when I mingled in the traders' camp. I couldn't put my thoughts to rest. Alexander's dealings with Bluidy must have compromised his beliefs, even if it was only for a couple of days. I shoveled out the last stall into the manure wagon and put down fresh straw. The smell was on me, so I hurried to the communal shower and put on fresh clothing before heading to Alexander's for the meeting and dinner.

A large white tent sat in front of Alexander's house. Windowless, the entrance faced the gate to the stadium. A canvas wall blocked the view of the village from anyone who tried to enter. Bluidy and his men would see only the canvas; this had been the arrangement since the first trading days, years ago. Several people, including Deena, sat at the festival table inside the tent. Madelyn was on her right, and she saved an empty seat to her left for me. We faced across the table from the entrance, giving us a perfect view of the guests as they arrived. Villagers, both men and women, were busy setting the table with large trays of food. Glasses of wine and beer sat on a table across from the festival table to be served upon request. After greeting many of the attendees, I took a seat beside Deena. She looked lovely, and I told her so. She gave me a slight grin and continued her conversation with Madelyn.

Except for the traders and Alexander, everyone sat down. We sat in wait. Benjamin leaned across his wife, who sat beside me, and whispered, "This is normal. They always make us wait."

Alexander entered with the aid of his sons. They held him steady as he limped on his fractured legs and took a seat at the head of the table. Everyone went silent as Alexander's oldest son stepped into the tent and announced Mr. Bluidy Gragam. The boy stepped aside as Bluidy and his small entourage entered. Bluidy raised his arms in a gregarious greeting. Everyone sensed his charm and charisma. The room filled with a strange energy, a different harmony hard to resist. He greeted the village leaders and their wives as they had risen from their seats to greet him. The commoners in attendance remained in their seats as the greetings progressed. Bluidy made a joke about Alexander's broken legs, and everyone laughed, even Alexander. I didn't see the humor or a reason to laugh, and Deena also refrained. Everyone took their seats; I expected Alexander to offer a blessing before we ate, but he told our servers to bring the food. As we filled our plates, Bluidy addressed Deena. He'd spotted her when he entered the tent. I saw his eyes fall on her several times during the greetings, but he waited until he sat before saying anything to her.

"Well, Alexander, I see you have a new face among you." He stared at Deena. "She is lovely. Her features are so fine. What's your name?"

I glanced at Deena's flushed face; she offered an impish grin. Was I jealous? Why? I had never viewed her as anyone except someone I promised to protect. Never did I imagine . . . But in truth, her grin in response to this barbarian stirred my emotions. I couldn't believe she was showing an interest in him. If he was what she desired, I had nothing to say.

"Deena . . . my name is Deena."

"Oh, beautiful name, very fitting," Bluidy said.

"She going to have a baby," I blurted. Why did I say that? The words were no sooner out of my mouth than I knew I had blundered.

Bluidy never took his eyes off Deena, nor did he blink as he spoke. "That explains your radiance. Do you have other children? The world needs children. I have many."

Deena's grin faded. She'd enjoyed the attention for a moment. Too long of a moment, I thought. When her grin left her face, Bluidy broke his stare and called for a mug of beer and continued to talk to Alexander and Benjamin. The tent filled with laughter, jokes, and camaraderie as Bluidy bragged about his exploits and adventures. He bragged about all the goods he would offer the village. He no sooner finished one beer than he demanded another. The meal went on for an hour and a half without any pause in the chatter. I said nothing after my blunder. My mind couldn't shake the embarrassment I had caused Deena. She would never forgive me. I knew it. Guilt-ridden, I caught glances of disapproval from all the others. I wanted to leave, but I was frozen in my chair.

Bluidy gave me a death stare. He was drunk and dangerous when he called me out. "So, who are you? You with the mouth?"

"Atanase."

"Atanase? You say little. You are too quiet. I don't like you or trust you. Quiet people are dangerous, they think too much. What do you think about?" Bluidy said.

I didn't respond, other than to tense up in my seat, ready to defend myself. Deena's hand came to rest on my knee under the table. The whole tent went silent. Alexander and Benjamin both went on guard, ready to come to my defense. I remained still and prayed. I worried maybe they would side with the traders. After all, I had nothing to offer them. Deena squeezed my knee tight. Bluidy always got his way, never backed down, I had been told. He broke into laughter and chugged another beer. Half of it spilled down his chest. The conversations and laughter continued, as did my thoughts. I no longer felt the need to find out information from the traders about my siblings. Nothing any of them could tell me about them mattered; I would find out for myself. I would never compromise my beliefs and commitments to interact with these thugs. Accusers and mockers might call me a coward, but I knew I would take on any threatening advances by these traders.

The festivities lasted into the night, and I sat without saying a word. Bluidy would glance in my direction to let me know I occupied his thoughts and the festivities weren't distracting him. Deena refrained from looking at him and focused on conversations with Madelyn and a couple of other women. If Deena stayed, I would stay, and she showed no signs of leaving. My blunder left me too awkward to suggest leaving, so I remained seated in my place. Deena and I both refrained from drink and were the only ones not intoxicated. Witnessing the drunkenness proved difficult, and people's character dropped in my eyes. Bluidy had influenced everyone, and this disheartened me.

My thoughts of leaving the village solidified, and I knew Deena and I must prepare to leave soon. I grabbed Deena's hand to get her attention and whispered, "Come with me. We need to get out of here," I said.

"I've been waiting for you to say it," she replied.

We stood, and no one appeared to notice. Conviviality and distraction consumed them. We made our way across the back side of the table, our backs rubbed against the canvas wall until we came to a slit and disappeared into the night. We slipped away from the festivities and climbed onto the wall of the stadium, looking down at the traders' camp—a scene wilder than the one in the tent. No villagers were taking part, just the traders. The scene encompassed every depravity known to man. Bands played in several locations. Hard to describe as music. Band members screeched, tortured their guitars, all to the pounding of drums. I held Deena's hand, guiding her through the dark along the wall to the far side of the village. We wouldn't sleep in our beds tonight. I led her to a shelter filled with bales of straw. We climbed the bales to the top, which stopped four feet from the roof. In the distance, we could see the chaos and partying. I broke open a bale, spread it out, and we snuggled into it. There was enough warmth to comfort us during the night.

"You thought I flirted with him, didn't you?"

Without a word, I kissed her. I couldn't help myself. We snuggled. We felt safe and honest in our silence.

TWENTY-TWO

Atanase & Deena

A morning chill kept us from wanting to crawl from our nest, and our position obscured the village's activity. The village commoners woke early to trade. They were fresh and energized. Two inches of snow had fallen during the night to reflect an intense sun in a cloudless sky. The revelers would find the light most annoying and painful to their eyes. A well-deserved punishment, I thought. Deena and I hurried to the edge of the straw bales to lie on our stomachs and observe. Deena more on her side, due to her condition. Neither of us trusted anyone and wondered who might be in search of us. From this vantage point, we saw most of the village, but it was improbable anyone would spot us.

"We can't stay here forever. Do you think it best for both of us to go down and investigate what is happening?" I asked.

"Bluidy scares me, and don't take offense, but you are no match for him," Deena said.

No offense taken. Even with a sling and stones, I would fail. Fear wasn't what Scripture taught me. Have no fear, God tells us. He will deliver us if we face the enemy. Deena is no weakling. She's quite capable of handling whatever comes our way, with strength and courage. Our best chance was to face whatever came head-on. We just needed a plan.

"Together, and with God's intervention, we can do what we need to, to overcome. I think we both need to go retrieve our hiking gear and leave this place. The longer we wait, the more those derelicts will recover from their drinking," I said.

"What if they grab me and threaten to harm me? You'll have to comply with their demands," Deena replied.

"If you let fear control you, it will control the situation," I said. "Let's lie here a while longer and gather ourselves. Focus. If we can get to our crossbows, we will be unstoppable. At any rate, if we're given a choice, it's best if we fight to the death. We can't stay here forever, and if we leave without our gear, we will die of exposure. So what's our option?"

Deena was silent, observing the village's exchange of merchandise. None of those people were a threat to us. Our threat lay with Bluidy and his men who did not roam the village unless they felt a threat or betrayal had occurred. Deena needed some time, so I waited a while before I shared my thoughts. Her response was a sly smile, accented by eyes showing agreement. After a brief pointed praise and prayer, we slid off the edge of the bales and climbed down to the stable level. No one was tending the horses, and I stopped to give mine a pat on the neck.

"We need a couple of horses, at least until we get far enough away and out of reach. You be a look-out as I saddle a couple and position them for an easy mount," I said.

Deena walked to the stable's double door and checked for anyone approaching. With the horses saddled, I tied them to a post at the far exit of the barn. This exit offered a run for the far gate, which opened to the old cemetery and fairgrounds where the village kept their livestock. Horses would give us an advantage to gain time and distance, but a disadvantage when it came to hiding from aerial surveillance with their large infrared images. Everything is a trade-off; we were taking a chance. Bluidy wanted Deena last night. Perhaps he'd changed his mind by now. Or maybe he didn't think pursuing us in a chase would be worth the risk. His safety net was his group, a group known to those he bribed.

When we ventured to the old airport, the drones and AI had identified us as targets. The same fate would befall Bluidy and his men once separated from their camp and involved in a chase into the countryside. The State, or AI, didn't allow for much leeway. All carbon units were to be eliminated, if traveling unauthorized and not identifiable. To the AI in charge, humans represented flawed works, nothing more than carbon.

Deena and I walked through the village giving regards to all we passed, and they returned our good cheer. Nothing was amiss as we approached the temporary tent set up for last night's festivities, which blocked the normal path to Alexander's and Benjamin's homes. We entered the tent where the tables were still covered with the remnants of last night's party. The table where Bluidy had sat lay overturned, surrounded by shards of glass. A shattered chair lay beside it. We walked to the far side of the tent and slipped through a slit, which allowed us access to the dwellings with our sleeping rooms. When Deena and I entered Alexander's home, Madelyn was working in the kitchen.

"Oh child, where have you been? You need to be careful. When you disappeared last night, Bluidy exploded. A berserk outburst, such as none have ever witnessed. We fear for you," Madelyn warned.

"I'm here to gather my things. We're leaving," Deena said.

"You must hurry. I'll help you."

Madelyn and Deena proceeded to Deena's room and collected all her belongings, and I departed for Benjamin's residence. When I entered, no one was home, and I was quick to gather all my things. With my backpack strapped on, crossbow in hand, I ran back into the tent, anticipating Deena's presence. I waited but a minute before she appeared with Madelyn through a slit in the canvas.

"Hurry, you must leave. Don't delay," Madelyn said.

Deena and I ran from the tent into the busy crowd of villagers, who carried trade goods to and from the main gate. We no sooner started running than Deena stopped and dropped her backpack to the ground. Why? She searched in the two outer pockets of her backpack.

"What are you looking for?" I asked.

"It's not here! I forgot it." She wailed.

"You forgot what?" I asked.

"Ellen's Bible!"

"Forget it. We must get out of here. There's no time to waste," I commanded.

"Waste? Ellen's Bible was a gift. It's a gift from Jim."

As I stood with all our gear, she dashed toward the tent and vanished into the canvas.

Some inner sense told me to follow. Unable to carry all our gear, I left it to follow her. When I reached Alexander's dwelling, my heart stopped. Bluidy blocked the entrance, his back to me.

Deena appeared in the doorway from the bedroom to the kitchen, the Bible clutched to her chest.

While I evaluated the situation from behind Bluidy, he pushed Madelyn aside in a charge toward Deena. As he reached her, Deena leaped into the air, legs extended, and with a swivel of her hips planted a foot in a spot which took away Bluidy's wind. As he staggered backward, I grabbed the nearest heavy object, a lampstand, which I swung as high as I could. The lampstand cracked against his head, and he fell to the floor. Alexander, hearing the struggle, stumbled from his bed into the kitchen, where he steadied himself against a chair.

"Bluidy always gets what he wants. He's been obsessing over you since last night. Both of you need to leave. He's going to be crazed when he comes to," Alexander said.

Bluidy lay writhing on the floor, an easy kill if any of us had the acumen, but none of us were cold-blooded enough. We hugged all around briefly before we ran toward our packs and the stables. The horses were in wait as planned, and soon we were at a gallop across the old snow-covered cemetery and fairgrounds, cattle and sheep scattered in our wake. We rode hard until Route 22, where the landscape transformed into a rural setting of pastures and remnant farm dwellings. We crossed Jordan Creek just beyond an old high school using the bridge on North Cedar Road but left the road to travel cross-country.

The sound of drones put us on alert, and we sought refuge at a deserted farm under a pavilion. Never had I seen so many drones in formation, their path headed due south toward Allentown. Several minutes passed before the drones were out of sight. The sound of thunder echoed from the direction they had traveled. I tried to picture their destination, from all my travels, but I would never know. Someone had betrayed Bluidy's special status of protection, I suspected. It is the way of corruption. The thoughts of us being chased faded, although we would remain vigilant. No longer under pressure, we remained under the pavilion for a time. The drones never returned, and we continued at a gentle pace, always on the lookout. We traveled across open fields until we came to an old no-name bedroom community, now deserted.

Old farmlands lay on the other side of the community. Once plowed fields, they now gave way to stands of saplings. The small trees offered us cover but also inhibited our sense of direction and vision. Before long, we came upon a huge open-pit strip mine and lake. Large "Danger" signs stood in our path; the land was so barren we knew the soil was toxic. A smaller sign warned of lead and other metals. We backtracked south.

Alexander had told me about the mines and suggested we stay well to the west of them. To the east, in a town called Egypt, lay the heavy population of Acceptors he warned me about. Deena and I speculated this area to be the launch point of the southbound drones. The strip mines offered their own sort of danger, but the Acceptors' danger was more acute.

Our route lay south of a deep pit mine, west to Quarry Road; then we chose the left branch onto a less traveled road along the lake shore. We moved past old industrial ruins into fields and woods, observing dwellings from there. We had plenty of cover from trees and shrubs as we picked our way north. When we came to a road, we crossed as fast as possible, disappearing into the woods. The area offered plenty of deserted farms and farmland. Evening found us on the banks of the Lehigh River in a thick wood after we crossed the Delaware Lehigh Trail. We set up camp for the night and sat on the bank to observe the river flow. Even though the evening was chilly, we didn't dare risk a fire.

In the morning, we rode along the Delaware and Lehigh Trail until we came to a bridge. We dismounted and led our horses through the woods. At the top of the low ridge, along the river, was a field that offered us a view of the road crossing the bridge. We monitored the road for over an hour, and not a single vehicle passed. Mounted, we took the bridge in a rush. Once on the other side, we stayed on the road until we observed a large swath of uninhabited land to our right and again disappeared into the brush and trees. We saw the Blue Mountain Ridge in the distance, our destination. During our day's travel, the snow had melted under clear skies and a bright sun. The Appalachian Trail ran along the ridge, our goal, and we had found our way toward the mountain, avoiding all inhabited areas.

At Lehigh Gap, we found an abandoned farm with several outbuildings. In the main barn, we dismounted and removed the horses' saddles and bridles. We placed the saddles on some racks designed to hold them and hung the bridles on hooks. With the barn door opened wide, we slapped the horses on their rears and gave a shout. The horses ran from the barn but stopped within sight. They were free. Horses were of no use to us anymore. The climb to the top of the ridge was steep and rocky, not horse friendly. We set up camp away from the farm's outbuildings, in a small stand of pine. The horses must have stayed near us all night because in the morning they stood in our camp. After we packed our gear and shouldered our packs, we petted the horses on their necks and thanked them for bringing us this far. To go away from them proved difficult, yet essential.

As we approached the Appalachian Trail, shock overtook us. Hundreds of people were descending the mountain trail into the river valley. The closer we came, we realized how ill-equipped most were and how blank their stares were. It was as if each person was just following the one in front of them. They didn't appear to be a group, but rather, individual wanderers. Deena and I warily approached the trail until we could observe them pass. We ventured to ask them about their destination, but none answered. Their eyes were hollow, cheeks sunken, and their bodies emaciated from hunger and physical stress. Some wore rags tied around their feet in place of shoes. Few possessed backpacks or sleeping gear. It was a death march. When the last one came down the trail, Deena and I began our ascent.

She claimed her foot didn't hurt at all, but the trek ahead on loose stones would offer a test. This part of the trail shreds good shoes and injures healthy feet. All four limbs are required to climb this section of trail. Deena proceeded first to set the pace. In sparse encounters, we passed others in descent. All looked like the hundreds we'd encountered at the start of our ascent. Without a spoken answer, we figured them as a southward migration of people stranded without utilities in the northern regions or perhaps something more sinister was routing them. The depleted looks on their faces made them look soulless. The nine-hundred-foot vertical rock scramble out of the valley taxed us after our horseback ride across the rolling plain. We knew we had a climb ahead of us, but the challenges were a little more than expected. At one overlook, the alternate route came into view. A blue-blazed detour for those who desired an easier path, one which avoided the rock scramble. It had a steady single flow of hikers. We figured we could use all fours to ascend, delighted to bypass the crowds of refugees and reach the top.

At one point, we stopped our climb to rest and take in the view of God's creation. The quilt work of abandoned farms stretched beneath a blue sky filled with white puffs of clouds rolling toward the horizon. It was nice to forget the pain and suffering humanity had brought upon itself for just a moment. Such beauty. How is it that humans treat each other in such vicious ways?

Deena and I shared some water, stale bread, and the warmth of the sun. From our position, we watched a stream of migrants cross the bridge over the Lehigh River. Several people collapsed to the side of the column, but no one stopped to give aid as they lay motionless. There appeared to be no compassion for their fellow travelers. I imagined these people were at one time productive citizens living in towns and cities going about routine lives in family settings. The throngs of migrants looked endless and hopeless.

Deena and I rose to our feet, brushed off our clothes, and proceeded on our climb. To our horror, we encountered bodies along our way. They were in various stages of decomposition based on when they'd died. Some were skeletal, while others with rotting flesh produced the worst aspects of nightmares. We held our breath and hurried past, attempting to avoid more than a fleeting glimpse, yet the images seared into our minds. We knew it would never wash away.

At the summit, a long way from the trail, the view stretched forever, and we sat on a boulder in the middle of a meadow. It offered a cleansing break. There was no hurry in either of us to stumble into more grotesque sights. Apparently those who send out the drones weren't interested in this ragtag stream of humanity. We needed a long rest. With no compulsion to move on, I suggested we camp in place. Deena was quick to agree. The area looked secure, with good visibility to detect anyone's approach. We nestled our tent at the base of the rock where shrubs offered some camouflage. We had hours of daylight to enjoy the views and sat on the rock to observe the sunset and the stars fill a blank sky. A full moon rose above the horizon, larger than any moon I had ever seen. I told Deena it was a Wolf Moon, but I wasn't sure. I remembered Father mentioning the name one winter when I was a boy.

Morning offered another sun and blue sky. Awakened by the expectation while it was still dark, we ate and gathered our sleeping bags to climb up onto our boulder. We sat shoulder to shoulder, bundled up to observe the glory of dawn. Deena's head rested against me as the sun crested the eastern landscape, the sky filled with thin red, pink, and yellow clouds against a blue backdrop. We sat there until the sun was three fists high over the horizon; then we packed our gear. On reaching the main trail, we saw migrants strung across the ridge as far as the eye could see. The same blank faces, in single file, in some sort of trance. None of them spoke or looked at us. They walked with their heads bowed; they stumbled and dragged their feet.

One very animated figure blocked their path. He faced into the line, holding a Bible high above his head, and confronted each passing soul. He repeated his words over and over, but none of them responded.

"Repent! Repent! Do you know Jesus? Repent! Come with me. I have water and food."

Even with an offer of water and food, people ignored him. People bumped into him, stumbled, caught themselves, and continued their walk. Deena and I walked up behind him. When I spoke, he jumped, then spun around to face us.

"You startled me. I have been here three days and never heard another human voice."

"Who are you? Why are you here?"

"I'm trying to save souls, Pastor Kevin from down in Palmerton. These poor souls have been passing through here for five days. Something bad must have happened up north. They act like their brains got sucked out. It's impossible to get through to them."

"This is Deena, I'm Atanase, on our way to New Hampshire, but seeing this migration makes me wonder."

"Ha, counterintuitive, heading north in winter. You are welcome to shelter in my church down below. New England winters are not to be taken lightly. The weather gets rough on the trail. Your wife looks like she's going to have a baby."

"Thank you for the offer, but we have a plan and will keep walking north."

"Suit yourselves, but if you change your mind, you are welcome in my church."

"Thank you."

Deena and I continued north, walking just off to the side of the trail to avoid the migrants. We hiked past the old Blue Mountain ski resort where the slopes filled with tent campers. We kept on the move. The sun warmed us and there was no wind. Gaps in the groups of migrants occurred, so when there were none, we used the trail. Whenever we found a shelter, long-term residents occupied it, and trash littered the surrounding area. At nightfall we would leave the trail to camp at a distance from the crowds. We pushed hard and covered about twelve miles, then wandered south off the main trail before reaching a place called Delps. We found a meadow with a grand view of the flats to the south. The horizon appeared to be fifty miles away, and again we could see remnants of abandoned farmlands and villages. Deena perched on a boulder as I set up camp. While I collected firewood, she read Ellen's Bible, as was her routine wherever possible. As the fire blazed, she called me to her.

"This passage gives me chills," Deena said. Then she read Jeremiah 51:13–16 to me: "You who reside by abundant water, rich in treasures, your end has come, your life thread is cut. The LORD of Armies has sworn by himself: I will fill you up with men as with locusts, and they will sing the victory song over you. He made the earth by his power, established the world by his wisdom, and spread out the heavens by his understanding. When he thunders, the waters in the heavens are tumultuous, and he causes the clouds to rise from the ends of the earth. He makes lightning for the rain and brings the wind from his storehouses."

"Do not worry, nor fear, believe with all your heart," I said.

"But I was a part of it. You weren't." Deena wept.

I sat beside her, and we praised the Lord and glorified him. Then both of us, in silence, reviewed the sins we knew we had committed and accepted responsibility for them. We sought forgiveness for all those involved in our mistakes. We also took responsibility for sins we failed to recognize. The sun set in the distance and the temperature plummeted. Deena drooped in weariness of all the trauma. Her pregnancy likely also affected her emotions. We sat by the fire and looked across the landscape as other campfires were lit. The stars lit the sky, and the wolf moon rose again. As our fire smoldered in a red glow, we slipped into our tent for the night.

I'm not sure of the exact time when the ground trembled and I awoke. I heard distant thunder as I crawled from the tent into darkness; the stars and moon had vanished. Deena called to me, and she followed my voice until seated beside me on the boulder. The darkness was absolute; we could not see each other or our surroundings. The ground continued to tremble, as did the distant rumble of thunder, but there was no lightning. To the east, a streak of light appeared, unlike a shooting star. The streak remained in the sky, growing steadily wider.

Deena moaned mournfully and fell back onto the boulder. I backed away and stood in awe. Her body became phosphorescent for a mere second as the light hovered then dispersed above her. She didn't move during the episode, and once the light left, I no longer saw her.

"Deena!" I called. When she didn't respond, I knelt down and reached for her. My hand touched her face and checked for breathing. I put my head to her chest and found no vital signs. I cried out again, "Deena!"

I pulled her into my arms. The baby! Time became critical. I opened her clothing to feel her abdomen for the baby and felt a kick. It was still alive. After a brief prayer, I pulled my hunting knife from the sheath on my belt. All by feel, I walked my fingers down the blade, guessing at the proper depth I would make an incision. I left just enough steel protruding between my fingers. My blade was sharp as a razor. My work would be by feel, for I still couldn't see anything. As I moved the blade toward Deena's abdomen, the knife handle caught on my coat. The blade slipped from my fingers, and I heard the knife strike the boulder before falling to the ground below.

"Oh, Lord! Why?"

In the absolute darkness, I knew it would take too much time to retrieve it, but I had no other option. The baby had no other option but death. As I laid Deena down and slid toward the edge of the boulder, I heard a gasp. The sound of a drowning victim surfacing for one final breath. I scrambled back to Deena's side as she arched her back off the rock in another gasp, locked in place. Her body trembled, not in spasms but in harmony with the tremors I felt in the earth. Their frequencies were a perfect match. Her body relaxed, and I lowered her from her arched position into an embrace. With my fingers beneath her nose, I sensed her breath, weak yet steady. I placed my ear to her chest and heard her heart beating in perfect rhythm. Her clothing restored, I held her to comfort her and waited for her to regain consciousness.

Then my body's trembles became apparent, in synchronicity with her and the earth. I hadn't realized this awesome, unbelievable fact in all the commotion. Now, in the absolute darkness and silence, it brought me peace. A peace I had never known.

In the distance I perceived a glow where I imagined the horizon might be. The glow didn't climb skyward. It rolled toward me. It spread without pause. The red glow appeared as a fire. As it approached, wonder overtook me. I had no fear of it. I just watched it roar toward me, engulf everything around me, and continue past me. The entire world looked ablaze, but I experienced no heat. I realized not everything was burning. This fire, like the one on Mount Horeb, consumed only discordant elements. The frequency increased in all God's creation not in harmony, until all reached a state of pure energy.

The goal of our spiritual journey is to become one with God. This harmony protects us. This is our salvation. What a revelation. Shekinah Glory. When Jesus returns to earth, I am a witness.

"Deena, wake up, Deena. You need to see this. Please wake up. It is like a dream; I need to know I'm not the only one witnessing this." I whispered.

There is no way to tell how long the fire burned, a long time, or maybe an instant. It was surreal. I doubted everything prior, and yet I didn't doubt the power behind these flames. The flames dimmed when Deena spoke.

"Atanase, what happened? My baby just kicked."

"Everything is perfect. Look. The world has been on fire while you slept."

"I didn't sleep. It was . . . I can't put it into words. Do you sense the peace?"

"I do."

The flames died out, and once again we were in total darkness but still held the harmony and peace. In an instant, a strange light came over the world, a mellow light. Unlike the sun, the light came from everywhere, not from the sky. The light had a quality we had never seen before because there were no shadows, no dark or shady spots. The light soothed us as the vibrations both inside us and in the earth quelled.

Deena turned to me. Never have I seen an expression or quality on anyone's face like she had. "Atanase, this is the beginning," Deena whispered.

***

. . . "It is done! I am the Alpha and the Omega, the beginning and the end. I will freely give to the thirsty from the spring of the water of life. The one who conquers will inherit these things, and I will be his God, and he will be my son. But the cowards, faithless, detestable, murderers, sexually immoral, sorcerers, idolaters, and all liars—their share will be in the lake that burns with fire and sulfur, which is the second death." Revelation 21:6–9

About the authors

Bill and Dale Ann have hiked and motorcycled through much of North America, Europe, and the Caribbean islands. Their works include several short stories and novel-length fiction creations, one of which involves a haunting—inspired by a house they lived in. *Above and Beyond: radio silence* is a creative nonfiction account of Ed Wright's WWII service as a radio operator on C-47s. *Instead, by Grace: from dark to light* is a true story, written from a journal kept over the course of a year of invasions into an idyllic lifestyle. When not writing, the Wrights are gardening, bicycling, caring for family, and supporting Grove City Alliance Church through missions near and far.

Reviews on Amazon and Goodreads Appreciated

Please visit

https://braveknightwriters.com/

for our blog and links to other works

Find us:

https://www.pintcrest.com/braveknight62/

Facebook- William Wright and Brave Knight Writers

Made in the USA
Columbia, SC
07 May 2026

82434303R00173